DUPONT CIRCLE

PAUL KAFKA-GIBBONS

DUPONT CIRCLE

A NOVEL

HOUGHTON MIFFLIN COMPANY

Boston   New York   2001

For information about permission to reproduce selections from this
book, write to Permissions, Houghton Mifflin Company,
215 Park Avenue South, New York, New York 10003.

Visit our Web site: www.houghtonmifflinbooks.com.

Library of Congress Cataloging-in-Publication Data

Kafka-Gibbons, Paul.
    Dupont circle : a novel / Paul Kafka-Gibbons.
        p. cm.
    ISBN 0-395-86932-3
    1. Dupont Circle (Washington, D.C.) — Fiction.
2. Women law students — Fiction.   3. Same-sex marriages
— Fiction.   4. Fathers and sons — Fiction.   5. Gay male
couples — Fiction.   6. Gay men — Fiction.   7. Judges —
Fiction.
        PS3561.A362 D8   2001
        813'.6—dc21   00-054126

Book design by Anne Chalmers
Typefaces: Janson Text and Copperplate 31bc

Printed in the United States of America
QUM 10 9 8 7 6 5 4 3 2 1

To my wife, Patty, with love,
and our son, Gabriel, with joy

The right to marry the person we love, the person with whom we want to share our lives, is one of the most fundamental of all our human and civil rights.

—Susan M. Murray, Beth Robinson, and Mary L. Bonauto, attorneys, brief to the Supreme Court of Vermont
March 1998

If gay people can't marry, straight people can't decorate.

—Henry Alford, "My Gay Wedding"

APRIL

The Still Point
of the Turning
World

JONATHAN ALLARD walks toward the fountain at the center of Dupont Circle and, Jon has always thought, of the capital itself. Jon's theory that Dupont Circle is a paradise in the heart of the city and the nation goes this way: In Dupont Circle poor meets rich, old meets young, gay meets straight, native meets new arrival, and the peoples, styles, and languages all squish together to form America. Love begins here during morning rush hour with a glance. At midday, political and religious evangelists stop passersby with a few words, a petition, a holy book. In the afternoon, solo figures pursue venture capital and real estate deals using tiny phones. In the evening, dogs approach or snub one another. People find good food nearby, designer and regular ice cream, coffee simple or embellished, newsstands, movie theaters with smallish screens. All of this, in Jon's eyes, is persuasive.

But what conclusively distinguishes Dupont Circle from its Parisian ancestors and Washington cousins are the dozen bookstores within a few minutes' walk. Bookstores enough to gladden any newly published author's heart. Bookstores chain and independent, specialty and general; large stores inventoried via satellite and corporate projection, small stores inventoried according to individual whim. Bookstores filled with thrillers and self-help books that sell like hotcakes, and bookstores obstinately maintaining law, philosophy, literature, and social history collections. Stores where books are as surprised to find themselves rubbing up against each other as the people who crisscross great Dupont Circle itself, queer theory thrust into a briefcase alongside military biography, genetics text squeezed into the same well-worn backpack with epistolary love story.

Dupont Circle, Jon maintains to friends when they complain that the place has become commercialized, gentrified, Metro-station dominated, is still perfect.

❄

He settles on one of Dupont Circle's inner row of benches. The fountain in front of him resembles a flying saucer, held aloft by two Greek women in flowing robes and one scantily clad Greek man blowing on a conch shell. Water pours from the saucer in a silky curtain into the basin below.

Jon scans the crosswalks to the north and east for his husband, Peter, and their little girl, Nita. Jon knows he has five minutes, Peter punctual with a self-righteousness Jon finds, after nine years, overly emphatic. Peter will, as always, wear that expression that says, *Yes, I'm exactly on time once again.* Jon himself is often late for dinner parties he and Peter are hosting, or bike rides with his training buddies, or even, once or twice a semester, seminars he is teaching. Jon is always sorry and promises to try harder.

Peter and Nita will arrive from either of two directions. Northwest lie Lambda Rising, Kramerbooks, Kulturas Books, and Jon's sister Valerie's beautiful, sunless house on Decatur Street, where Valerie lives with her eight-week-old, Sam. Nita, a big seven-year-old, is Valerie's first child. Jon and Peter have raised Nita since she was a baby, when Valerie once again became an inpatient at Chestnut Lodge in Rockville. Peter may have taken Nita to see Valerie and Sam. Nita needs to get to know her baby brother. It is possibly only a matter of weeks before baby Sam comes to live in Peter and Jon's Church Street row house. If they come from Valerie's, Peter and Nita will appear on Connecticut, among the crowd emerging from the Q Street Metro exit, crossing from coffee corner toward the necklacepod trees.

On the other hand, Peter may have skipped Valerie's — who can blame Peter for shying away from Jon's sister without Jon along to help? Peter may have gone to Bailey's, Jon's father's house, just about the last of the lovely patrician townhouses on O Street not yet converted to condos, offices, or stores. On Friday afternoons, Bailey and Nita often bake cookies and play gin rummy, while Peter slips around the corner to Second Story Books, or upstairs to Bailey's own library to daydream, nap, read, or perhaps even write a word or two in his current notebook. If they come from Bailey's, Peter and Nita will appear from the west, by the drugstore or the elliptically curved office building. Jon scans both lines of approach. He waits for the tulips to open.

❋

Whereas a moment before Jon was content, sunning, his legs stretched in front of him, suddenly he is aware of how lonely he has been. Nita spots him and comes running, Peter almost keeping pace, his chin up as if to counterbalance the downward tilt of his long torso. Jon lifts Nita, and kisses her. "How," Jon asks them, as if it's been weeks, not hours, "goes?"

"We made cookies," Nita reports. "I beat Grandpa five games to two."

"We had a nice afternoon," Peter says.

"Cookies?"

"Oatmeal chocolate chip," Nita says, pillowing her head on Jon's shoulder.

"I'll just try one now," Jon says, reaching into the bag Peter carries. He munches and lugs Nita off toward home. "What did you do in school?"

"We practiced minuses with checkers. Ms. Schwartz read us *Mrs. Piggle-Wiggle's Bad Table-Manners Cure*. We had mac-and-cheese for lunch. We played Bombardment outside. We did Quiet Drawing. We got New Words." And on and on, through the day, omitting no part of her program. Ms. Schwartz is the sort of elementary school teacher adored by all. She never raises her voice. She is not large of stature, and she has bangs. The worst troublemakers, those who reduced the first-grade teacher to tears, reform instantly when they reach the second grade, so potent is Ms. Schwartz's magic. "We made pipe-cleaner art. I made Voltaire. I want to put him in The Gallery, for five dollars."

Nita takes after Peter. She loves nothing more than telling her whole story and selling her art. She has her own gallery space in Peter's home office and, of course, a Web site. Peter helps Nita price her paintings, drawings, sculptures, and books. Voltaire, the tawny tomcat, is often Nita's subject. Relatives and friends regularly buy her work. Peter, a novelist himself, insists this whole process is vocational training.

"Bailey got a call from a second-year," Peter says.

"Does he sound all right?"

"It's a woman."

"Oh," Jon says, setting Nita down and taking her hand to cross to P Street. He and Peter decided that Bailey could use a student in the house, currently occupied by only Bailey himself. Bailey, now sixty-six, has long suggested that there should be other occupants, or that he should sell the place. His children and grandchildren all want the house to stay just as it is, with him inside it. Jon assumed Bailey would find a man. A

6

young woman living in the house with his father disturbs him.

"I don't think Caroline would object," Peter says.

"She'd be all for it," Jon says. His mother has been dead for eight years. "What did Bailey tell you about her?"

"Louisa. He says she sounds very businesslike and responsible. She's an early riser. They're meeting tomorrow."

A Disagreeable Man

THREE COCKER SPANIELS, goofy and caramel colored, tumble over one another as they cross leashes and H Street to the George Washington Law campus. The judge walks tall and serene, just behind the dogs. *What kind of man has three cockers?* Louisa thinks. The sight of so much activity makes her head hurt. This is the first morning in three weeks through which she could have slept, the last of her papers behind her. Instead, here she is on campus, coffeeless. The dogs will no doubt be part of her job. Louisa doesn't have a good feeling about this.

"Leo and Virginia Woof," Bailey explains. "Given to my wife and me by diplomat friends. Our friends realized they were going to be on the move and would have to put the Woofs in quarantine every few years. That one's their son, Henry." Bailey points. Leo and Henry run and nip at each other. It is the pre-class hour. Students reach to pet the dogs. Henry sniffs the base of the statue of George Washington and strays into the rose garden.

"Come," Louisa calls with authority. Henry halts, tail poised, runs to her. Leo follows slowly. Louisa pats Henry, tugs his silky ears, which he appreciates. Leo and Virginia sit by Bailey, who rests his fingers on Virginia's long forehead.

"You know dogs."

"My father bred Gordons," Louisa tells him. "Mom and my brothers kept the line going after Dad died. Now Mom only has one brother at home, and four dogs. My other brothers are out of the house, but in-state." Even after two years Louisa is aware of the distance, cultural and geographic, she has traveled from Montana. After college, she earned a bare living as a journalist on the *Missoulian* environmental beat.

"What brought you to GW?" Bailey asks.

"They gave me some money," Louisa says, which is part of it. "Also, I had this idea that people out here knew something I didn't."

"Is it true?"

"I think so. I'm learning how to operate in a crowd. I know how to operate solo."

"You sure you want to share a house?"

"If it's big enough."

"Oh, it's big," Bailey tells her. Louisa learned of Bailey's housemate search from the student notice board in Burns alcove. She had just picked up her International Intellectual Property seminar paper from her 2L folder in Stockton. The grade was good. Louisa gave a victory hoot, alarming a cluster of first-year students in the lounge. She floated down the hall toward the library and there on the notice board was a letter, handwritten in the palest of blue ink, on moonlight-white stationery. The note stood out from the xeroxed conference announcements like a watercolor. "Greetings, Law Students," read the precise hand.

I am an antediluvian with a cavernous house in the neighborhood of Dupont Circle. I wonder if one of you would like to live here, rent free, in exchange for holding a mirror to my lips once a day. As a sitting member of the DC Circuit, I might afford you a glimpse of one of many dismal fates awaiting you upon completion of your studies. Sean Harper will vouch for my disagreeable character.

The letter was dated that Monday. Louisa read it on Wednesday and called as soon as she reached her apartment, a cramped L Street share she needed to be out of in a week. She reached a secretary at the courthouse, who put her through to a clerk, who asked her who she was and why she was calling. By the time Allard himself finally picked up the phone, Louisa was flustered. She agreed to meet him, and his *walking companions*, at eight-thirty the next morning.

"Why law?" Bailey asks. His chin is tucked down and held in his left hand, as if he's cradling a violin. His one trained dog, Virginia, looks Louisa straight in the eye.

"I like to argue and write," Louisa tells them. "I want to make some money, at some point. I'm an activist, in a lazy sort of way." Bailey has a quality of alertness, of listening to exactly what Louisa says, that surprises her in a man of his generation. She senses that he has room for her, not only in his house but in his mind. And the males appear trainable. "Tell me about this housemate situation."

"No rent for you, peace of mind for my children. I look forward to having someone around the old place. You're welcome to set up breakfast on weekday mornings. This will be a method of ascertaining that I've made it through another night." On weekends, he goes on to say, his children will just have to phone, if they want to check his pulse. He is healthy, except for mental oddities that have plagued him since childhood. She raises an eyebrow. Nothing much, he assures her. An inability to leave books turned upside down, open, on tables. Even strangers' books on restaurant tables. A minor case of dog-human confusion, which leads him to talk to his three cocker spaniels more intimately than is customary in our culture. Speaking of which, would Ms. Robbins be so good as to walk the dogs on court mornings? Bailey never arrives at chambers before ten, but on court mornings, he just has time to wake himself up (at Yale he was known as Bailey Conscious), scan that day's bench memos, and slip into his robe. Do second-years at George Washington have those Socratic interrogations before their eyes open? How is it that Louisa happened on Bailey's advertisement? Is Ms. Robbins a student of Sean Harper?

"Whoa," Louisa tells him. "Call me Louisa. I took Harper's course last year. Only a few professors still use seating charts and grill everybody after the first year. As far as breakfast goes, I can try. I'm not usually awake enough to check on anyone. Look," she says. "Let's just take this one step at a time. I'll come see the place. We'll talk again." Bailey leans down and speaks to Virginia. Virginia sniffs Louisa's knees, looks into her eyes once more. Bailey straightens up and takes Louisa's hand in a strong grip.

"Virginia believes that you have the necessary qualifications for judge- and dog-sitting. Whether or not we meet with your approval is another matter. How's tomorrow at six? I'll show you around. You can meet my son, my son-in-all-but-law, and my granddaughter, whom they are in the process of raising."

"Tomorrow is fine."

"Boys?" Bailey shouts. Leo and Henry eventually return from their wanderings and stand, wagging. Bailey leashes them and leads his entourage off.

Lucky Charms

"LOUISA?" With a shy smile, Jon ushers Louisa into the foyer of the tall house on O Street. "I'm Jon. Bailey asked us to come give you the tour."

"Peter," says Peter, coming out of the shadows of the front parlor. He is tall, with thick, dark hair and gold-rimmed glasses. He holds a bowl of Lucky Charms in his left hand and extends his right. "I don't usually eat these. Nita was having some."

"I do," Louisa says. "Listen. I don't mean to be pushy. It's just that I've only got a week left on my lease. The judge asked me to come today."

"The judge," Jon says, shaking his head. "Haven't heard anyone call Bailey that since I was a kid. Nellie used to call Bailey 'the judge' and me 'Mr. Jonathan.' Of course, Grandma called Nellie and Ollie 'the help.'" Jon wanders through his childhood house, switching on dim lights. Peter ushers Louisa forward. A second- or third-grade girl with a nest of light brown curls sits with her back to the wall. She's eating cereal with a soup spoon that she has to open her mouth wide to engulf.

"This is Nita," Jon says. "Nita, this is Louisa. Bailey apologizes, by the way. One of his grandnephews has a bad throat. His parents didn't want to leave the little guy with a babysitter."

"So they called Bailey to sit a five-year-old and a two-year-old. Typical," Peter says. "You're mastering this family tree, I hope. Bailey has three kids: Jon here is the middle one, Bess the eldest, and Valerie, Nita's mother, the youngest. Thing is, Jon and I, who are about as married as two men can get in this part of the country, are raising Nita. Don't worry about Bailey's great-niece and -nephew right now. But Stevie's the one with the cold."

"When's the quiz?"

"In a year. By the way, your being here is all my fault," Peter says. "I think Bailey needs someone here in the house. He's not getting any younger, though the whole family treats him as if he's fifty. And frankly, it offends my proletarian sensibility to see one man living in a place this size."

"The sewing room," Jon announces. The room holds an enormous desk, in the middle of which stands a computer. Dark wood cabinets line the walls. An ancient office chair stands high and robotic by the only window. "No one's done any sewing here in a while. My mother did her writing here. She died just before Nita was born, so Nita didn't get to know her," he adds. Nita, who has followed the men, rolls her eyes, as if she has heard about not getting to know her grandmother a few too many times. She balances the cereal bowl, a shallow old china piece, high in front of her.

"What did your mother write?" Louisa comes into the room and runs her fingers over the desk. The wood is polished to a high sheen.

"Politics for the *Post*," Jon tells her, and walks on through a door in the back of the room. Louisa waits for more, but Jon doesn't elaborate.

"The Allards think we ordinary citizens learn their family names in junior high history class," Peter tells her. Louisa flashes him a smile. He's such a husband. Jon, ahead of them, clears his throat.

"I write, too," Nita says.

"Do you, now," Louisa says.

"My biggest book is *The Dragon That Created the Sun.*"

"I'd like to see that."

"You can order it online for three dollars. It's in The Gallery. I printed out twenty-five copies and sewed them with red thread. I'll read it to you, if you want."

"What's The Gallery?"

"It's where I show my art in my house," Nita says. Peter looks on proudly.

"The front room," Jon tells them. The front room is about midway back in the Dupont house. Louisa knows just enough to know that the porcelain lamps, the red-lacquered tables, and the giant Chinese vase in the corner are ancient. Also, nice to look at and run one's fingers over. Jon walks onward, turns on the light in the next room. "The parlor." Two armchairs oppose a TV. Behind the chairs, under a fishhook lamp, stands an old radio with elaborate wooden scrollwork and large, false-ivory knobs.

"You can picture people in here listening to *War of the Worlds,*" Louisa says. Is it all right to be irreverent? She looks to Peter, who smiles happily, as if he's had the same thought for years. Jon leads off down the hallway to the dining room, where harp-backed chairs surround a table beneath a modest chandelier. A swinging door leads to a pantry with glassed-in cabinets, a beige tin breadbox with a red lid, high shelves crowded with cans of soup and vegetables. Beyond, painted sunshine-yellow, the kitchen is as large as the dining room. A monumental stove with two ovens, two pie warmers, and a bread warmer covers a good piece of one wall. Past the kitchen is yet another room, with an ordinary kitchen table and chairs from the era of aluminum tubing and sparkly gray upholstery.

"When I was a lad, the dining room was used for dinner every night," Jon tells her. "Now it's mainly for holidays."

"Mint chip?" Peter asks, from the freezer. "Or perhaps a bowl of Lucky Charms?"

"Would it be possible," Louisa asks, "to sprinkle a few Lucky Charms *on* some mint chip?" Peter sets her up. Jon fetches himself a bowl of ice cream, straight up. Nita tops off her milk with more cereal. All sit on the sparkly upholstery. It's six-fifteen in the evening. Louisa feels that she already lives in the house. She picks out her yellow crescent moons and green clovers. There is so much money, like a fieldstone foundation, under the house. Generations have lived beneath these high ceilings. But to Louisa, the nearly empty place is the opposite of ghostly. The house is a quiet carnival of what was, and what might be again.

"Where are the Woofs?" she asks.

"Out back," Peter says, tilting his head. "They have a red brick bungalow with double-glazed windows and forced hot water."

"Oh, please," Jon tells him. "Don't start that the-dogs-live-better-than-some-people routine."

"I've seen your name. You teach at George Washington," Louisa says to head them off.

"History," Jon says. "You're just finishing second year at the law school?" Louisa nods, spoon handle rising and falling.

"You should go down to the courthouse and see Bailey sometime. On the bench he's like God," Peter says. "Except liberal."

"What do you do? Wait. Let me guess."

"Please don't," Peter says. "I'm a novelist. Yes, I'm published. No, I don't earn much."

"What kind?"

"I don't do trailer-park realism. I don't do thrillers with words like *covenant* and *sanction* in the title. I don't do horror or porn, at least not intentionally. I do the other stuff."

"His characters tend to have complicated domestic situations and identifying physical gestures and speech markers," Jon says, twitching his head to the right and drawing out the last word to "maarkers." He pours himself another bowl of cereal but doesn't add more milk.

"What is that kind of stuff called?" Louisa asks Jon.

"Literary fiction."

"Let's talk about Jon," Peter says. "The kindly professor who spends too much time on his students. Whose office is cozy but disorganized. Do the what-I-do number for her."

"Whoa," Louisa says. But there's no stopping the men.

"I write about social history," Jon says. "Usually nineteenth century. For the last five years or so about marriage. I'm interested in how marriage changes as a legal and social institution. More generally, I'm interested in why people marry, what they think marriage will give them. I'm interested in what other people expect married people to contribute, and why some groups and governments try to stop people from marrying."

"Like pale people being told they can't marry less pale people," Peter elaborates. "Like daughters being told they can't marry anybody daddy doesn't tell them to. Like gay people being told they can't marry each other by straight people. Where are you from in Montana?"

"Creston. Near Kalispell. How did you know I was from Montana?"

"Bailey—" A thump comes from the back of the long, narrow house. Henry skitters onto the linoleum, attempts a turn, sprawls on the kitchen floor, recovers, and stands, wagging. He is followed by a young woman in black riding clothes with a short haircut and three earrings in her left ear. Also Leo and

Virginia. "—told us," Peter finishes. "Bess and TJ's daughter Dee, another of our nieces. Bailey's granddaughter," he adds sotto voce.

"Hi, Uncles," says Dee, twenty or so. "Hi, Peanut," she greets Nita, kissing her forehead. "You must be the Bailey sitter," she says to Louisa.

"Louisa Robbins." Louisa rises and offers a little curtsy, spoon to one side.

"Deirdre Jensen. Pleased, I'm sure," Dee says, bowing. She looks at Louisa's ice cream and Lucky Charms sundae. "Bailey told me to come meet somebody I'd like. Nobody told me there was going to be dinner."

✳

When they have finished, Jon suggests that Dee show Louisa the rest of the house. "We'll just stay here, clean up," Peter tells Louisa, "and have a discussion." Nita has been gazing at Louisa with the kind of affection that seven-year-old girls suddenly develop for pretty twenty-six-year-olds with long, auburn hair. She and the dogs follow Louisa and Dee to the front hall. Leo and Henry start up the steps, until Dee smacks her riding crop against her boot. The men in the kitchen begin bickering about something in a married kind of way.

"Heel," Dee commands. Leo and Henry tumble back and sit, trembling. All the females head up to the second floor. Louisa slides her fingers over the smooth banister. Leo and Henry whimper, as if they've just chased all the girls up a tree. The men can just be heard, talking about who was late and why.

"They're not having an argument," Nita says. "That's a discussion. There's not supposed to be a winner, but Peter's always more right."

"Jon and Peter are Peanut's parents for all practical purposes," Dee explains. "Grant, Nita's dad, divorced Valerie when Nita was born and Valerie cracked up again. He started a Stepford family in Leesburg with Cookie, the golf princess."

"Her real name is Regina," Nita tells Louisa.

"Is she nice?"

"She's really nice," Nita says. "But she calls my dad Daddy, even though she's not his daughter. I'm his daughter. They're married."

"Okay," Louisa says. "Valerie's your mom. Jon's other sister, Bess, is Dee's mom. Grant is Valerie's former husband, Nita's father, currently residing with Cookie. Your father," she tells Dee, "is TJ." She feels like she's fallen into a Russian novel and hit the ground running. "And you ride horses."

"Theodore Julian," Dee says. Nita has the riding crop and is smacking herself experimentally on the bottom. "I ride. I teach riding. Do you ride?"

"You could call it that. I travel on the backs of horses. Come," Louisa commands, unable to tolerate the whimpering any longer. Leo and Henry charge to the second floor and begin circling. "Sit," Louisa says. They sit.

"Well, you know how to manage dogs," Dee observes. "I'll take you riding sometime. Valerie does the best she can. But she's got like a milkshake of bipolar, schizophrenic, and borderline disorders. The bottom line is she can be really great sometimes, or really out of it. She can also be mean. We love her, but we have to watch out. Right, Peanut?"

"I don't always love her."

"That's the way it is," Louisa says. "You can love a person and not love them all the time."

"You'll have a great summer here," Dee says, heading down the hall. "I'd live here myself, but my squeeze Kelley and I are housesitting for his sister Kathy, who's on the Sardis expedition." More names for the genealogy, Louisa notes. Kelley, the boyfriend; his sister, Kathy.

"Does squeeze mean boyfriend? What's Sardis? When are

you going to move here?" Nita asks. The second floor has even higher ceilings than the first, and more rooms than Louisa can keep track of. Dee turns on the lights, which have an on button and an off button. Louisa has seen this type of switch once before, in the Conrad mansion she visited in Kalispell with her sixth-grade class. Her mother was a field-trip helper for the overnight trip, back before her father died and her mother started working in town.

"A squeeze is a boyfriend," Dee tells Nita. "Sardis is a place in Turkey, the country. Kathy digs up really old art, dusts it off, and puts it back together."

"I'm thinking about living here next week," Louisa says.

"Grandpa's nice," Nita tells her. "He knows how to play gin, casino, and spit. Heel," she shouts. But the dogs wander, sniffing the wainscoting.

"Try making your voice lower and steadier," Louisa advises Nita in a low, steady voice. "Say 'come.' Then say 'heel.'"

"Come," Nita says, lower. The dogs saunter over, sniff the crop. "Heel." They sit. Nita looks amazed.

"Want to see my promise ring?" Dee offers her hand. Louisa studies the ring in the dimness. Even with the lights on, there are no brightly lit places on this floor. Louisa adores this. She wonders in what peaceful, shadowy room she will sleep.

"How did you get all the pieces to stick together?"

"Soldered them. The baguettes kept popping out. Don't you love how, in French, *baguettes* means both 'diamonds' and 'bread'? Bailey has about a hundred of these little guys in a shoe box." Dee's ring is made of tiny pieces of cufflink, earring, hat pin, and watch chain, clipped down to diamond-enclosing nubbins and sealed together. *Leftover diamonds*, Louisa thinks. *That's different.* "Kelley's at the ag school. We met in metal working," Dee tells her. "Kelley believes that tool-and-die and engine knowledge are essential for a farmer. You want to choose your area?" Dee pulls Louisa down a hallway, her riding boots thonking. "This was Claire's room." She swings open a door. "I died right after she was born. She made these," Dee says, opening a closet full of knitted bedcovers in rose and pale green wool, lined in satin. "They smell great." She and Nita bury their noses in the bedcovers. Louisa gives them a sniff. There is some rich perfume embedded in the satin, which is cool against her cheek.

"You mean *Claire* died right after *you* were born," Louisa says. "Who was she?"

"That's what I said."

"No, you said—"

"I know what I said. Claire was Bailey's mother, my great-grandmother," Dee says. *Whatever,* Louisa thinks, as she and Nita follow Dee across the hall.

"Dee has a word thing," Nita whispers, "where she says things wrong and doesn't know."

"Okay," Louisa tells her. They enter a bedroom lined with bookcases—Hardy boys, Junior Britannica, spy books, an acre of paperback science fiction. On top of the cases is a collection of artillery pieces. Wide shelves hold easily a thousand soldiers in formation—Napoleonic, Confederate, American and German World War II, and some ornate, antique models Louisa can't identify. The desk is hidden beneath a detailed log fort, possibly Revolutionary, on a plywood base.

"Jon's room. He's a war geek," Dee says. "That's how he got into history. We did a war two Christmases ago. I was the Royal Welch Fusiliers. I always sleep here when I stay over."

"Want to see where I sleep?" Nita asks. She takes Louisa's hand and pulls her back into the hall. Louisa experiences a slight thrill at this. They head to a small room with tennis posters on the walls and a trophy shelf of little golden players in dresses. "This is Aunt Bess's room. She's famous," Nita says.

"Mom was good," Dee says. "She's not famous. Let's show Louisa where she should stay." Dee leads Louisa still further back into the house. "This was Caroline and Bailey's area, while Claire was alive."

"They all lived here together?"

"Yup. Caroline and Bailey could have had the front, but they let Claire use it. Can you believe grown people lived with their parents back then? Now Bailey lives up front. You should take this whole part." Dee says. "Caroline was great. We all miss her, but Bailey's still in love with her. It's romantic, but a little spooky. Like Heathcliff and Catherine in *Wuthering Heights*."

"What's wuthering heights?" Nita asks, still holding Louisa's hand. "Is Grandpa spooky?"

"Wuthering is getting blown by the wind. Heights means hills. It's spooky to love somebody too much after they're dead. Bailey's just supposed to remember Caroline fondly. He gets a little carried away."

"How?" Louisa asks.

"He talks." Dee says. *Talks to whom about what?* Louisa wants to ask, but resists, not wanting to be too much of a seven-year-old herself. Dee leads Louisa and Nita into a long room with French doors opening above a garden. A high bed faces an armoire fronted with a tall mirror. Bookshelves occupy two corners, and a chaise longue stretches beneath an impressionist landscape. Behind and above the tall double bed stands a deco swan's-neck lamp with a pleated silk shade.

"Come see where the dogs live," Nita says, pulling Louisa to the window. In the twilight Louisa sees the sturdy brick doghouse, under a maple that screens the yard from the neighbor's house.

"Keeping this place up must be expensive," Louisa says. "I don't mean the doghouse."

"We're rich," Nita says. "Can I braid your hair?"

"The house has been Bailey's since the dawn of man," Dee says. "It's not like there's a mortgage or anything. There are still property taxes and upkeep, but repairs on old houses are tax deductible or something. Do you have a sweetie?"

"Do my hair when we go downstairs," Louisa tells Nita. "I have a boyfriend in New York. I need to ask the judge, I mean Bailey, how he feels about Chris staying here sometimes."

"Is Chris a good guy?"

"He's not a thief or an arsonist. We've been going out for two years."

"No problem," Dee says. "Bailey's cool about sex. He has girlfriends."

"Lorraine," Nita chimes in. "But they're just friends now. What's an arsonist?" Louisa feels her heart sink, but doesn't know how to take account of this. Why should she mind if Bailey has girlfriends? The question is whether he minds if she has a boyfriend.

"A person who burns buildings down on purpose," Louisa says. "I thought you said Bailey was stuck on Caroline."

"I said he talks to her," Dee says. "You can catch him if you sneak up on him. But he's trying to live his life. Men just keep doing it until they drop. Women, too, sometimes. I will."

"Doing what?" Nita asks.

"Having sex," Dee says.

"I know what sex is."

"Not my mother," Louisa says. "She's of the Never-Will-I-Find-Another school of widowhood."

"Your dad died?" Nita asks.

"He had a heart attack when I was fourteen."

"Doesn't that suck," Dee says.

"Jon and Peter won't die. They're young," Nita says.

"Of course they won't," Dee says. "Well, Bailey's handsome and—you've met him—charming. He doesn't have old-man breath, and he rows his shell twice a week and rides his bike to work. I bet he's a sack animal."

"What's that?" Nita asks.

"Somebody who's good at sex. Marsha has been after Bailey for years. She was Caroline's best friend, which is probably why Bailey is holding out on her. *If* he's holding out on her. Bailey didn't date at all after Caroline died. Then, I guess it was like four years ago, Jon gave him a talking to. Use it or lose it. Since then Bailey's made up for lost time." Louisa feels her spirits drop. She's disappointed to discover that Bailey might be another womanizing judge, a William O. Douglas type, enlightened on the bench, benighted off it. She's heard so many stories about out-of-control old men. She thinks of Bailey's letter. Was that only two days ago? "Prof. Harper will vouch for my disagreeable character." For the first time, Louisa has serious doubts about moving in.

"Use it or lose what?" Nita asks.

"Sex appeal," Dee says, then turns to Louisa. "Don't get me wrong. There's only been like one a year. The one who lasted longest was Nancy—"

"What's sex appeal?"

"It's when other people want to have sex with you. Nancy was only thirty-four. They all fall in love with Bailey and want to marry him. He has to jettison them gently," Dee says. "Is your Chris guy serious, or just recreational?" They sit on the bed, Nita in the middle. Louisa discreetly tests the mattress with the heel of her hand. Not bad.

"Kind of serious," Louisa says. "What do you mean jettison gently?"

"Give them their walking papers. He hates to do it, you can tell, but one holiday he's got Sally—"

"Sally laughed even when nothing was funny," Nita reports.

"—or Nancy on his arm, and the next he's alone again. I think he's still waiting for Caroline to come back. Rap on the second-floor window in the middle of a storm, Bailey runs to her, she kisses him with icy lips. That kind of thing. What do you mean, Chris is kind of serious?" Louisa gives Dee the abridged history of Chris, how they met through friends when he was in med school at Georgetown, how they almost broke up but didn't when Chris left for New York. How he's in orthopedics, in his residency. Louisa will move up to New York when she finishes law school. Nita, Henry, and Leo wander off, leaving Virginia. But here Louisa is in DC, ready to start a second summer at Arnold & Porter. Why is she in DC if she needs to find a New York firm? Why doesn't she spend the summers with Chris? It comes down to how little he requires her. He agreed too quickly that, since she had found a job at a better firm in DC than in New York, she should stay for the summer. He doesn't give her the confidence to be a little bit of a fool for love. Dee nods.

"Sounds like Brad. He was a runner. Of course, we were in ninth grade."

"Chris isn't a runner. He's a surgeon."

"Work-oriented. Want to see the third floor? You could take it, but you'd have too much space. You'd never see Bailey." *Too much space*, Louisa thinks. As far as never seeing Bailey, it will be her job to check on him.

That, at least, is what she tells herself, back downstairs in the sewing room, while Nita braids her hair. Nita tugs gently, making a loose braid, which pulls to the right. In the den, Dee, Jon, and Peter are watching television.

"I'll live in Caroline and Bailey's old area," Louisa tells Nita.

"Yeah," Nita answers. "At night you can open your window and talk to Virginia."

Love Versus United States

"LOOKS LIKE we've got a live one," Max says, strolling into the conference room with his peculiar, loose gait. He's smiling.

"Well, now," Bailey says, rubbing his hands. "Bring it on."

Max's shirttail hangs free behind his blazer. He has a patch of yolk on his tie. His glasses are opaque with dust. Yet Max, a bookish Ukrainian American, is one of the sharpest legal minds Bailey has ever employed. Both his clerks are exceptional. Bailey can't tell if his growing reputation is luring better clerks this decade, or if the job options on the outside are driving them his way. Certainly there's money to be made in a law firm, but the hours are endless and the prospects of making partner slim.

"Two men married in New Mexico about a year after the high court decision. They came back to DC, where they reside, and paid their taxes. The IRS says they underpaid because their marital status is determined by the state of residence and DC says one boy plus one girl doth a marriage make, end of story. So the fellows paid the taxes and sued for a refund in the district court. They won in the district court and got an injunction ordering DC and the IRS to treat them as a married couple and refund their overpayment. The IRS and DC appealed up here."

"Wait a minute. They had to pay *more* because they were married?" Bailey asks. "What about the marriage penalty?"

"They're one of those big income–tiny income couples. They actually paid more taxes as single men than they should have as married men."

"I see," Bailey says. Max has a habit of summarizing and advising as if he himself is the judge and Bailey his clerk, an attitude Bailey encourages. Bailey's chambers consist of a central room, where Amelia the secretary reigns; to Amelia's left a short hall, off of which are the clerks' small offices; to Amelia's right the conference room, where Bailey and Max are now; and beside the conference room, Bailey's office. Bailey's office and the conference room offer a view of the Capitol building, which looks like a nineteenth-century etching of itself. Most often Bailey works in the conference room, where a large oak table serves as his desk and two leather armchairs face the windows. One wall is hidden by bookcases of Supreme Court reporters. The opposite wall holds court of appeals reporters. "I should talk to a few people before docket meeting. Maybe I can get my mitts on it. What's it going to turn on?"

"When we look beyond the motion to the merits, DOMA," Max says. "And Full Faith and Credit. DC Counsel enacted a resolution in favor of same-sex marriage. Congress shot it down."

"Defense of Marriage Act," Bailey says, head tilted, chin in left hand. "Interesting."

"You haven't heard the best part. Guess the names."

"Tell," Bailey says. Bailey has a theory about everything. His theory about toast, for example, is that it must be thin so that the amount of untoasted bread is minimized, but not so thin that it dries out in the toaster. His theory about successful appeals cases, which he has elaborated to his clerks, is that, like pop songs, they have to have a good caption. If a plaintiff has the right name, he or she will have a better chance of being heard by the high court and remembered by legal scholars. Max slaps the folder down and spreads his arms wide.

"Mr. Wilson," Max says, "and Mr. Love." Max grins at Bailey. *Love and Wilson v. United States* passes the name test with flying colors. It will be *Loving v. Virginia* all over again.

"Where's Eve?"

"She has a doctor's appointment," Max says. "She'll be here pretty soon." He mumbles like a schoolboy, eyes on his splayed feet. Eve and Max have been seeing each other since at least late fall. One chilly November evening, Bailey forgot his scarf and turned around at the bike rack to fetch it. He caught his clerks hotly necking in one of the leather chairs. *Max and Eve are perfectly mismatched* is the way Bailey explains their mutual attraction to Caroline. He tells her about them as he rides his Schwinn to and from home. Bailey's theory about couples is that either the two people should be very similar, or they should be quite different. When they are only somewhat similar, they bore each other without agreeing on anything. Max is comical in his physical progress through the world, but devilishly quick in the head. Eve is witty and encyclopedic, Max's match intellectually, but entirely superior from the point of view of comportment and grace. Together, they have an odd charm. Eve, a wealthy girl from Richmond, stylishly dressed, coifed, and bejeweled, stands beside disheveled Max like a noblewoman greeting a peasant in a Renaissance scene. Now Eve's at the doctor's office, and Max doesn't look worried.

"When do we close for last month?"

"Yesterday," Max says.

"I'm almost there on the possession and food stamps cases. Anything else?"

"Only lunch."

"Sushi?" Bailey always buys. It's one of his clerks' perks.

"Sure. No," Max says, mumbling again, "maybe not."

"Why don't we just ask Eve, when she gets in?"

"Yes," Max says, and ambles toward the door, head down, feet dragging.

⁂

Even the conference table is confining this morning, perhaps because of the sunshine, which splashes onto the wide sidewalk beyond the window. The armchairs facing the street are a better place, but still not right. Bailey arranges his materials there —his notes and Eve's from the case of the urban farmer, two opinions, clipboard. It's a brisk, lovely day, a day not for work but for a hike along the canal with the dogs. Bailey shifts in the chair, drops his head back, and scans the sky, absently rubbing his forehead with the fingers of his right hand.

He should be walking the towpath. Perhaps he could persuade Louisa to join him. They could get to know each other. Bailey pictures her striding the path beside him, the dogs ahead. He has enjoyed having Louisa in his house this last week, even though he knows she feels awkward there. They bump into each other. They exchange a few words, often about the dogs. Bailey finds himself listening for her, timing his own trips to the kitchen so that they will meet. They had one evening chat in the den, over ice cream. They watched the ten o'clock news, said good night.

After their first meeting at the law school, Bailey missed showing Louisa the house. His grandnephew Stevie had a sore throat and a fever. Bailey calculated that Louisa would be reassured to meet part of his family, so that she wouldn't worry about locking herself up in the big house alone with the old man. He and Louisa spoke on the phone the day after her visit. Louisa announced her intention of moving in. She was almost cool. He wondered what Peter, and especially what Dee, had said about him. No doubt stories about Bailey's alleged nocturnal adventuring, but wouldn't Louisa find that reassuring, in a way?

His children and grandchildren believe him to be something of a ladies' man. The truth is simpler and sadder. Bailey hasn't slept with a woman in two years. After Jon sternly took him to task on the sixth anniversary of Caroline's passing, Bailey went on dates for a time, and climbed into a few beds. But what that activity led to was the melancholy of reawakened senses and heightened memory. On the other side of the bed, the younger women wanted to marry. He could see that in their eyes, feel it in their caresses. He could hear the broken dreams in their voices. He had to tell them he was not the man they were waiting for.

There is no casual sex. He wonders if there ever was. Bailey never wanted more than to be a father and a husband. Caroline perhaps slept from time to time with the man she almost married, who had never married and never gotten over her. She and Bailey never spoke of it. If Caroline was sportive, she was true to Bailey in her fashion. For his part, Bailey had no desire to be with other women. Marriage was tailor-made for him. He was Caroline's. That was all.

Bailey straightens up in his chair and decides to get to work, but his mind moves to the case Max just brought in. Finally, a viable gay marriage challenge. Long before his son Jon and Jon's love, Peter, married in a ceremony conducted by Jon's renegade Catholic priest, Rick Wood, long before Jon and Peter became the de facto parents of Nita, Bailey was on the lookout for such a case. He always wanted to be the maverick judge, the history-maker, with Caroline behind him, quietly marshaling her army of like-minded colleagues in the press. The idea of gay marriage becoming federal law in Bailey's time seemed unlikely, even when the states began ruling in favor of gay couples at century's end, first Hawaii, then Vermont, later New Mexico, which went further than Hawaii and

Vermont, actually issuing marriage licenses. The prospect of New Mexico's ruling was distant on the political horizon when Bailey and Caroline began outlining their campaign. Now the battle has come home to Bailey's court, but his chief ally and advisor is far away. Caroline left him. Well, she died. Yet he felt at the time, and less strongly after eight years, that Caroline abandoned him unnecessarily, certainly prematurely. He knows this is childish. He begs Caroline's forgiveness as quickly as he accuses her. Mostly, he wonders where exactly she is. He makes no effort not to talk to her when he is alone.

Now, for instance, he quietly chats with her as he works. He shares with her choice bits of the opinion he's in the middle of writing on Mark Beggs, who sued the District for denying him food stamps. Beggs farms on top of his building in Northeast, and District regulations allow no depreciation for farm equipment in calculating food-stamp eligibility. The man has a complicated irrigation and drainage system on his roof, as well as thermal insulation for his seedlings, and he has yet to show a profit after five years of raising herbs and vegetables. Beggs's attorney argues that the District has incorrectly extended the restrictions of the Food Stamp Act. Caroline would appreciate the farmer's plight, and his location. Eve's knock sounds on his door.

"Come in," Bailey says. "Are you all right?"

"I'm pregnant," Eve tells him. "Besides that, I'm ducky." She is smiling and pale, and her dress betrays no bulge. "I'm not going to take leave till this fall, when you have new clerks. If I have to exit the courtroom during arguments to go puke, blame Max." Bailey rises to his feet, extends his hand.

"Congratulations. You will be magnificent parents."

"Yeah," Eve says. "I guess we should get married. I was thinking maybe you could officiate."

"I would be honored."

"When do we start on the gay marriage case?"

Suddenly, Caroline doesn't seem quite so far away.

The Great Room

"I DON'T WANT a new room," Nita says, looking first at Jon, then at Peter. They have just finished breakfast and have about ten minutes before Jon has to take Nita to school.

"Sure you do," Peter says. "You've been saying you wanted the big room since you started sleeping over at Andrei's house. You said you had to have leopard curtains just like Andrei, that as soon as the room was ready, you'd move in. Well, it is ready."

"I said I'd *think* about it."

"Monkey, think about it soon. Because Sam's going to be spending more time here, and we need to be able to hear him when he cries at night before he wakes *you* up. That means he should be in the little room, and you should be in *the great room*." Peter is not above a little real estate double-talk to try to move Nita along. Jon, as usual, says nothing and looks back and forth between husband and Nita, with the same dispassionate air as Monsieur Voltaire. Jon's definitely a judge's son, Peter thinks, preferring to wait until all the arguments have been presented, go off for a long think, and only then conduct a tidy mediation. The worst of it is Peter finds himself waiting for these decisions to be handed down instead of simply saying to Nita, *You're seven. What I say goes.* Not to mention the fact that the curtains took forever to hem.

"Sam is Valerie's baby," Nita says, and again looks from Peter to Jon. "He lives with her." Nita loves placing her parents in this position, in which Jon would prefer to toe the party line and Peter insists on speaking truth. Peter folds his arms across his chest and looks at Jon in the international parental gesture meaning, *Well?*

"Valerie might get sick again," Jon says. "Then Sam will come stay with us." Peter looks out the window and rattles his spoon as he stirs his coffee. Valerie *might* get sick again? Peter finds this fiction, that Valerie will suddenly throw off the shadow of illness and become a capable mother, like some kind of Oliver Sacks cover girl, a bit irritating. The woman has been under twenty-four-hour supervision since he and Jon met nine years ago. For the first few years, Peter thought the hope-that-will-never-die thing kind of sweet. Then Nita was born, Valerie went out to Chestnut Lodge, and Peter became a father overnight. He and Jon had moved in together all of five months previous to Nita's arrival and were just figuring out, without the benefit of a legal wedding to focus them on the task, what their relationship was. And then here was this three-week-old, Jon had exactly no experience with infants, and were Peter not the second of six kids, had he not more or less raised his twin sisters when they were born and he himself was eight, things might have been pretty difficult on Church Street.

As it was, Peter became primary caretaker overnight, without ever having decided if he wanted children (fortunately, it turned out he did), without the usual ring on his finger, deed to a house held in common, or other reassurances for which one traditionally gives up all of one's independence and time. Fine. No problem. Peter adored Nita, his Love Monkey who never really looked like a monkey except for her bright lemur eyes, big for her thin, thoughtful face all through infancy, eyes dark brown and curious, following every motion, reading adult expression with uncanny accuracy. Nita understood her own complicated situation before she could do more than crow, knowing somehow that the woman who came and went, who held her, talked to her, sometimes sang lullabies and other songs, not necessarily so soothing, by her bassinet, had to be treated delicately. Nita didn't ask Valerie for anything. She would turn, in her mother's arms, to Jon or Peter and let them know if she needed a change of scene or a change of diaper. Valerie, in turn, didn't always remember her daughter's name.

One morning, Valerie was driven over to Peter and Jon's house by Bailey, who kept insisting that if Valerie would only spend enough time with Nita, she would become well enough to mother her daughter in her own house. At the door, Valerie asked, very politely actually, *Where is it?* That was when Peter understood he was Nita's and Nita was his, not for a few months or a year, but forever. Bailey, for all his learning and common sense, has a father's unreasoning belief that, someday, Valerie will be healthy and happy. Jon never really challenges his father's faith, and perhaps deep down he shares it. Meanwhile, Peter has raised one of Valerie's children and will soon, it appears, be raising another.

"Why does Sam have to live in *my* room?" Nita addresses this question to Peter. Nita knows where babies come from but has an understandable uncertainty about her own parentage. She realizes that Valerie is her mother and Grant her father, but she feels this is more of a formal than a biological bond. It's as if, for obscure legal reasons, Valerie has the title *mother*, whereas Nita knows her natural parents are Jon and Peter. Obviously neither man has any connection to the birth of Sam, whom Nita considers a nuisance, though not yet a major one. Something on the order of the chores—picking up her toys when her room becomes unwalkable, keeping Voltaire's water dish full—that she must perform in order to receive her allowance.

"We don't know who Sam's father is," Jon says, which is

certainly true. *We know he's tall*, Peter has to restrain himself from commenting, as Sam is already twenty-five inches in his tenth week. All that is certain is that, on a balmy night the previous May, Valerie snuck out of her house when Lucy, one of her two caretakers, wasn't looking. She met a tall man and spent the night with him at the Marriott in Woodley Park, where she was found, confused but unharmed, by the house staff at check-out time. The mystery man, who had paid in cash for a deluxe suite and given a bogus name and address, was nowhere to be found.

Peter did get a few minutes alone with Valerie one afternoon toward the end of her second trimester. He did what he has always done, talked to Valerie as if she weren't crazy. This produces mixed results. What, Peter asked when he finally got the chance, was the man she met and slept with that one night *wearing*? Did he have a *creative job*? Was he *bald*? Peter was anxious to know all he could about Sam's bio-dad. Valerie looked at Peter as if she, too, had been waiting for this chance, Bailey and Jon out of the room. "He meditated," Valerie said. This, while candid and possibly an avenue for further exploration, was not terribly revealing. Did he chant? Was this before or after? During? No further clarification was forthcoming.

That's the difficulty with Valerie—well, one of them. She never answers on the right level of abstraction. If you ask her what she wants for dinner, she might well say food. If you then ask her what kind of food she wants, she might say salty, without intending to be difficult. On the other hand, if you raise her baby girl for three months while she's at Chestnut Lodge, she might well come screaming into your house with her father behind her, saying that you've "stolen her baby" and that she's "going to kill you."

Life as Valerie's brother-in-law is not dull, and moments spent with her occasionally take on a Tennessee Williams pathos. Valerie is as beautiful as her brother, in much the same fragile way, the thin bones, the delicate skin, the silky, light brown hair. She can be calm for hours at a time, smiling gently, speaking softly, occasionally entering the conversation with an eerie remark or two. That was how she got laid so quickly whenever she slipped her keepers. Men think she's introspective and attractive when they come across her in a public place. Peter can only imagine how their perceptions change when, in the afterglow, Valerie starts speaking about this and that.

"I think Sam should live at Grant's," Nita says.

"Finish your waffle," Jon tells her. "We'll talk about it in the car. Carol, I mean Ms. Schwartz, is going to lock us out again." Nita attends a school so progressive it believes in old-fashioned discipline, not canings but strict Kantian ethics reinforced by group discussion. If children are late in the morning, they and their parent must wait in the school office until the next activity begins. Then, child and parent are asked, by one or another seven-year-old, to consider the impact of their behavior on the class as a whole. Jon, Mr. Can't-Mind-the-Clock, finds himself in the surprising position of beseeching second-graders through a locked door, while all fourteen of them and their teacher listen unsympathetically to excuses about car batteries and traffic. It is an effective behavioral modification tool, Peter thinks. He should have employed it himself on Jon, years ago. Nita hasn't been late in almost two weeks.

"She's got a point," Peter says, when Nita is upstairs with Voltaire, getting her extensive library of schoolbooks together.

"You don't want Sam to come here?"

"Jon," Peter says, standing beside his chair. "Are you asking me if I want to have another baby?" It's been so many years the men have almost forgotten the difficulty of their position, fresh once again. They had never intended to become urban parents of two.

"Come here," Jon says, pulling Peter onto his lap. "Do you want to have another baby?" Then comes the persuasive kiss, not coercive, lightly loving, as if to say, *Who can refuse me anything?* But Peter holds back.

"I don't know," he tells Jon. "I really don't. It's been a long time since we've had a baby in the house."

"It will be good for Nita to have a bro—"

"That's true," Peter says, kissing Jon this time, to forestall the reasonableness, the good son, good brother, good father reasonableness. "But do I want to raise another child? I don't know." Nita comes banging down the stairs, Voltaire a step ahead, his ears pointed backwards above the place on both sides of his forehead where the skin shows through, as if the cat, like the other males in the house, had a receding hairline.

"We don't have much time."

"I won't be pushed into this," Peter says. "I mean it." Jon looks at him and sighs.

Framers

SEAN HARPER pulls up in his powerful little car and toots the horn. Bailey works his long legs into the passenger side and closes the door. "What's the program?" Bailey asks.

"Weed, tunes," Sean tells him. "Dana's in Paris." He dodges traffic to Rock Creek Parkway, races along, working the gearshift. The top is down. Sean's graying hair is blown back along his temples. Very like Sean to call on a Thursday when Bailey is about to bed down. *Ready?* he asked on the phone, as if he and Bailey had a plan. *Sure*, Bailey replied. They reach Lulu's in the middle of the first set and take the only table left, too close to the stage and in front of a trombone. Sean's cigars are laced with pot. They drink scotch.

"So what do you think of Louisa Robbins?" Sean asks during the break. "I talked to her a few times last year, when she was a prisoner in my course." Sean and Bailey have been friends since college. Caroline met Dana when Dana ran for but didn't quite make City Council, before she went to business school. It was Caroline's idea to introduce Dana and Sean. They married. Now Dana keeps tabs on Bailey.

"Western, no nonsense," Bailey tells Sean. "She liked your class."

"She did journalism out West. Tendency to close down questions a little quickly." Then the tune overpowers the conversation. By the time the next long number ends, Bailey has a pronounced buzz on. "What's new at the office?" Sean asks.

"Couple of gay men trying to get the feds to recognize their marriage."

"Here, here," Sean says, raising his glass. "About time. What's it turn on?"

"Income tax," Bailey tells him. Sean chuckles.

"Nice." Law for Sean is theater. "Lovers against tax collectors. Family-values gays versus Bible-thumping accountants. Caroline's going to hate missing this one." Back in the old days, Caroline and Sean helped each other think and write. "When I'm king," Sean says now, "I'm going to make a few changes. First, this advocacy idea. Not always useful. The premise that if gay marriage gains, straight marriage loses, as if the whole thing is a football game—this is not helping. I blame many of this country's sillier disputes on advocacy."

"What's second?" Bailey asks. But the band is playing the next number. Sean and Bailey leave at two and walk through the neighborhood. In the cloudy night, Georgetown looks colonial. Cobbled streets, brick houses on a scale for short people in short beds.

"Second is this business about the framers," Sean says. "I love it, God knows I do. Let's base our justice system on what a collection of wig-wearing, slave-owning, Rousseau wannabes may or may not have thought, based on their quill scribblings on pieces of leather. Makes Borges's wildest invented universe seem like Tarrytown, New York. But when you come up against a real question, whether Rob can marry Steve, and you've got think tanks full of earnest traditionalists carrying on about how marriage is the union of boy and girl because the framers said so in 1787, the whole thing gets a little twisted. Imagine," Sean says, stopping and turning to Bailey, "we're talking about house framers instead of constitution framers. Imagine we can only live in buildings that the framers of those houses either built, thought about building, or thought somebody should build. Now you want to put up the new East Wing of the National Gallery. Your job is to prove that the framers of that house" — Sean points out a particularly lovely house — "had in mind that someday someone would build a place with no right angles. Or," Sean says, walking again, "your job is to assert, with a straight face, that the framer wouldn't have liked the East Wing at all. That is where this constitutional reverence gets funky. When I'm king, I'm going to put the brakes on it. Run for it," he adds, turning and heading off toward the car. The sky has just opened up.

Rain

THAT SHORT NIGHT Bailey dreams of Caroline. The rain continues long after Sean has dropped him off and roared away. In bed, eyelids fluttering, Bailey attends the coo and purr of the copper gutters of his O Street house. Rain has been his lullaby here since he and Caroline moved in the year they were married. Now Bailey rocks himself in his dream, watches leaves shimmying on New Hampshire birches. He is on his way back to Dartmouth, parted from Washington six weeks after meeting Caroline.

There. On the men's staircase at the Press Club. The speaker drones on in the hall above. Caroline is leaving early, Bailey arriving late. She's already a working woman, scouting from the landing with her air of a safari leader, square shoulders, elbows warning all comers. Warning Bailey, a summer intern, a college kid, to step to the banister. Through forty-five years, Bailey looks into her eyes as he makes his way upstairs to hear the speech about whatever it was. He just asks Caroline if what's-his-name has said anything of interest. Caroline says, no, nothing of interest.

For days, Bailey scrutinizes that stairwell moment, reenacting both parts with inflection and gesture. Studies his heart competently. Makes inquiries among friends. Begins to lecture everyone he knows on the subject of Caroline Taylor, journalist. He speaks of her confidently. He hasn't had another word with her. His analyses are his only solace. She's engaged, he's found out. She's twenty-six, an older woman. She will not answer his calls. He goes back to Dartmouth. He writes letters, these, too, unanswered.

Bailey crosses his arms on his sleeping chest. Sighs Elizabethan perplexity to the spring night. He had all but given up hope, he broods beneath the rain, a story above O Street. At home in February he runs into Caroline and her fiancé in the doorway of a bar. The situation is worse than he has pessimistically calculated. The fiancé is handsome in love, prosperous, unruffled by challenge. State Department. He is almost kind to the college boy who greets Caroline with his heart on his sleeve. Caroline, too, is merciful. Have the letters touched her? Bailey wanders wet-footed through melting snow, one among the throng of Caroline's soon-to-be-forgotten suitors. He courts Caroline by phone until the end of his break. She goes out with him once, to a movie. Pity? She kisses him at the door of her building. From his New Hampshire dormitory, Bailey writes to her each midnight—journal, love poem, weather. Willingness to become hers at a whistle.

He does not come to Washington for the summer. Her wedding is in July, by which time he is in the White Mountains, wielding a chain saw. Each windstorm provides a month of work. He writes her from his tent, sends and receives mail once a week. As June turns into July, Bailey, eating dried food, smelling of gasoline and wood smoke, feels his heart dry and crack open. Fire danger is moderate around him, high within. Caroline has mysteriously passed from the state of being engaged to that of being nearly married. He composes one last letter for the collection he imagines accumulating beneath

Caroline's bed. *Goodbye*, his hand insists. *I will always love you.*

Weeks pass. Bailey cuts and hauls like one of the damned. He understands that he is aging at a terrible pace for one just finishing college. Suddenly he comprehends the way an unfulfilled life passes, knows why he has seen on even the faces of young, unmarried men a narrow insistence that all is well. Caroline arrives on the fifth dawn before her wedding day. She has hitched a ride from Boston, hiked the last three miles with a map from the trail maintenance office. In the first light, when he hears her ripping open the entrance to his tent, Bailey thinks she's a bear. *Go ahead*, he murmurs. *Eat me.* Caroline pushes into the tent. *What?* she asks. She strips off her clothes in the cool morning. *Do you want me?* she demands. *Or did you just want to write letters?*

Now, stoned, asleep, Bailey's laughter spills across the swell of his bedding. She chose him, a boy. For more than three decades he became the man Caroline saw in him. Then she left and he turned back into a boy again.

He lifts his head from his pillow, reaches up to her. "I want you," he tells naked, twenty-seven-year-old Caroline.

No, After *You*

LOUISA LIES IN BED, trying not to feel undeserving. Bailey's footsteps recede. She knows he has left her coffee on the small table outside the door of her area. For the first six days she lived in the Dupont house, she managed to make her way downstairs, start coffee, and set the table for breakfast. She laid out the everyday china, a creamy white set with ivy leaves around the rim, and the silverware, silver, heavy, slightly too big for the hand. Polished, along with the rest of the house, on Mondays and Thursdays by Ethel and Becca, the seventy-something-year-old cleaning woman and her middle-aged daughter. This, too, makes Louisa feel like a slacker. She lies in the crisp sheets, looks across the room at the dusted windowsill and into the standing wardrobe, where the women have arranged her shoes.

For six days Louisa set the table, poured orange juice, placed Bailey's toast in the toaster in the pantry, took out the butter, then went back up to bed and crashed for as long as she could, before rushing out of the house late as always. On the seventh day she rested until seven-fifteen or so, and it was then that she hard Bailey's footsteps in the hall, the quiet clink as he set a tray with a red-plaid thermos beside the Friends of the National Zoo mug, sugar bowl, and spoon on the little telephone table. Later that day Bailey assured Louisa he didn't need her to prepare breakfast, that she could check his metabolism just as easily by noting whether or not he brought her coffee—"black, sugar, isn't it?"—each day. Fine, Louisa tells herself, let Bailey take care of *her* if that's what makes him happy. *The rich*, her mother always said, and anyone who breeds dogs knows the rich, *are not odder than the rest of us. They just have more time for it.* So Louisa isn't going to worry about the coffee any more than she will worry about the rent she would be spending on a share were she not Bailey's housemate.

Yet, as Bailey's footsteps lightly depart, Louisa feels once again that she is taking advantage. Perhaps, she thinks, she can break the ice if, on this second Saturday, she actually sits down with Bailey. She will have to go to work in the afternoon, but she certainly doesn't intend to get there in the morning. She hits the bathroom, dresses. She finds Bailey reading the paper at the table in the pantry. He starts to rise, as if she is his guest. He thinks better of it, sits down, only to pop up again.

"I made eggs. I didn't know if you would like a couple. How do you—"

"I don't want any eggs. I mean, no thank you. I'll make my own, if I want any," Louisa says, wondering why everything is so awkward, and why she sounds rude, when all she wants is for Bailey not to put himself out.

"Fine," Bailey says, sitting again. "Paper? I've just about finished—"

"No. Thanks. Maybe I will scramble an egg or two."

"How about an English muffin? I'll make myself another one."

"Listen," Louisa says, wincing at her tone. "Can I say something?" Bailey nods emphatically. "I think I need to just sit down and drink my coffee. Then maybe I'll think about breakfast. Also, please don't take your paper apart. I don't want to mess up your routine. Just pretend I'm not here." Bailey's face falls.

"I'm sorry. I didn't mean to be a bother." He sits and plays with his wedding band for a minute, turning it, then reads. Louisa feels worse than ever. *This isn't going to work*, she thinks.

But then it does start to work. Louisa scrambles three eggs the way she likes them, what most people would consider too dry. She toasts and butters her muffin and finds, of all things, huckleberry jam in the refrigerator.

"Huckleberry," she says, bringing her plate in. Bailey looks up brightly. "We have a big patch—well, it's on our neighbor's ranch, but we can pick there. We always have a day with my cousins, my dad's brother Alex, his wife, Lauren, and their kids. We make crumble, then jar the rest. We only end up with a couple jars, but it's a great day."

"I'm afraid I just buy mine," Bailey says.

"Delicious. Can I have the Metro section? Let's read," Louisa says. "Okay?" Bailey nods, again with a degree of enthusiasm that Louisa tries not to worry about. She feels better than before, though still a little bossy. She is bossy. Her brothers call her "Sarge," have since she was a girl and began issuing instructions to them. If only Bailey can learn to ignore her, or stand up to her, Louisa thinks she might be able to stay.

Motherhood

"MY EYES HURT," Valerie tells Jon. She sits up in bed at home on Decatur Street, holding Sam and a pacifier. The curtains are drawn against the afternoon light. "I don't sleep at all. I'm still sore. I don't know why I decided to have another kid," she says, "except that he's such an *angel.*"

Valerie, Jon thinks, listening to his sister, is no different from anyone else, except in degree. She says what she knows she's supposed to say, from having heard others. She didn't *decide to have another kid*. She just ended up pregnant.

"What can we do to make things easier?" Jon asks. He has always been Valerie's protector and helper. In grade school, when it became clear that she couldn't get along with other kids, he played with her for hours. When at twelve she first went to the mental hospital in Rockville, he visited her with Bailey and Caroline, brought her magazines and books, helped her keep up with schoolwork. He asked to have a separate line connected to his bedroom so Val could call him whenever she wanted. Bess, three years older than Jon and five years older than Val, never really let Val get in the way of her activities. Jon often wonders which of them, he or Bess, is more useful to Val. Bess, like Peter, provides Val with ordinary interaction, not *care*. Jon asks himself if he is unintentionally keeping Valerie in the role of disturbed sister, or if she just *is* the disturbed sister. One thing is sure—when Valerie couldn't raise Nita, it was Jon and Peter's job to take over. Bess didn't consider taking Nita in, and no one thought to ask her. Now Val has Sam, but for how long?

"I'd love to go out."

"Of course."

"How about tonight? Just to Nora's. We can bring Sam."

"I don't know, Sis. We've got to pick up Nita in a bit."

"Let Peter pick her up. I never get to see you." Jon comes on Wednesday evenings and Sunday afternoons, without fail. Sam nurses hungrily. When Val can concentrate, as now, she has what Peter calls *good baby hands*. Bailey's right, Valerie does look better. Maybe she will be able to keep Sam, with Lucy and Roberta's help, for a few months.

❋

Sam needs a bottle. Jon says he'll take care of that. He heads to the kitchen where Lucy chats with Peter. Lucy goes to sit with Valerie. Jon hands off Sam to Peter and makes up a bottle.

"We've got to take Sam out of here," Peter says. "Lucy is exhausted. Valerie was catatonic yesterday. Sam looks—"

"He looks fine," Jon says. Sam has managed to focus for a moment on Jon's face and is making funny shapes with his lips.

"How can we leave him here?" Peter asks. "Babies need connection. They need consistency."

"Val's doing pretty well," Jon says wearily. "Lucy and Roberta are here."

"So we just go on like this?" Peter asks. Jon pauses in the middle of counting out scoops of formula.

"Look," Jon says. "There's something to be said, don't you think, for Sam spending a little time with Val? As much as possible, with Roberta and Lucy right here?"

"Sure," Peter answers. Jon sets the bottle in a saucepan of

47

warm water. Sam, on Peter's lap, lip-synchs to a song only he can hear, while pumping his right arm up and down to the beat. "I just don't think this makes sense."

"I can see why you wouldn't," Jon says. "For one thing, Val's not your sister. For another, you're going to end up with this boy one of these days. But you don't know when, and that's wearing you out. For another thing, we haven't really decided if we're going to raise him. It's bad enough that we, that I, take for granted you will be Sam's daddy. It's even worse that I'm putting you on hold like this. But what can I do?"

"Jon. I don't know if I can handle this." Jon hugs Peter, on the side where Sam isn't. Peter weeps silently. Sam wiggles. "It's okay when I'm not here," Peter says. "I pretend Sam's all right. But when I'm here and I see what he's getting, and not getting, and I know we're going to leave in half an hour, I can't pretend."

"Roberta and Lucy are excellent. We should all have been raised by Roberta and Lucy."

"Sam needs us, Jon. He needs me."

"Yes. He does."

Let No Man Put Asunder

"LASKIN ROBBED a bank. He needs to go away for a long time."

"Wally, there's no call for that."

"He told the teller he was going to start killing people if she didn't hurry up. I call that an express threat." The eleven judges of the DC Circuit meet informally every other month to plan the docket. Bob Lipscomb, chief judge, runs the meetings, at which he decides which three judges will hear, and which one of these three will preside, over oral arguments of upcoming cases. Technically, the cases are assigned randomly. But the judges like to have a say, letting Lipscomb know about conflicts of interest that would make them recuse themselves or putting in bids for cases they know about from ruling on motions.

"Well, I want him," Wally declares. "My clerks have clocked time on this." Wally's favorite trick is to sic his clerks on a case he wants but that hasn't yet been assigned. Then if Bob doesn't give it to him, the clerks' time and taxpayers' money is wasted. The court doesn't get many cases about a fellow who actually walked into a bank and asked for stacks of fifties and hundreds. His attorneys are appealing the terms of his sentence, the district court having sentenced Laskin to sixty-four months' incarceration and three years' parole. Laskin contends the district court erred by applying a two-level enhancement when the evidence failed to show an express threat of death, and by failing to consider the accused's ability to pay before ordering restitution. Wally likes this sort of thing better than several of the other offerings, one involving misrepresentation of hard money in a congressional election, another the expansion of a cable company into telephony.

"Oh, what the hell," chimes in Reg. "Let Wally have Laskin. If he wants him that badly, why should the rest of us miss lunch?"

"A couple of doubles is not lunch," murmurs Maurice, who was to preside on Laskin before Wally started yelling for him. "I'm not going to let Wally bully Bob again."

"I'm just trying to be useful," Wally says. "I've only got a year or two left. By the way, I'd like the name of your cardiologist, Mo."

"Cut the violins," Maurice answers. "You don't need a cardiologist. You need common sense." The conference room looks like a corporate boardroom crossed with a museum. The judges at the long table are surrounded on three sides by busts of their predecessors, who gaze outward in perpetual, stony disapproval from their pedestals. The table reflects the current generation's necks and shoulders, puny and pale in the modern overhead light.

"You haven't said a thing, Dick."

"I'm waiting for my robber baron."

"Foerster is no robber baron," Reg says. "He's just a cable contractor who wants to start a phone company."

"Phones today, the world tomorrow. From what I read, in ten years you're not going to be able to wipe your ass without broadband."

"Wally," Bob tries again. "There really is no call for that kind of language."

"Whatever happened to the benevolent monopolies of our youth?" Mark asks, his dreamy tenor reverberating off the high ceiling.

"Black phones with dials," Dick echoes him. "Operators with the enunciation of schoolteachers. Exchanges with words at the beginning. Technology with a human face."

"While Dick's on memory lane," Jerry says, rising, "I'm going to go play nine holes."

"Sit down, Jerry," Patty says. He sits. "Let's focus on the docket, please." Of the eleven judges in their padded chairs, Patty is the only woman. Twenty-two years younger than Bailey, nine younger than Bob, Patty arbitrates. She cuts short the men's feuds and, with the slightest changes of expression, regulates their grossest improprieties. Bailey, in conversation with Max and Eve, calls Patty "Civilization." *Civilization held the barbarians at the gates,* he'll say. *Civilization is teaching Marty to think.* Bob gives Laskin to Maurice, Reg, and Dick. Bob hasn't stood up to Wally in some time. He hurries to the next matter, the most important, *Love and Wilson v. United States.*

"Are we really going to pass this one upstairs?" Wally asks. In the silence, Harmon, unmarried, perhaps gay, but private to the point of mystery, keeps his eyes on the papers in front of him.

"There are challenges pending in Connecticut, Wisconsin, and Florida," Bailey reports.

"That may be. But a couple of boys exchanging rings in a sweat lodge is not holy matrimony."

"That's enough, Wally."

"I'll take the case," Bailey says to Bob. "I heard *Radnor.* I'm up on contested status."

"That you are," Wally says. "How's your son?" Thick silence. Patty turns to Wally, but this time, Wally does not immediately yield to her. "Bob, you're not honestly going to let Bailey hear this case. Hell, why not let me have the next Brady challenge?" Several judges allow themselves a brief chuckle. Walter is NRA.

"I believe you heard *Duffy* in eighty-four," Bailey counters.

"My God, Bailey, you've got a memory like my wife," Wally thunders. "What the hell does *Duffy* have to do with this travesty?" Harmon lifts his eyes from the papers in front of him.

"Your daughter was divorcing at the time," Bailey quietly observes.

"I almost shot that son of a bitch," Wally says. "Imagine that he could contest, after what he did to her." Wally's hoarse voice trails off. His eyes fill with tears. Bailey speaks in the same steady tone.

"You didn't recuse yourself, even though *Duffy* turned on" —Bailey hesitates—"domestic violence."

"No." Wally looks chastened. He sighs and runs his hand through his thinning hair. "I didn't."

"Let's go ahead on this, Bob," Patty suggests.

"Bailey will preside," Bob says. "Patty and Marty will hear." Wally opens his mouth and leans forward. Harmon, directly across from him, looks Wally in the eye. Wally closes his mouth and settles back in his chair.

Will You Marry Me?

"OOPS," Max says. Red wine splatters his faded beige cords below the knee. He stoops to pick up pieces of broken glass and cuts his thumb. "Ouch."

Eve pulls him to his feet. She rinses his cut under cold water. She improvises a dustpan out of newspaper and collects glass, using another section of paper as a broom. Max sops up the wine with a dish cloth.

"I have a broom," he says.

"Don't."

"What?" Max asks, smiling beatifically. He wipes his bleeding finger across his shirt.

"Don't get blood on your shirt," Eve says, her tone revealing just a hint of the ocean of irritation and despair she feels. "Put on a Band-Aid."

"Don't have one, Cupcake," Max says. "But I've got paper towels and scotch tape." Max searches his cupboards. His finger dots blood on everything he touches—canned soup, coffee filters, a stack of stoneware plates, a pack of bendable drinking straws, a cracker box. Max's cupboards betray no arrangement or pattern. Food and dishes occupy the same shelves. In the cabinet on the other side of the refrigerator are a partial stack of more stoneware, an open loaf of pumpernickel, a jar of pistachios, sake cups.

"Okay, then toilet paper and masking tape," Max says. He steps on a fragment of glass, which splinters. Again, he beams at Eve, then shuffles across the dining room. Eve slides to the floor, far from the wine pool, her back against the refrigerator. Max's feet, in their winey Wallabees, leave faint prints. A breeze and the growl of a motorcycle reach Eve from the window open to Biltmore Street. A cool end-of-April night, a night for sleeping under the comforter in her own quiet apartment. She tries to grapple with the simple truth that she must give up her solo existence and try, soon, to create a baby-safe house with Max. Max is a one-man hazard zone. She rests her head against the refrigerator. Who organizes cabinets without separating food and dishes? Who shuffles through life, smiling mysteriously, leaving tracks? Who wears Wallabees in this decade? Max.

Dr. Alice Shapiro, Eve's therapist, asked Eve only yesterday if Max made Eve feel that she would have to be the adult in the relationship, that Max was in some way childish, and if that was the underlying source of Eve's anxiety about marriage and parenthood. *Of course that's what scares me*, Eve snapped. *Max is a baby himself. How can I have a baby with a baby? Well,* Alice continued placidly, neither the nearly silent nor the easily intimidated type, *what exactly is it that you expect from Max? Help,* Eve told Alice. *The making of things easier. Money. Understanding. Structure.* Eve free-associated herself into a fairly tight corner. *He gives you many things you have talked about,* Alice suggested, *and other things. Friendship, laughter. Security.* Eve was of course crying. She has been crying for almost a year now, ever since she graduated from sitting in the chair to lying on the couch. That's all right, because crying makes her feel she's getting somewhere. But since her pregnancy, she's been crying *outside* of Alice's office almost as easily as during her hours. Is this progress? Is this what she's paying for?

"Mr. Brawny!" Max declares. He drops the tangle of toilet paper onto a dining room chair and grabs a three-pack of paper towels from on top of the television. "Mr. Brawny was hiding. I adore the Brawny man. He's expensive, but I must have him. He's the Marlboro man without the tobacco. He's Mr. Clean without the body shave. Dumpling, you two must be starving," he tells Eve. "No more delays. I'll have you and Imogen fed before the next cell division. That's a promise."

Eve is always hungry and nauseated. She used to think these states were mutually exclusive. She is not acutely ill in the morning, just punk all day long. Max helps her stand up. He kisses her tenderly. Slowly Eve's sense of hopelessness evaporates. Max assumes their baby is a girl and calls her Imogen. Eve also "knows" her baby is a girl but refuses to accept this as more than a guess. Why a girl? Why Imogen? *Why not?* Max counters, almost every day. Imogen for a girl, Eugene in the unlikely instance of a boy. Either way, Gene at home. Imogen and Eugene are both good dress-up names. As in, *This year's Nobel Prize is awarded to Imogen (or Eugene) Broido-Rosen for her (or his) outstanding contribution to astrophysics.*

Eve lets Max escort her the three steps to the dining room table he inherited from his roommate, Zeke, before Zeke married Angela and moved out. The table has not fared well under Max's care, the varnished surface scratched, ringed. Eve thinks of her own beautiful mahogany table, once her grandmother's. Eve will have Max's baby. But does she have to live with him? For one thing, she doesn't want to leave her elegant apartment on New Hampshire. The place is way too small for a male presence, with or without a baby presence. She loves the apartment, which is her own in a way that no other home has been. She chose it and everything in it. The storage space is perfect for one, inadequate for two or three.

Eve tries to imagine a bassinet by this bed, a changing table next to her desk. This is as difficult as picturing herself in a few months, her belly taut and round, with that brown stripe from navel to crotch, above swollen ankles. But she does picture an old cradle, one she saw at an antique store in Manassas. What Eve cannot imagine is Max's Wallabees in her closet beside her Kenneth Coles. His threadbare slacks beside her black and gray wool from Saks and Bendels. No.

Max serves lasagna noodles with clam sauce he makes from a can of clams and one of peeled plum tomatoes. Why not either a white sauce or a red sauce? Why not linguini or corkscrew pasta? The same qualities of mind that serve Max so well in Bailey's chambers—his instinct for new territory, his fearless ability to improvise—are liabilities in the kitchen. He combines whatever is at hand. His dishes are collections of found objects. He does not consult cookbooks before setting oven temperatures. He has a mad scientist's notion of nutrition, although Eve must admit that this is now often curiously in accord with her own cravings for unusual combinations of foods. Max brings in the pumpernickel, sets out Eve's lemon seltzer, pours himself another glass of wine, and settles beside her.

"Eat," he urges. But when Eve reaches for her fork, she can't find it because she can't see through her tears. How is she going to live with a man who makes everything up as he goes along? "Happy or sad?" Max asks, placing the fork in her fingers. "Or we-don't-know?"

"Frightened," Eve manages.

"Tell Max," Max says. "But first, you and Imogen have a few bites."

Eve's head points to the bottom left corner of Max's bed. A tangled sheet loosely wraps her hips. Holding her, Max sleeps, his arms and belly a circle of warmth in which Eve resides. She always preferred lean muscular men, men of linear résumés, cogent remarks, and understated ties. She cannot at the moment remember their names. Max's round belly complements the curve of her consciousness, in which two ideas float lazily—first, that she can't get pregnant because she's already pregnant, and second, that she likes it here in Max's randomized house. Clothes and books loom in the light through the closet slats, along with a briefcase and a pile of papers. Max and Eve like to view each other in a romantic glow of the closet light when they make love. Eve is afraid to leave a candle burning, lest they fall asleep and burn up. She has a fear of open flames, even a candle on a plate, far from fabric. Max understands. Max accommodates. Max's plants are a rain forest beneath the open window, the hibiscus highest, its yellow blooms open over the middle canopy, where orchids float like blue flags on poles above a ground cover of fuzzy purple violets. Max is a good fairy to flora. Max's friends all bring their suffering, downtrodden plants. Max dries out soggy root systems in his botanical Betty Ford, welcomes masses of yellowed leaves, greens them, and usually gives them a permanent home.

Eve wakes him now by kissing. Another peculiarity of Max is that he awakens in good humor, if anything better than the humor in which he falls asleep. "I was wondering if you could get me some water," Eve asks, and when Max starts to rise, she stops him. "Not yet." The bed is king-size. In the night, making love, sleeping, Eve and Max pivot together like the needle of a compass until the furled sheet falls from them. Now, under the influence of Max's caresses, Eve is soon on the verge of something—not another orgasm. She doesn't come twice in one night except during the week after her period, and it's been a long time since her period. That's when she feels a hot, wet ring slide onto her ring finger. In the closet light she sees a band of gold inset with a solitaire in a platinum bezel. There is a wide open ring box on Max's chest beneath her. He is a tricky man.

"Will you marry me?" Max asks.

"Yes," Eve tells him. Then she's coming, and bringing gentle Max with her.

MAY

Planet Sam

"Excuse me," Peter says. "Can *I* scream now?" But nobody hears him. Nita's hiking boots pound the stairs and then her door slams. Sam laments in the front room, needing what? Not a diaper, not a bottle. Burp? Another circuit of the house on Peter's chest? Jon's soft knock on Nita's door is met with "Go away!" and desperate sobs. So Nita's not happy about Sam's unexpected arrival five days before, Roberta having called on Wednesday at six in the morning to say that Valerie was "speeding up," that she and Lucy would have their hands full with the mother that day without having to worry about baby Sam. Since then, Sam occupies the room that just two weeks before was Nita's. Nothing has been taken from her, neither her book at bedtime, nor her wake-up rubs and kisses, nor her input into what she wants for weekend breakfasts or school lunches. Nothing in Nita's routine has changed, yet all is altered.

Peter is tired. He doesn't have the energy to indulge Nita when, for instance, two minutes ago, she didn't like any of his suggestions for how she might spend her Sunday. Peter sticks to the rules—Nita must come up with a plan for lunch that doesn't involve going to Andrei's house for mini-pizzas. Peter walks Sam around and around. How did the kid get so motion-dependent? Must have been Roberta, carrying Sam all around Valerie's house when she was on night duty during his first three months. Peter circles from front room to den, kitchen, Jon's office, living room, front hall, as he has maybe fifty times in the last twenty-four hours, singing, "Inchworm," "Baa Baa Black Sheep," "The Farmer in the Dell," "Twinkle, Twinkle, Little Star," and best of the Beatles. Peter's standards have all been reissued for Sam. Nita doesn't like hearing Peter sing *her* songs to *him*, as she still calls Sam when she's angry. Several times since Sam arrived, Peter has let Nita give Sam part of a bottle, Sam on Nita's lap, Nita sitting on the floor, Peter close by. Nita's hugs are too hard, her kisses like surprise attacks when Sam is dropping off to sleep. When Peter calls Nita on this, her protestations are so unconvincing that Peter must force himself not to frown judgmentally, but instead to explain, once more, how delicate Sam is.

The novel? *Oh, that,* Peter has thought once or twice an hour for the entire five days, while driving to pick up Nita, Sam strapped into his car pod in the back seat, while getting break-fast, lunch, or dinner on the table, while doing another load of laundry. *The novel,* he has thought while taking a hurried crap before everybody wakes in the morning, while reading a page, the same page as the day before, of someone else's book. The thing about novels, Peter often says in his own head, where most of his adult conversations take place since Sam arrived in Jon's arms and Valerie started back on stronger meds — the thing about novels is they require steady application. They're not hard to write, in the sense that if one manages a thousand words a day (four manuscript pages, an hour on a good day, three hours on a terrible day) for a hundred days, one has a medium-length novel. The trick is to produce four pages that bear some relationship to the previous and successive four.

The trick is to end up with a sheaf of pages which are *about* something—interconnected lives, a coherent plot, distinct characters. Many parts of the novel-making process, such as editing passages, outlining upcoming chapters, and reading factual background, can be undertaken in ten-minute intervals snatched in the middle of the day, while Sam naps and Nita is at school. But there remains one aspect of the writing process that requires longer intervals of concentration, two hours, say, when one is rested, not hungry, not worried about what is happening down the hall or across town. This is composition, the making of shit up. The filling of the blank screen with winking new words, unexpected even to the author, that add up to a new scene, the filling out of a character, the elaboration of an idea. The last time Peter wrote a brand-new paragraph was the day before Sam arrived. Go figure.

Peter hoists the quavery voiced, self-winding Sam higher on his shoulder and walks him one more lap. Sam's lament tapers off as Peter heads from the living room through the arched doorway into the entrance hall, with its unseasonably laden coat tree, its framed but legally meaningless marriage contract, its family photos, and its last-chance-on-the-way-out-the-door mirror. He and Sam continue into the front room, with Jon's cluttered desk, Nita's low drawing table, the love seat with the squashed cushions, the coffee table buried under periodicals, the TV, and Voltaire's tattered scratching post. On the straightaway from den through kitchen, Sam stops crying. Voltaire's tag, like Tinkerbell's invisible note, can suddenly be heard as the cat trots upstairs. Sam smacks his lips and looks nearsightedly up at Peter, like a drunk waking up after a bender. *Where am I? What was all that noise?* Upstairs, Jon's super-reasonable voice coaxes Nita.

"What happened?" Jon asks.

"Nothing," Nita answers.

"Why did the baby suddenly wake up and start to cry?"

"I don't know."

"What do you want to do this afternoon?"

"Nothing."

"Do you want to go grocery shopping with me?"

"No," Nita says.

"What's Andrei doing?"

"I don't care."

"Let's call and find out."

"No."

Peter misses his novel. Sometimes he visits it late at night, flipping on the computer and wincing at the machine's little noises, though they are not loud enough to wake Sam. The novel looks like it could use a little more love and affection. Peter feels he should visit each day, including—no, especially—government holidays and weekends. *You said you'd come see me*, the novel whispers. So, during naptime, Peter manages a hurried half-hour. He fixes a word here, moves a paragraph there. Then over the baby monitor he hears Sam making I'm-about-to-cry noises. Hurriedly, Peter backs up the few new bytes he has managed to produce. *I'll be fine*, the novel says with false cheer as Peter leaves. *Sam needs you. Later, you'll have more time*, the novel insists. The novel is manipulative.

In Peter's arms, Sam blows bubbles and looks profoundly thoughtful. Peter has settled himself cautiously into an armchair in the den. Sam is a philosopher and a grunter. "*Grr um tfft*," Sam says. He is working out a theory of everything, Peter is sure. About the third day after Sam's arrival, Peter realized he was entirely taken up with him. He sees Sam whenever they are apart. He listens for Sam with or without the monitor. He mentally charts Sam's intake and output. Peter has also begun to adopt Gruntspeak, and not only to Sam. Friday morning Jon reminded Peter about a tune-up appointment for the Saab and Peter answered with a few grunting syllables. "What?" Jon asked. Peter elaborated with some exasperation that he would take the car in if the shop promised to have it back that evening.

Having a new baby is similar to falling in love. One's entire consciousness is taken over. There is little room for any business unconnected to the baby. The days and nights are taken up with baby care, or simply baby adoration. Time becomes fuzzy. Mornings, afternoons pass in duty and contemplation. What has one accomplished? Everything, not much. *When I am hungry, thou shalt cease in whatever occupies you and come and feed me, even unto the second bottle. When I am awake, thou shalt bestir thyself, though darkness reigns upon the land. Thou shalt cavort and make merry with me, giving thyself over to jiggling and renditions of "Blackbird" from* The White Album. *Thou shalt carry me on high, though the people mock and pity thee. Thou shalt not envy thy spouse, though his job permitteth him to leave the house wearing natty clothing and to speak in complete sentences, other than Gruntspeak, to people who admire him. Thou shalt not covet his suit, unadorned with milk and drool, nor his wearing of lace-up shoes and a wristwatch.* Fatherhood is a country that no one else can see, not the friends who come for an hour of congratulatory ogling before skedaddling with just a hint of panic. Not one's parents, who don't remember having charge of an infant and who, one suspects, didn't actually parent in contemporary terms but rather ran something like a dorm in which one lived a life of quiet self-sufficiency.

Peter settles down onto the sofa looking out over the front yard. Sam blinks in the daylight. The front hedge needs trimming. A shopping bag is trapped, fluttering, in the dogwood. Nita's voice is softer now. She and Jon plan the day together, though Jon is still doing most of the talking. Peter can think of no one he would rather raise children with than Jon, yet the prospect of Sam staying is daunting. Not even Jon fully understands what Peter took on last week. Jon imagines that when he makes it home "early" at six-thirty, his self-esteem and batteries fully recharged, to "contribute," to "do his part," to let Peter "have a break"—Jon imagines that everything is fifty-fifty. Alas, one need only observe Jon at two last night, handing Sam to Peter and climbing the stairs to go back to sleep, to know this is not so. Peter and Sam are the sole permanent residents of Planet Sam, just as, seven years ago, he and Nita were the principal inhabitants of Nita Land. That's ironic in so many ways that Peter just shakes his head and leans back against the cushions, Sam warm on his chest.

"Ironic," he says to Sam. "In many ways." Peter tries not to fall entirely into Gruntspeak. He makes a point of using his ordinary speaking voice with Sam, as he did with Nita. He has a horror of shrill, false, Muppetlike delivery in parents. If he talks to Sam in a voice like a duck's, how will Sam learn to answer him like a person? "I always thought," he tells Sam now, "that I was doubly insured against just this sort of homemaker existence, first by being gay, then by being an artist. I figured as a queer I was unlikely to father a child, and not likely to adopt one, because, no offense, I just didn't want to. Plus"— Peter shakes his head and smiles, and Sam focuses directly on him for a moment before going back to gazing at imaginary beings flitting over Peter's head—"I had this idea that being an artist meant I was probably never going to have any money, but that I would have lots of time to work."

"*Gpvuj*," Sam says.

"Well, yes, I was young," Peter says. "And I hadn't met Jon." Peter struggles up from the chair and carries Sam out through the kitchen into the diminutive backyard. A weed whacker whizzes a lawn away. There's hammering from the renovation across the alley. Sam nose-breathes noisily and looks as far as he can to the left. Peter turns to accommodate him, but Sam still wants to see as far to the left as possible. It's as if there's a corner that keeps moving, around which Sam wants a view. When Peter came to DC to take his first and as it turned out only creative writing faculty position, he wanted to be single for a while, maybe a long while. Within a month, he met Jon. Jon was just the sort of man Peter hadn't been with before, a catch, ready to be serious, yes, to marry, but also willing to let Peter go, if that's what Peter wanted. Jon was the man Peter had been avoiding, intentionally or not: a well-adjusted intellectual, playful, trusting, and, as it turned out, loaded. Peter's bachelor days were over. "You see," he tells Sam, "now I have money and love, but not so much time."

He walks back inside and sets Sam in the bouncy chair. Sam's mauve eyelids flutter. His eyes are an opaque blue that cannot possibly remain. *Baby contact lenses*, Peter calls them. Nita appears, sniffling, at the head of the stairs, Jon behind her. When the pair reach the ground floor, Jon heaves Nita up onto his shoulder. She smiles reluctantly.

"Nita wants to call Andrei and teach him to play tennis."

"No, I don't."

"But first she wants to help make a picnic. She's very concerned that the sandwiches have enough mayonnaise, and that they be cut properly along the diagonal."

"I don't care." Nita, Peter remembers, was a squeaker, not a grunter. She emitted long, complicated squeaky noises, like the tires of cars in movie chase scenes.

"Where's Pooper?" Jon asks. Nita giggles.

"In his bouncy chair. He just fell asleep," Peter says, trying not to give Nita a warning look. "We'll just leave him be."

"Sure," Jon says. "Let's find some chips and cut the pickles, shall we?" He bends his knees to carry Nita into the kitchen, she leaning back like a limbo dancer. She smiles upside-down at Peter under the door frame.

Professional Confidence

LOUISA RETURNS to the Dupont house after nine, hauling her litigation bag, as wide as a pilot's flight bag, into the entrance hall. She carries her work shoes by the straps in her other hand. She is dressed for Arnold & Porter—pantyhose against the polar air conditioning, skirt suit, fake pearls. She commutes home in her running shoes, and the May evening has brought a sheen to her cheeks.

"Ice cream?" Bailey calls from the den. Louisa smiles. The awkwardness has passed. Turned out the first few weeks at the Dupont house were not unlike those at the firm. The tension had as much to do with newness as with anything else. Bailey is nice. He is lonely but not too lonely, and a most considerate housemate. She finds she counts on her minutes with him in the morning, and anticipates her longer conversations with him in the evening.

"You didn't finish the mocha?" she asks.

"No," he assures her. His chair creaks as he rises and heads for the freezer, where he keeps the bowls. He has a theory about cold bowls, which delay melting times. Louisa hears the hiss of aerosol whipped cream, which Bailey believes to be one of the world's significant technological advances, the clink of pecans on the cookie sheet for toasting, and the microwave warming the chocolate sauce. She runs up to her area, puts on shorts and a T-shirt, and pads barefoot down the cool wood stairs to the den. Her sundae awaits her. Also a tumbler of cold water.

"How's the factory?" Bailey asks.

"Still playing catch-up."

"What are you working on?"

"We've got to prepare our embezzler for trial," Louisa asks. "I can tell you, can't I? He won't come to your court. He's up in New York."

"What bank?" Bailey asks, waving his spoon reassuringly.

"Citi. Acts like he didn't do anything out of the ordinary. I met him today."

"How much did he sneak?"

"A million four. Says he knew he'd get caught."

"Course he did. The embezzler is a child trying to punish someone—a boss, a spouse. But they must get caught first." Louisa's line rings upstairs.

"Chris was supposed to call me at work." Bailey nods and reaches for her bowl so he can store it for her in the freezer. This will keep the ice cream from melting but will harden the chocolate sauce. The only way around it is to remove the chocolate sauce for reheating. "Not so fast." Louisa settles back in her chair, taking little bites, continuing to talk. "I waited. For him all. Afternoon he missed. His chance I'll talk. To him tomorrow. Tell me why. White-collar criminals want." She swallows. "To get caught."

"You mustn't divulge any of this to anybody et cetera," Bailey says. "Daniel Love and Thomas Wilson got married out in New Mexico two years ago. They came back to DC, where they live, and filed a joint tax return. The IRS said they weren't married in DC so they couldn't file jointly and had therefore underpaid."

"But I thought married people paid more than single people," Louisa says.

"Not if the discrepancy in their incomes is large enough," Bailey says. "The men paid the higher taxes, sued for a refund, and won in the district court. The IRS and DC appealed, and now we're going to hear it."

Louisa settles back in her easy chair and feels fortunate. It's not every woman not yet out of law school who has the opportunity to talk about a significant case with a federal judge, especially in the comfort of an elegant old townhouse. The pale walls and the neatly scrolled moldings reflect the golden lamplight. From the living room comes Glenn Miller's "Stardust." Bailey plays certain records every few days, actual LPs on a turntable with a delicately floating arm. Louisa's good fortune in landing here is only now, after a few weeks, becoming clear to her.

"I went to a wedding in Taos during the Great March," she says. "My best friend from college, Terry, and her lover, Wendy." Bailey nods. The Great Wedding March, so christened by the press, took place immediately following the New Mexico high court injunction requiring the issuance of licenses to same-sex couples wishing to marry and meeting all former criteria—age of majority, unmarried status, nonconsanguinity. In the first year about eight thousand couples, who had been waiting for just such an opportunity, flocked to the state to be legally joined. The second year the number was up to eleven thousand, with only nine thousand the third year. The fourth is still in progress, continuing the slow tapering trend.

"Aren't there lots of gay marriage–related cases coming up on appeal?" Louisa asks. "Wills, custody, inheritance, citizenship?"

"Yes," Bailey says. "But ours might be the one to reach the

Supreme Court first. This case has certain advantages."

"I thought the DC Council legalized gay marriage. I read about it just before I came out here."

"They did their best," Bailey says, his chin settling into his hand. "That's part of what might make *Love and Wilson* fly. Just after the New Mexico decision, the Council passed an act to accept New Mexico's and any future state's same-sex marriage licenses. They stopped short of calling for DC to start issuing its own. Then Congress reviewed the act and knocked it down, effectively barring gay marriage here. Still, it is unusually difficult for the IRS to claim that there is a *deeply held public belief* against same-sex marriage in a city whose representatives voted to accept it."

"These pecans are so sweet."

"Then there are the intangibles. At the time of the Court ruling against Virginia, sixteen states had laws prohibiting interracial marriages. Gay marriage has the same aura of permanence about it today. Prejudice codified as law always has this double quality, just before the sea change."

"Did Jon and Peter go to New Mexico?"

"Jon and Peter were married here years ago, not legally of course. They hold property in common, have named each other as beneficiaries. George Washington extends Jon's benefits to Peter. I suppose they'll get out to New Mexico one of these days. I keep warning them that the state referendum may end the March. They don't listen to me. They never have. That's usually for the best."

They talk on, Bailey explaining nuances of Full Faith and Credit and congressional authority. Louisa asks questions, feels insightful. Then she carries the ice cream bowls to the kitchen and rinses them in the deep, square sink. She passes back through the den.

"Good night," she tells Bailey.

"Good night." Ascending the staircase, Louisa thinks, *What a civilized man is Bailey Allard.*

71

Through a Glass, Darkly

"DARLING," Max tells Eve, "we're going to have a sea horse." Eve and Max are on the gynecology floor of the George Washington University Hospital. They look into the screen suspended over reclining Eve. The technician, Heather, runs the ultrasound monitor across the transparent goo spread on Eve's belly. The little creature moves suddenly, like a microorganism in a biology class film. It does look like a sea horse, the head equine, the body a paisley. "Dr. Davis," Max says when the obstetrician reenters the room. "There seems to be some confusion. We were planning to have a human child."

William Davis has almost enough time and patience to tolerate Max, but not quite. He explains that the budding limbs and large head-to-body ratio is perfectly normal. Eve doesn't listen. She studies the creature inside her, who looks a bit like Tessie, her grandmother on her father's side, after a trip to the salon. Something about the forehead and nose bud. Heather stops running the magic wand across Eve's belly. Eve asks her to do it again. Yes, there is her baby. That's what the fetus looks like to her: not a sea horse but a baby, with dramatic features and a rich internal life. Curled up in an introspective C, she or he looks like she's reading a book held between her, or his, fragile elbows. Tears spring to Eve's eyes. Max takes her hand.

"Max, look." Again Max and Eve watch the shifting, opalescent form, at once two-dimensional and full-bodied, talking to them in rapid semaphore. She or he is a witty creature, confident, humorous. Only a very brilliant, sweet girl or boy talks like this.

"Bunny," Max says, squeezing Eve's hand, "she's perfectly perfect. And we made her at home. You just grew her, in between throwing up and working. Now you've got her partying inside you. You're like her private Club Med—fun activities all day long, no bills till the end."

"Or he," Eve says, determined to keep their imaginings gender neutral. Either the nurse or the doctor could read the cursive shorthand of Imogen's or Eugene's anatomy, but Eve doesn't want to know. Max had a dream in which Imogen had already been born. He was holding her, looking into her eyes, and she was a girl. That settled it, as far as he was concerned. "Talk to her, Max. Tell her we want to meet her in person, but she should take her time, and not forgot to develop any of her parts. Or his." Max leans down and conveys all this to Imogen in an earnest whisper. Then he straightens up to talk to Eve.

"She says she's not going to rush things. She's just going to put one fin in front of the other." William and Heather have retreated as far as the small room allows. They prefer couples to be quietly moved, silently awed, and then to ask a few simple questions. Max and Eve are engaged in something closer to a séance. "May I wiggle the thing?" Max asks them, taking the transceiver from its stand and nudging it into the transparent gelatin on Eve's belly. "We don't have to put in another quarter, do we? We're Partners Plus." Heather hurries forward and takes the wand from Max.

"It doesn't hurt the baby to have those sound waves bounced off her?" Eve asks. "Or him?" William frowns. Eve, lying on the table, her blouse hiked up to her bra, her Liz Claiborne slacks, a tawny khaki, tucked down to her hips, watches the screen. Heather draws figure eights around her navel.

"No danger at all," William says in his mission-control voice. "The fetus can't hear this. Even if it could hear, ultrasound is not in the audible spectrum."

"Did I mention," Max asks William and Heather, "that I started Imogen on the Well-Tempered Clavier? She's going to be a conductor and composer, a pitcher for the Mets, and a labor organizer. Aren't you, my little chordate?" Max makes a clucking sound, eyes turned to the monitor mounted on a swinging arm above them. "Recapitulate phylogeny. That's a good girl." He places his hand on Heather's and moves the transceiver in enticing circles. Heather freezes, then continues.

"That tickles," Eve tells them. "Not so fast, Max. You don't have to trick her into pouncing. She's not a kitten. Or him." William removes Max's hand from Heather's. He makes a few summary statements about how everything is going well, mentioning the measurements of this and that, rhythms of fetal activity. He looks at his watch, asks if there are any questions, then leaves the room definitively. Heather grimly prints out images from the monitor.

"I wish we could send *her* a picture of *us*," Eve says, drying her tears with the back of Max's hand. "Or him." She takes the strip of black and gray pictures from Heather. "I bet she wonders what we look like. Or he does."

"Heather," Max says. "I know we told you not to tell us, but level with me. Imogen's a very little girl, isn't she?"

"You would have to ask Dr. Davis. Should I ask him to come back?" Heather asks, pressing her lips together.

"No," Eve says.

"All right," Max says. "Let's be scientific." He takes the transceiver, places it, and leans until his lips are almost kissing the goo. "Imogen. If you're a girl, wiggle yourself in a clockwise direction. If you're a boy, take this pen"—Max holds up a pen with his free hand—"out of my hand, float it across the room, and write *I have a penis* on the wall." He moves the transceiver over Eve. The image on the screen wiggles twice in no particular rotation. The pen remains in Max's hand. "We paint the nursery pink," Max announces. "I buy the Shetland pony."

❀

"What do y'all want for breakfast?" Max asks, steering Eve through the hospital door. He often refers to Eve as *y'all*, an allusion to both her plurality and her Southern roots.

"We all had breakfast at home. How about you buying us some lunch?"

"Whatever you folks hanker after. I told Bailey we'd mosey in when we felt good and ready." The day, which began coolish, is getting steamy. Max and Eve walk 22nd Street to the Brickskeller, technically not open yet. The manager gives them sodas and pretzels to nibble while they wait for the cook. They talk about *Love and Wilson*. Bailey is going to preside on the panel and Eve is writing the bench memo, which is an elaborate set of crib notes for Bailey so he'll know what's what before he hears oral arguments. Max is Eve's sounding board and editor. She's reading the briefs that have been filed by Love and Wilson, and by the government, which lost in the district court and is appealing. She's also reading the district court's decision.

"Brundage added up Hawaii, Alaska, Vermont, and New Mexico, and divided by four. It's a little cumbersome."

"Wait," Max says. "Let me do this. Hawaii was sex discrimination. Baehr and Dancel were discriminated against on gender since, had either been male, they both would have been granted a marriage license." Eve nods. "Vermont was equal protection for gay couples qua couples. The high court directed the legislature to give the couples either marriage or an equivalent status, with the benefits, protections, and responsibilities appertaining. To everyone's surprise, the legislature came up with civil union in a couple months. *Brause v. Alaska* decision"—Max pauses, sips his Coke—"said marriage is a fundamental right, denial of civil marriage licenses to same-sex couples is discrimination based on sex as in *Baehr v. Mike*, and therefore the government must show a compelling reason for withholding a civil marriage license from a gay couple."

"Correct," Eve says. She has finished the basket of pretzels and is blindly feeling around in it for strays. "New Mexico?" A waiter arrives, takes their orders, and brings them more pretzels.

"*Martin and Wesler v. New Mexico*. All I remember is the injunction," Max says. "Immediate issue of license, referendum or legislative directive be damned."

"The remedy was the big news. Actual marriage licenses to be issued forthwith. But equally of note was that the court took on *Bowers*, arguing that in New Mexico, sexual acts of consenting adults in the privacy of their own homes are not subject to scrutiny, and that therefore gay couples are indistinguishable on grounds of conduct."

"They went for the whole enchilada. Anybody ever figure out why?"

"Not really. McWhinney was no surprise. Beaumont was near retirement. Barsugli actually *is* gay. Not that that guaranteed anything."

"So I know it's too early to talk about this, but what should Bailey decide?"

"We don't want to lean too heavily on the best-interests-of-the-child argument is my feeling," Eve says. "That kind of policy can backfire. We've got to erase parenthood from the equation. I like Vermont, especially with monetary damages. That's all-American. Marriage is close enough to a fundamental right to be one. We'll go back to Douglas in *Griswold*."

"Eh," Max waves his hands. "You make it sound delicate. Equivocation makes everybody rambunctious. Look at integration of the armed forces. You have the Gillem Report in forty-five, and Forrestal backtracking in forty-eight. Nothing happens until after Korea, when Truman tells everybody,

'Look, these are the rules, all colors of people get to be commanding officers, no separate showers or barracks, live with it.' The delicate stuff goes away. What's delicate is when power is ambiguously withheld. No one's sure whether they're in charge or resisting. Tell people they don't have the option of telling other people who they can love and marry, and they'll mind their own business."

"Hawaii high court reversed, after the referendum. Also, you've got Denmark, Sweden, Norway with domestic partnership but no right to adopt."

"Scandinavia's a special case. It's dark half the year. My sense is they're tolerant during the sunny months, but when they're trapped inside all winter they get the shack nasties. Vitamin-D-deficient tolerant people act differently than confused intolerant people, which is what we have here."

"People weren't sun-deprived in Hawaii. They still voted down gay marriage."

"That's archipelago-type intolerance," says Max vaguely. "I still don't think we can go with fiscal inequity. We make it all about money and taxes, and people will miss the point. Marriage is about love and freedom."

"Onions," Eve says, sniffing. Onions are cooking in back. "Bailey will probably have a few ideas about what kind of opinion to write."

"Granted," Max says. "Bailey's pretty lively, for a judge." The waiter opens blinds and adjusts tables. He and Eve do some smiling at each other.

"When's your baby coming?" the waiter asks. He turns out to be Irish.

"September," Eve says. She pulls the strip of ultrasound images from her purse. The waiter studies them.

"Fine-looking girl," he tells the two of them, then moves more tables around.

"Told you so," Max says.

Bigfoot

"WAIT," Dee says. "What do you want to cut all that off for?"

"Vectoring," Kelley tells Dee and Louisa, who are setting the table and arranging the bagels Louisa brought over. "Focuses the plant's energies."

"It's a squash, Lamb. Not a bonsai."

"Same principle, shorter season," Kelley tells her. He turns back to the garden and resumes nipping. The land behind the Reservoir Road house teems with dusty green abundance. Louisa was pleased when Dee called and invited her over to meet Kelley, eat, and read the Sunday paper. The night Louisa and Dee had met, Dee had said they should get together. But then a few weeks passed and Louisa had begun to think Dee was too disorganized to become a new friend. Turns out Dee had been in Maine at a women's sailing course.

"Kelley is this new kind of farmer: part futurist, part Luddite," Dee says. "He picked up all these books on ecosystem transformation and alien species introduction at Reiter's and Pathfinder Books. He's been doing radical shit to his sister's garden since we got here. How's it going with Bailey?"

"I like it," Louisa tells her. "I felt like a bitch at first because Bailey's so polite. It was like living with Cary Grant. I got over it."

"I remember when I was in my impossible teens," Dee says. "Bailey was so understanding, even when I did really stupid and mean stuff. I finally just gave up trying to rebel against him and let him help me rebel against my folks. For instance, I took my boyfriends to his house when he was at work. I lost my virginity in Jon's room, with his Prince Albert's Hussars standing guard."

"What?" Kelley says. He's on the edge of earshot.

"I said we should go to Virginia Beach sometime. We can get frozen custard."

"Virginia Beach for Dairy Queen?"

"I hear it's beautiful. Plus, I can sail. I need to show off."

"Cool."

"He doesn't know you weren't a virgin?" Louisa whispers. "Or about the hussars?"

"He knows. But boys hate to hear about that stuff more than is absolutely necessary. Why ruin his day? Isn't he da bomb?" Dee asks. "Come on. Have you ever seen a guy cuter than that?"

"He is very attractive," Louisa says, which is an understatement. Kelley is slender, noble, unselfconscious. Tan, with long brown hair tied back, and the most vertical posture Louisa has ever seen. He is a male beauty, and no one has exactly prepared her for this. Kelley washes himself off with the garden hose and bounds up the stairs to the deck. As they eat, Kelley tells Louisa what he has done with the garden since coming down from Ithaca.

"Improved soil with bog humus and volcanic sand. Colonized with *Bacillus thurengiensis* to control Mr. Potato Beetle. Introduced *Reduviidae*, commonly known as the assassin bug, who sports razor-sharp spines on his hind legs, to manage aphids, caterpillars, and other miscreants. Did I mention that once the assassin latches onto the victim, he pierces its body with his beak and injects a paralyzing venom? Could you pass that scallion cream cheese? I also threw in a hundred green lacewings to deal with the mites and blew a couple gallons of seaweed spray to control that embarrassing damping off problem I was having with my spinach."

"Has Kathy signed off on the assassin?" Dee asks.

"British worms, *Phasmarhabditas hermaphrodita*, to control slugs, and a dozen grade-A large eggs, beaten and sprayed, to discourage Mickey Mouse and his friends. But a whole posse of rodents kept visiting, so I bought a quart of assorted large cat scat from the National Zoo. Turns out," Kelley says, taking a huge bite of bagel and wiping cream cheese from his lips with the back of his hand, "big cat shit terrifies insectivores and herbivores, from mole to moose."

"It's sort of like how we would feel," Dee says, "if we went out to shovel snow and saw Bigfoot tracks." Louisa laughs for a little longer than she can account for, except that the company of Dee and Kelley makes her giddy.

"What time do you do class today?" Kelley asks.

"Four. Oh, Lamb," Dee tells him. "Don't worry."

"I'm not worried. I'm just—what?"

"Worried."

"About what?"

"Rex, the graphic artist, who draws me fabulously and asks me out after every session. You're worried he'll steal me from you."

"But he won't."

"Never," Dee says, going to Kelley's side. "I'll accept his drawings, and he can gaze at me, but that's all. I'm deeply monotonous. Yours and yours alone."

"Monogamous," Kelley corrects.

"That's what I said," Dee says. Kelley turns to Louisa.

"Dee has substitism," Kelley explains, "a condition in

which one word or phrase is unconsciously substituted for another."

"Nita told me," Louisa says, glancing at Dee. Dee doesn't appear to hear them. "Doesn't she know she has it?"

"That's not how it works," Kelley says. "Nicko, my roommate who's a psych major, told me about it. The speaker never believes they have misspoken, even when their voice is immediately replayed to them on tape or video."

"I don't have substitism," Dee says.

"Okay," Louisa says. "Tell me about the modeling job."

"It's fun. Fifteen an hour."

"Not bad."

"You should try it. It's like nude dancing, only slower and without the pasties. They need somebody for mornings. I don't do standing poses and I don't do mornings. I could give them your number."

"Louisa's almost a lawyer," Kelley says. "She doesn't need to strip."

"How much do you make at Arnold & Porter?" Dee asks.

"Six thousand a month, give or take a couple hundred in perks."

"And no rent."

"I know. But I have," Louisa tilts her head back, calculates, "twenty-three thousand in loans. I'd have a lot more if I wasn't a scholarship baby."

"Ouch."

"Yup."

"Are you always completely naked?" Kelley asks.

"That's why they call it life drawing," Dee tells him. Kelley frowns. Dee ruffles his hair. "You don't want anyone else to see me. That's sweet."

"I can't argue with fifteen an hour," Kelley tells Louisa. He explains their finances. Dee models and is a riding instructor at her old stable. Kelley digs footings at a construction site in Northeast. His site opens at seven and shuts down at three, so he's home by four and gardens into the cool of the evening. Dee and Kelley live the inconsistent life of one rich woman and one working-class guy nearing the end of college. Each is trying to learn how to pay his or her own way in the world, and to share expenses. But Dee has her impending fortune, and surprise money keeps coming in. This makes budgeting less urgent. Her sailing course was a Christmas present from her parents.

"If I didn't want to break even this summer, I wouldn't have to model," Dee tells Louisa. "But Kelley wants us to make ends meet. He's worried that if we get married, my money will make us fight. When I turn thirty, I really get a pile of it. In the meantime, Bailey keeps giving me chunks."

"I want to have a working farm," Kelley says. "I don't want to have a hobby farm." He goes back to gardening and Dee takes off her clothes and sunbathes. She has little round breasts with dark nipples. She has a layer of baby fat on her hips that makes her waist less distinct. That and the sweat that pools in Dee's belly button makes Louisa a little weak with diffuse desire and a sense that it really is summertime. She takes off her own clothes, except for her boring blue panties (it never occurred to her to wear party panties). Kelley can't see Dee and Louisa from the garden. They are in girl world.

"How's it going with Chris?" Dee asks.

"Fine," Louisa says. "I'm heading up next weekend."

"Will you do tons of New York stuff?"

"Will we ever. Chris is Mr. Organization."

"Do you just fuck your brains out, after like two weeks like that? Isn't that the best, when you're all pent up?" Louisa rolls on her side and looks into Dee's green eyes. There's a line of sweat droplets across Dee's mustache, which another girl might decide to bleach.

"No, I don't like it," Louisa says. "I try to pretend

we've been on a regular schedule. If not, I expect too much."

"He just comes, right? Since he's been waiting."

"Yup," Louisa says.

"Hold him, Newt. He's headed for the creek." Dee laughs, and Louisa with her. "Kelley wasn't so great either. It took me forever to train him. But his problem was slow, not fast. He had a bad case of I-am-not-worthy. You know, nibbling and touching ever so lightly for hours on end. As if maybe I could just come by being tickled and knowing how much he loved me." Louisa smiles and settles back to the deck.

"God, I remember that. Chris is all business, but my high school boyfriend, Ed, used to play with my breasts—correction, with just one breast—for half an hour. Then he'd move on to the other one. As if each was a separate, unfathomable mystery."

"Can I ask you something?" Dee asks, after a minute.

"Shoot." Louisa lays her elbow across her eyes to block the sun.

"When you talk about Chris, it's like you're talking about a baloney sandwich."

"It is?"

"You never really say, 'Oh, Chris is the most amazing lover,' or, 'He's the sweetest man,' or whatever. It's like you're just settling for him. So my question is, how do you know you love him?"

"I don't think," Louisa says carefully, "I do know. He's smart, funny, kind. He takes care of people, not just at work. He's sexy. I don't think I'm just settling for him. When we first met, I felt like this clumsy Montana girl, unsophisticated. Chris had this knowledge base that just blew me away. He knows about pretty much everything."

"So Chris was doing you a favor? 'Cause he was an Easterner and smart?"

"I don't feel like that now. But I did then. Now, I'm not

sure we fit as well as I think we should." She lifts her arm away and squints over at Dee. "What about you and Kelley?"

"I just love him completely. Kelley's the only guy I've ever wanted to spend more than a year or two with. I've been just crazy for him since our first night, welding."

"Sigh," Louisa says.

"He's this adventure I never thought I'd have. He's such a guy, but he's a human, too. He's definitely woman's best friend. He really understands fun, strange activities. The night I got back from Maine, we stayed up all night gluing Bette Davis mobiles. I had found this Bette Davis book for a dollar. We cut out the pictures and put her on a scooter and stuff. I'll show you the mobile before we turn over. Anyway, I thought all my biggest adventures were going to be solo. But now I think about making the farm with Kelley. We're looking at land north of Albany. Kelley's been planning and drawing maps. I'll probably get a teaching degree and teach middle school kids in a little town. I love middle school kids. Everybody's down on them because they're so emotional and they talk back. I love that."

"You'll be great."

"And I want to have three children."

"I can see you and Kelley with all your kids. Your farm will have a bunkhouse, where they'll sleep."

"You're wonderful. I say you decide quick about Chris, because if you're not in love with him or he's not wild about you, you should test-drive other guys."

"A guy who's gentle, worldly."

"Rich. Good in bed. Not too fast, not too slow."

"A martini drinker," Louisa says to the sun. "A door opener. An ankle appreciater." She finds herself thinking about Bailey.

"Young, handsome."

"Handsome," Louisa says. "I've done young." The

women sunbathe in silence. The sun is warm, but not too. Louisa is asleep when Kelley's voice comes to her from across the garden.

"You know what I can't figure out?" Kelley calls.

"What?" Dee answers.

"Why anybody would want a low-acid tomato."

The Skinny

THE FOUNTAIN at Dupont throws a crown of water upward into the breeze. White sheets of water pour from the upper basin to the collecting pool. As Bailey strides beneath the sycamores in the long evening sunlight, a fine mist reaches him. He settles beside Dana and sets down his bulging Olsson's bag.

"How was Paris?" he asks. "Where's Sean?"

"Paris was tiring and lonely. Sean's cooking." She rummages through Bailey's shopping bag, pulls out Bruce Chatwin's *In Patagonia*. "Can I borrow this?"

"Sure."

"We're supposed to talk. I'm supposed to urge you to fall in love with the girl."

"My pulse-checker?"

"Yes," Dana says.

"Why," Bailey asks, "would a silly old man do that?"

"Sean says she's just right. I know she's young. But Sean's friends thought I was too young."

"You were a shocking twenty-eight. He was thirty-nine. You broke the ten-year rule. This is another order of magnitude."

"My friends also thought he was too white."

"His friends thought you were both very advanced and brave." They smile to think of it, one decade's social revolution becoming the next decade's commonplace.

"You're supposed to raise objections about Louisa. I'm supposed to point out that Sean and I are a good couple, despite everyone's objections."

"Louisa is one of Peter's best ideas. She humors me and walks the dogs. We all find her excellent company."

"Listen," Dana says. "Before I convince you to go for her, tell me she doesn't play up to you. *Mr. Judge, I'm just a little girl law student. What should I think?* That might be hard to be around."

"Nothing like that," Bailey says. "She sees me for what I am. The way Caroline did." On the bench beside him, Dana gives a little start. Bailey looks at her. "Oh, I see. My mentioning Louisa and Caroline in the same breath."

"I didn't know you felt strongly toward her," Dana says.

"I like her. By the way," Bailey says, "you're not the one to persuade me. You have divided loyalties."

"No," Dana says. "It just never occurred to me you might compare her to Caroline."

"Memory," Bailey says, "is comparison. But Louisa's all but engaged. We're friends. Amazing, isn't it, what they can do now?" With a gesture of his chin, Bailey indicates a skateboarder in baggy shorts and a neon shirt. The kid jumps a curb, loops lazily toward them, springs onto and off of the rim of the pool. A few yards from where Bailey and Dana sit, he whirls, the back of the board scraping, then glides off. His shaved scalp is tattooed with a Masonic eye.

"All but engaged?" Dana asks.

"She doesn't wear a ring." Bailey pulls out and crumbles a stale dinner roll. Pigeons unenthusiastically rally.

"Sean didn't even say she had a beau."

"Why does Sean think I should fall in love? I try not to call him more often than he calls me."

"When you don't call for a week, he becomes impossible. He's convinced you're angry with him."

"Sean and I share social paranoia."

"He wants you to be happy."

"I was happy. Then I was sad," Bailey says. "Now, I'm fine." Dana looks over Bailey's shoulder. Bailey turns to see why. Two of the afternoon's best-dressed men are on a collision course. The first crosses confidently from New Hampshire, the second saunters over from 19th Street. Two has the better physique; One, the better clothes. Dana inclines her chin minutely toward One, his profile accented by his sideburn and close beard. Two sports a charcoal black suit and a cream shirt. No tie, shoes as black and dimpled as old change purses. At the last moment, Two yields an inch of concrete to One. Bailey tosses a confetti of bread crumbs into the air. The pigeons shake the falling crumbs from their iridescent wings. "She graduates next year," Bailey says. "Chris is in New York. She'll move up."

"He's not here."

"They talk on the phone, they e-mail. They meet every other week. Louisa is a lucky woman in the prime of life. Or almost in the prime of her life. I'm a relic. I have my children and my grandchildren." He produces his wallet. He hopes to cover the confusion he feels. He is infatuated with Louisa, but he thought that he and Caroline, with whom he has been discussing the matter openly, were the only souls who knew. He has said nothing to Sean to give himself away. That was his mistake, he sees. He should have made a casual reference to Louisa to throw Sean off.

"The newest arrival," he tells Dana, showing her Sam in his bassinet, looking preoccupied.

"Darling. How's Valerie?"

"Making it from day to day. Except for last week, when Jon and Peter took over."

"Are they going to raise him?"

"I think so. They've got the nursery ready."

"Same old story," Dana says. "Gay folks taking on the job when no one else has the patience, or the ability."

"You idealize gays. But I wonder what I would have done without Peter. Jon couldn't have raised Nita alone. She could have come to me. I would have hired someone to live in and take care of her. But that wouldn't have been the same thing. Not like having two parents."

"No," Dana says. "Jon and Peter are godsends. But you must have a center to your own life." Bailey starts to speak, but doesn't. Dana apparently knows everything in his mind and heart. Louisa has been in the house—has it been only seven weeks? Yet Bailey depends on her presence. He listens for her footsteps on the stairwell, watches for her smiles when she reads the comics.

"You're right," he answers. "Marsha called again—"

"Let's be serious for a minute," Dana tells him. Marsha is in their circle, another friend of Caroline's. "Louisa draws you. Sean has the feeling that you're happier than you've been in a long time."

"He said that?" As Bailey focuses his thoughts, his hand rises to his chin. "Suppose I do dote on Louisa a little bit. Where does that leave me?" He and Dana listen to the fountain, watch the commuters who worked late. Bailey explains how, a week ago, he met Chris. Louisa and Chris make a good young couple. They rely on each other, and young people, Bailey points out, are marrying again nowadays. For the moment, Louisa livens up his and Caroline's old house. That's all there is to it.

"We'll see," Dana says.

"Sean has lost track of time."

"Sean thinks you're a prize."

"I'm starving. What's he cooking?"

"Moqueca de peixe. By the way," Dana says. "I adore you."

"Well, keep telling me. Each time, I'll be thrilled."

"Caroline and I found the two best men."

"Am I really in Sean's class?"

"You're a bit more handsome, he's a bit more vain. You're both loving, but not clinging. Dependable."

"Louisa thinks I'm funny."

"Sean was right," Dana says, rising. "You do love her."

The Eastern System

JON WANDERS in nine-thirtyish, loiters in the history department office on the third floor of Phillips, pulling mail out of his cubby, gossiping with Cynthia, the secretary-by-day, folk-singer-by-night. Cynthia dresses like a librarian in below-the-knee skirts and sensible pumps. She has faint acne scars and gentle brown eyes, and the tilt of her head indicates that she is always trying to understand something deeper than what Jon is saying.

"How's Sam?" she asks.

"He's back at our house. He had a giggling fit last night. I thought he was crying. Scared the daylights out of me."

"Valerie?"

"Not so hot. We're hoping she'll be able to take Sam back in a couple days. But who knows for how long."

"Can you tolerate this on-off thing?"

"Have to," Jon says.

"Peter?"

Jon shakes his head. "He's losing it. He and I need to make a decision. I need to talk to Valerie."

"You need to talk to Peter," Cynthia says. Cynthia identifies with Peter as the stay-at-home spouse. Cynthia is a single mom. There was a husband in North Carolina, where she grew up. She doesn't talk about her twenties, except to indicate that there were choices she made, then, that she had to un-make as she rounded the corner into her thirties. Her son, Ted, is eleven. Cynthia drops him off sometimes with Peter and Jon when she has a gig.

"How was Baldwin's?"

"I didn't get on till ten," Cynthia says. "Nice people, lousy mixing board." Jon and Peter have heard Cynthia perform on small stages in restaurant/bars so crowded and noisy that only Cynthia's seriousness made it work. Cynthia has several CDs to her name, available at DCCD and online at folk Web sites. Cynthia is content with her following of a few hundred locally, maybe a thousand or two nationally. She says, *That's a pretty big crowd.* She says, *My people know me pretty well.*

"Well, good morning, Dr. Johansen," Jon murmurs as Asst. Prof. Linda Johansen comes in, sets down her book bag and purse, gets her coffee and mail. During her not-yet-tenured first years, Linda adopted Jon as a big brother. He became her interpreter of the sudden disapproval and the equally sudden adoration of the rest of the faculty. Linda has a lovely pink complexion and flaxen hair and is often smiling widely, as if a practical joke is under way. Jon and Linda carry second cups of coffee down the hall to Jon's office, on the east side of the modern, beige brick building.

"I want to go away," Linda says.

"You are away. You aren't teaching now or in the fall."

"Oh, right. Then why aren't I planning a proper sabbatical in the Rockies, hiking, making love to my husband, and drinking beer?"

"You're using the Library of Congress. It's a period of great intellectual ferment for you."

"That's it," Linda says. "I knew there was something."

"You're not pregnant?" Jon asks hopefully.

"No."

"You thinking about technology?"

"Two more months. Then we get pictures taken of all my overpasses and underpasses, and Nat does the sperm races. He's wearing boxers even as we speak."

"You'll get there. You just have to tap your heels together and say, *There's no place like maternity slash paternity*. Which there isn't."

"I know. My life will change completely, and there's nothing more wonderful. But I don't want my life to change completely, and I don't believe in pure wonderful."

"Fine. Let me just say this much. The mysteries will be revealed." They agree to meet for lunch and Linda heads off, leaving Jon alone with his two computers. On the fast new one, he answers two e-mails from his backlog, the first to his old friend Curt, who just got divorced. It is one of those situations in which everyone is surprised, having seen none of the cracks but being told that *things were never good*. Marriages are truly private in the sense that no one outside of them knows what is going on. This is perhaps why Americans since the eighteenth century have been particularly suspicious of state interference, Jon reckons. Apropos of which the second e-mail is to his colleague Brook in the sociology department, regarding a course they are developing on the history of marriage in America. He could call Brook or, heaven forbid, actually walk downstairs and across H Street to talk to him face to face, but that wouldn't be modern at all. They send e-mail every day. They are reorganizing the social history survey they coteach so they'll have time to cover the evolution of modern marriage law and custom from English common and ecclesiastic law. Ten-thirty-five. He calls Peter. "Hi," he says. "I miss you."

"I was just thinking about you," Peter answers so quietly Jon knows Sam is beside him, asleep.

"Thinking?"

"How much I love you. How good you were last night."

"Was I?"

"When Sam was giggling and you panicked."

"I thought he was crying."

"You made your mother's infinite-concern-and-compassion face."

"Empathy."

"Sam was talking a blue streak to the curtains this morning. Sunlight is apparently one of his friends."

"How's the review going?"

"I wrote it all in one long burst. Wonder if it makes any sense. The beginning and the end do. I'm not so sure about the middle."

"Good book?"

"Not as good as I say it is. I think I've made it out to be the best book ever written."

"You make them all sound splendid. As if not reading them constitutes a life poorly spent."

"I get enthusiastic."

"You weren't so enthusiastic about S's last one."

"True, but S is famous, and that book was numbingly dull. When are you coming home?"

"Core meeting," Jon says. "Then I'll shop."

"So, like seven?"

"Yeah. I took the list off the fridge. We need anything else?" Jon asks. A pause ensues.

"We need to keep Sam."

"We have him," Jon says gently, "for now."

"I can't do this over and over. You know that. Honey?"

"I know."

"Turns me inside out. Organize everything around Sam, then just go back to being visiting uncle. It hurts too much."

"I know."

"It's not just the logistics, which are impossible. It's not even how sad it makes me. The problem is it's not fair to Mr. Sweets. He's very little, and probably very flexible emotionally. But soon this will be damaging. Plus, I'm really getting to know him. Everything he needs and wants. To send him back to a house where he'll get about half of all that is not possible."

"No. We can't keep doing that."

"Just so you understand. I'm not angry."

"I understand," Jon says. Peter is weeping a little on the other end of the line. "Please don't cry."

"Okay."

"I love you. You're a wonderful man," Jon says, sympathetic tears springing into his own eyes. "So what do we need? Diapers? Cat food?"

"We're all set."

"I love you. Did I mention that?"

"You did," Peter tells him.

❀

Jon is reluctantly preparing for class when the knock comes.

"May I intrude?" Jim, advisee, is already pushing through the door. Male graduate students do not need academic guidance so much as recognition of their arrival on life's stage. Jim knows exactly what he wants to write, bridles when Jon makes even the slightest recommendation. The rage and ambition of the young man is a tonic for Jon, which is how he ended up advising Jim, whose topic is far afield of Jon's. The rest of the department is scared of the rarely washed young man. Jon finds the most ordinary talk with Jim, such as today's discussion of the best strategy for getting Jim a summer research trip to New Orleans, electric. The real problem is that Jim applied two months after the deadline.

"What's their deal?" Jim asks about the same faculty members, give or take one or two, who will have to approve his dissertation in a year. "They know the Acolapissa papers are in the manuscript room. I shouldn't have to beg for a few bucks to go look at primaries." But at this date he does have to beg, and Jon helps him craft a few paragraphs explaining why his topic, French hegemony in the Pearl River and Bayou Costine settlements, requires travel money. Another round of vituperation against the bureaucracy, and Jim's off. Jon feels five years younger. Bea arrives five minutes early for her appointment.

"It's no good, is it?" Bea asks, maybe half a minute after handing Jon her week's sheaf. Women graduate students generally work harder, and feel less deserving, than their male counterparts. Jon's method with his advisees is to ask them to bring him whatever they have written, just to hit Print and let 'er rip, every two weeks. For undergrads, every week. Bea has three double-spaced pages of text and a few single-spaced pages of notes. She is ashamed; she won't look Jon in the eye. This is partly because she is in love with him. The paragraphs she produces are of regular length and avoid obvious stylistic pitfalls.

"Good," Jon says, reads. Bea raises her eyes to his chest. She doesn't sleep enough. Her eyes are pink-rimmed and perpetually tearful. Her husband wants her to bear a child, that largest of homework assignments, soon. Bea wants to be Jon, she has led him to understand. A gay man like Jon, she believes, is free. She wants to be a gay male scholar with a stay-at-home husband, not a straight woman with a mathematician husband who believes in traditional roles for women.

"So the Irish and Germans are the cloth and pattern cutters," Jon says. "The Russian newcomers do all the sewing."

"It's an order-of-arrival hierarchy." Bea is writing about the way social divisions yield to political exigency in the needle trades in Baltimore in the late nineteenth century. Her eyes, with cautious lash enhancement, come to bear on Jon's own. She is ascetic and quick. She reminds him of his second-to-last girlfriend, before he realized there would be no more girl-friends.

"Phil Kahn says I. Freeman leaves the shop bosses alone," Jon says, reading. "Baltimore expands slowly anyway. Why?" Bea gets out her notes on industrial versus other jobs in Newark, Philadelphia, Boston. Jon congratulates, soothes. Sends Bea away, nominally for another two weeks, except that she will come see him the day after tomorrow with just one more question. In the end she will produce a dissertation clean as a whistle. Jim will get through, with a lot of histrionics and revision. The life cycle of the graduate student is a Greek tragedy in slow motion. Jon sees all, or almost all, in advance. He interposes himself between members of the department and his flock of advisees.

Linda fetches him. They walk down H Street to The Burro. It's sunny and cool, so they sit outdoors. Jon has a salad with so much grated cheddar, olives, and avocado that he might as well have had a burrito. He walks fast but arrives back in Rome, the building, five minutes late to teach his seminar, or rather to observe the male graduate students hijack it. Jon is like a referee in a pro-wrestling match, not really doing much except occasionally offering himself as a foil to be swatted across the room (an airless closet with loudly humming flores-cent lights) by students with monikers like New Historical Bane of Discourse, I Just Have One Point, and Critical Appa-ratus Going Berserk. Eventually the fracas dies down and the women get to talk.

Jon makes it back to his office at two-forty-five, desperate to pee, brush his teeth, and do a little writing. As he sits down at his newer computer, one of the undergraduates appears.

"Hey, Jon. 'Kai come in?" Craig attended a Waldorf school in Philadelphia where all the teachers were called by their first names. Jon has suggested to him that the university is different, but Craig still calls him Jon. Craig is majoring in business. In theory, this is a practical decision that shows how in touch with the real world today's students are. In practice, Jon finds that most of the business majors are intimidated by their parents, and slowly if ever figure out what they themselves might want to study.

"I read about you and your partner in the *Hatchet*. My mom's best friend is gay. He's a doctor in Austin." Every year or two, Jon is profiled in the student paper. He talks about Peter and Nita and explains that his interest in marriage is both academic and personal. Each new group of students assumes that he has just come out and is asking for acceptance from eighteen-year-olds. Craig thinks gay people are brave and admirable, especially ones like Jon, who act "regular." Craig is in Jon's lecture course and also in his discussion section. He comes to Jon's office once a week. Often he has a good question about that week's lecture.

"What kind of doctor?"

"Like a regular doctor. I brought my paper." Craig was diagnosed with a learning disability long ago, the result of which is that he works carefully, drafting his essays and getting extra help. Craig is comparing the two codes of marriage law in the early nineteenth century: the Southern "Biblical system," which allowed first cousins to marry but did not allow in-law marriages, such as those between a man and his deceased wife's sister (affinal marriages); and the Western American system, which proscribed first-cousin unions but authorized affinal ones. The accepted theory is that the Southern system helped sustain a highly stratified, family-centered economic order, whereas the Western allowed the expansion and distribution of wealth across family lines. Both served moneyed elites, but the Southern and Western systems signaled different strategies for acquisition and preservation. Jon reads:

In the south farmers managed larger properties but when they had children the properties were subdivided without analysis of efficiency effects. In the west farmers and ranchers tended to join ranches and farms together by marrying their kids to each other and this meant efficiency was maintained.

Jon marks nothing but points out to Craig that his main idea doesn't appear until the fifth paragraph. Jon asks him which system became the dominant one by century's end, and Craig says he doesn't know but he'll find out. Jon has no doubt he will. They talk briefly about Craig's summer plans—camp counselor, Craig's old camp. Jon is forced to look at his watch several times before Craig leaves.

Jon rolls over to the old, slow computer. His third book lives in it. His first book was an expansion of his dissertation, on the demography of Lee's enlisted men (no officers) at the Siege of Petersburg (June 1864 till the end of the war). How many in the ranks were property owners, professionals, what states they came from. Not earth-shaking stuff, but one of the few fallow corners of the field, and arduous to research, hence a good grunt-work topic for a dues-paying grad student and former Civil War nut. He met an editor from the University Press of Virginia at his second American Historical Association hoedown in Chicago, a woman as young and eager as himself, and soon he was rewriting the manuscript into a book. Had he not been terrified of becoming a rich man of no occupation, Bailey Allard's son who never amounted to much, he might not have completed the revision of the dissertation. But he did, and it landed him a job and he started to relax. His second opus, on Civil War women and social transformation, was a lot more fun and less work from inception through publication. *Ready or not, here I come*, was Jon's feeling as he delivered his first papers to what he thought would be territorial feminist historians in a small conference room in a large New York hotel. To his astonishment, the women were kind and welcoming. The second book earned him tenure and a brief flurry of name-recognition.

His third book, the one he is writing now in that almost-forty, post-tenure parental haze, concerns father-son relations in nineteenth-century middle-class families. The project grips him, perhaps because his own relationships with his well-known father, his dead mother, and his troubled sister are fraught with conflict, love, and overinvolvement. The nineteenth century saw the decline of the earlier post-Revolution patriarchal family, in which the father held all the power and each home was a miniature state. What emerged was a family in which women, children, and even servants were citizens, each protected in his or her private sphere. Family law was invented in the appellate courts during this period of social transformation. The son especially took center stage in a number of legal contexts. Jon's thesis is basically that breaking up is hard to do, especially when you're breaking up one idea of the family and building another.

Jon leaves his manuscript on the screen of his old computer and works on it whenever he can. His new computer is for all the rest of the flotsam and jetsam of the job, paper abstracts to be submitted, responses to abstracts submitted to him, syllabi, exams, memos. Sometimes his book is all Jon wants to work on; other times he is incapable of long thoughts. Sometimes he feels part of a chapter inside him like an alien about to bust its reptilian head through his sternum. Then his fingers leap over the keyboard, as if he were Dracula at the organ. Other times a bureaucratic frenzy takes him, and he rolls his chair over to the new machine that's online and flies through a score of student recommendations, book orders for next semester, e-mail to his department head on graduate admissions policy revision. His modem whistles high and lonesome, his printer clicks and moans, and his thinning hair tumbles across his forehead. There is a moment to every task.

Now no one comes to the door. He writes a few pages of the new book.

Working Relationship

LOUISA WATCHES Chris come through the arrival gate with the other shuttle passengers. He bounds toward Louisa, his sports bag held out from his running legs, his blond hair flopping, his smile embracing her before his arms do. He picks her up and whirls her around, sets her down and kisses her. Louisa loves the way Chris overwhelms her. She and Chris walk hand in hand through Reagan and out to the Metro station.

"You're scrumptious," Chris tells Louisa as they wait for the Washington-bound train. She's wearing her new work suit and her Cole Haans, carrying her briefcase. He kisses her and she goes limp in his arms, playing Carole Lombard to his Clark Gable. "Guess what?" Chris says. "We're meeting Scott and Beth at the Kennedy Center. Scott got tickets to the Kronos Quartet."

"Oh," Louisa says, trying not to look upset. Chris hates it when Louisa isn't spontaneous, when she gets upset over a simple change of plans. But she can't hide it.

"What's wrong?" Chris asks, his own face hardening. They're right back where they were when they said goodbye in Penn Station two weeks before.

"It's just. I thought…"

"I sent you e-mail last night," Chris says, as if that answers any objections. "Scott told me to check the Kronos Web page. There were three reviews of the Schnittke, all raves. I listened to the CD all the way down. It's wild. Here." Chris pulls his headphones from his pocket and plants them in Louisa's ears. He pushes a button. Shrill strings fill Louisa's head, a racket that might accompany a murder in a Hitchcock film. She bobs her head and snaps her fingers, as if she's listening to a pop tune. She tries to look cheerful.

"Nice." She pulls the inserters out. "I can't wait." To her astonishment, Chris believes her. She wants nothing more than to rush home, climb out of her clothes, into the shower, and into bed. Then, when she and Chris have made love and had a nap, she will take him to Amaryllis for a late snack.

"I know you don't like modern stuff, but I thought you'd have fun hanging out with Beth and Scott." Louisa tries to smile in an *Okay, it'll be fun* way. But why, since Chris knows she's not a fan of twentieth-century composers, is he dragging her to the Kennedy Center on their first evening together in two weeks? Only one answer presents itself. Chris wants to hear the concert and see his med school friends. What Louisa wants doesn't matter. As far as seeing Scott and Beth goes, Louisa longs to be indifferent to Beth but hasn't yet grown quite that fond of her. Scott's all right. He's one of Chris's only friends with whom she can carry on a conversation.

❋

Chris runs over to Scott and Beth at roughly the same pace as to Louisa at the airport. Chris and Beth complete their hugs and kisses, and Chris and Scott start punching each other's shoulders. As always when she walks up to the threesome, Louisa feels she is the outsider. She greets June, Scott's wife, and Randy, Beth's boyfriend of the month. Randy she's met once before, when he and Beth were in the, well, randy phase. He seems like a nice enough city planner, a little boring but pleasant and in awe, poor bastard, of Beth. June gives Louisa her hands-on-shoulders embrace. June's a lawyer at Dewey Ballantine and is a couple years older than the rest of the gang. She has the exhausted look of a woman who will eventually make partner, as if she's already been swallowed up by her endless hours at the firm. Deep down, Louisa fears that, when she and Chris marry, she will turn into another June, the aging spouse of the eternally young man.

Eventually Scott, who made it through med school with the rudiments of social graces still intact, asks how Louisa is. But when she starts to tell him that she's living in a wonderful old house off Dupont Circle, and that her summer job is going rather well, Scott is already distracted, his eyes drifting, his *uh-huh*s automatic. Beth's hair almost touches Chris's own as she leans to tell him whatever story makes him smile. They look good together, like brother and sister, close in temperament and coloring. They both turn to her.

"Love the suit," Beth says. "New image, right?" They make their way into the small theater and naturally Louisa winds up at the end of the row, Chris beside her, Beth on Chris's left. Chris holds Louisa's hand but continues his conversation with Beth, about people whose names Louisa has come to recognize but whom she has never met. When at last Chris turns to her, the concert is beginning. The difficult music fills the hall. Louisa thinks longingly of Bailey who, at this hour, is sitting back in one of the two overstuffed armchairs in the front room, listening to Tommy Dorsey and reading.

※

"Not there," Louisa tells Chris, too late. He tosses his bag onto the high, mahogany bureau. Louisa finds a scratch.

"Come here," Chris tells her, pulling her toward the bed, slipping his hands inside her clothes.

"Wait."

"I've been waiting all night."

"Wait longer," Louisa says, going back to the bureau and running her fingers over the scratch. "Please be more careful with the things in this house. They're not ours. We're guests here." But what Louisa is really thinking is that the beautiful old piece is hers, and that she doesn't want Chris near it. Chris is the guest in this house, and not a welcome one at the moment. He stares at her.

"You sound like my mother."

"You act like a brat. I'm taking a shower." Louisa lifts her bathrobe from the hook inside her closet door and goes down the hall. She is shaking. This isn't the way it was supposed to be at all. She and Chris should have been in bed hours ago, laughing, catching up. She doesn't love Chris. She knows this suddenly. But he has come to DC to be with her. They have three days. Maybe she's just tired. After the concert, the six of them met Brad, who was Chris and Scott's Princeton roommate, and they all went out for a late dinner in Georgetown. Beth dominated the table for an hour with tales of life in emergency medicine. Chris drank two beers and ate a blue-cheese burger with onions. Maybe that's why she doesn't want to kiss him. At least he could brush his teeth. God, what's happening to her?

"I'm sorry," she tells him, back in the room.

"No, I'm sorry. I try to fit in too many things. You didn't even want to go out tonight. I mean with friends."

"I wanted to be alone with you."

"You're awfully delicious. Can you forgive me?"

"Maybe," she says.

"I love you," Chris tells her, as easily as always. He sounds so good, he looks so good, saying it. She curls up beside him with her head on his chest. Everything will be all right, she tells herself. He trails his fingers between her shoulder and her hip. "Louisa," he says. "Don't let me lose you." They make love. As Louisa falls asleep, her back against Chris's broad chest, she remembers what he said. *Perhaps*, she thinks, *it really is all up to me.*

She smells coffee. She thinks of Bailey and smiles, before she remembers that Chris is beside her. When she opens the bedroom door she finds two mugs, an extra-large thermos, and a pitcher of milk beside the usual sugar bowl. *Oh, Bailey*, she thinks, opening the thermos and pouring her first cup. *How thoughtful, bringing extra coffee and milk in case Chris wants some.* Chris is sound asleep. Louisa puts on her robe, washes up, and heads downstairs. Bailey is reading the paper in the kitchen. He wears dark blue pajamas and his olive robe with the wide lapels. He takes off his glasses as Louisa enters.

"Good morning," she says, settling into her place across from him. She loves her seat because she can see Bailey and look out the window at the rose bushes at the same time. The two spend half an hour eating and reading the paper. Bailey prepares triangles of French toast with vanilla and cinnamon, topped with whipped butter and maple syrup. When Chris comes down, Louisa introduces him to Bailey, who puts Chris at ease with a few questions about New York and the life of a surgery resident. Then Bailey puts another round on the griddle and heads upstairs, to leave the two alone. His feet in their leather slippers climb the stairs. Louisa sits beside Chris. She pushes one bare knee up over his leg and settles in against him. She feels well, and prosperous.

"What do you want to do today?" Chris asks. "I was thinking we should check out the Modigliani exhibit. Tonight we could find this place I read about in Manassas, Whole Hog Barbecue. Scott invited everybody over for drinks. He said we can take his car to Virginia. It's only like half an hour."

"Interesting," Louisa tells him. But she wonders why he's

in such a hurry to get together with other people. She tells herself she should be grateful, the way he explores Washington with her. Hell, she wouldn't see anything if it weren't for Chris, and she loves barbecue. But she can't help feeling that his plans have nothing to do with her, that he would have the same day in mind if he were on his own. All she needs to do, she thinks, is talk to him. "I thought we could take a walk this afternoon," she says. "Go by Mystery Books so you can stock up, have a smoothie. Then come back here for a siesta. Then I don't know." She takes Chris's hand.

"I guess we could see the exhibit tomorrow. We don't need to go to Whole Hog."

"No. Let's go. Let's borrow Scott's car and skip the drinks. We saw everybody last night." Chris takes a deep breath. He is about to object, Louisa knows, when he catches himself. He lets the breath out.

"Good," he says carefully. He lets his head drop onto her shoulder. "That's a good plan." Louisa kisses him. "It's hard, isn't it?" he says after a while. "But we're doing better."

❊

The weekend passes smoothly—only one more little fight, no big ones, lots of good food, lovemaking, and sleep. Chris goes for his jogs. His mood is stable. Everything Louisa hoped for comes to pass. Chris appreciates the Dupont house, and he and Bailey get to know each other. Chris learns the Woofs' names and takes Leo and Henry with him on his runs. Sunday evening, Bailey, Louisa, and Chris spend an hour together. Chris's flight isn't until eight. They drink beer. Chris looks over Bailey's record collection and chooses a Hayden cello concerto. The sunlight is pale yellow through the high front windows. Bailey turns on the fan, and apologizes.

"We could put in a central system. It would cost a mint. But we've always made do with a few window units in the bedrooms, and the fans. I suppose I like to sweat in the summer and freeze in winter. Otherwise I'd do the sensible thing, and move to a condominium with eight-foot ceilings and a little communal garden."

"I can't see that," Chris says.

"No, I can't either," Bailey says. Louisa drinks and observes the two men. Bailey is taller, more slender. Chris emanates good will. He is charming, her boyfriend. Intelligent, knowledgeable, and above all curious, soaking up information about everything, music and art, old houses, law careers.

"And after Yale?" he is asking Bailey.

"SEC."

"How did you become a judge?" Chris asks.

"I was appointed. We moved down."

"Wait. Did you tell someone you wanted to be a judge?"

"I don't know what I told my friend Sean, but he decided it meant I wanted to move to Washington and be a judge. He told friends of his in the administration."

"Just like that."

"You'll see. The doctors who supervise you now and who see how capable you are will be running hospitals in twenty years. One of them will offer you an appointment in a medical school and teaching hospital. In middle age, people become exponentially more busy. They have children and administrative responsibilities, and they call on the people they know."

"That's just about as hard to imagine," Chris says, "as having enough money to give to alumni associations." Bailey has taken a chair by the window so that Chris and Louisa are together. All weekend, Bailey has promoted Louisa and Chris's closeness. Now Bailey steers the conversation away from his life to Chris's.

"Chief resident," Bailey says. "Quite an honor."

"It was a one-in-six chance. They had to pick somebody."

"I don't imagine the other five take consolation in that," Bailey says. "How have you found the job?"

"It turns out to be scheduling, mostly. I put together the

teams that round on the wards. The trick is figuring out which personalities work best together." Louisa spent a night on the ward with Chris. She marveled at how effective and kind he was. Louisa tells the story of that night.

"You are a lucky woman," Bailey tells Louisa, when she has finished. "And you," he tells Chris, "are a very fortunate man." Bailey shakes Chris's hand and heads upstairs so Louisa and Chris can spend their last hour alone. "Take the car," he says. "The keys are on the table by the back door." He disappears.

"Hell of a guy," Chris says, after a minute.

"Bailey?" Louisa answers. "He's all right."

Kitty Hawk

"STAY ON THE SIDEWALK," Jon yells. Nita swerves up a rounded curb on her small red mountain bike. A lot of bike for a seven-year-old, but Jon couldn't resist. Her training wheels ride a couple of inches off the ground on either side of her rear fork, only touching when she leans into turns, but Nita likes to know they're there. Last spring she watched her best friend, the courageous but slightly oblivious Andrei, turn the handlebars of his Sears special around and take a few layers of skin off his right cheek. Nita hasn't said a word to Jon about removing the training wheels he keeps adjusting further and further out of her way. She has seven gears but generally rides in either the highest or the lowest, so that she is either spinning fast or barely chugging along. Jon, on his Aeon with its tri-void boom tube and low forward pivot, hangs in ridiculously low gear himself, so he gets an aerobic workout, madly spinning along behind Nita. He's dressed down, having left his current favorite outfit—purple-side-striped Sugoi pants, marigold-yellow and chili-red Louis Garneau jersey—at home. Instead he wears old Pearl Izumi shorts and a faded Bubba Shuma jersey. Just dad out with daughter, not a semipro road racer on a training ride.

Nita turns to him and scowls. As far as she's concerned, holiday bike rides are her due. Jon has ridden with her in fair weather since she was out of diapers. But that was pre-Sam. Now she acts as if she's actually doing him a favor when, really, by getting out of the house on Memorial Day Monday, they're both doing Peter a favor. Jon tentatively imagines just how tiring, complicated, and satisfying Saturdays are going to be when Sam is back for good. Sam's been with Valerie for almost two weeks. She is better again, interested in taking care of her baby. But it's only a matter of time until Valerie has another spell and Lucy and Roberta call and say, "Come get the boy." Jon can picture a morning when he will take both Sam and Nita out riding, Sam in the racing chariot hitched to his back fork, Nita up ahead. Jon never planned to have a second child, but now that Sam is here, he's excited. His enthusiasm takes the form of thoughts about all the gear he can justify buying.

Nita turns left on R Street toward Connecticut. Jon has always lavished praise on her for her navigational acumen. "Slow up, Lizard!" he calls. Where did he and Peter come up with the endless nicknames, stretching back to infancy—Lizard, Leaper, Peanut, Professor Slurpy, and all the rest of the elaborate silliness? Jon and Peter like to list the nicknames backwards toward the very first two, Cricket and Love Monkey, uncovering the whole archeology of parenthood along the way. When Nita first came to them, she was Cricket most days, because of her articulate chirpings and always-working bony legs.

"I'm tired," Nita says. She's pulled her bike up to The Childe Harolde and stands, one foot poised on the stoop.

"I hear your Danish calling," Jon says. They ride on, passing between the buffalo on the Q Street Bridge and continuing into Georgetown. They lean their bikes against a tree and clack into Sara's Market on their cleats.

"What can I get you today, Precious?" the woman behind the counter asks. Nita points. Jon tickles her under her pointing arm.

"I'd like an apricot cheese Danish, please," Nita says.

"That's more like it," Jon says. "I'd like coffee and an orange muffin, please."

They sit on the curb by the bikes. Nita eats her Danish and drinks from her water bottle in silence.

"Are you having a grouchy morning?" Jon asks. Nita shrugs. "If I let you have some coffee, will you talk?" Jon asks. Nita nods. He reaches and brushes crumbs from her cheek. She drinks from his cup with a fervor that bodes ill for her. She will be a caffeine hound like Peter, as soon as she gets old enough to procure. She looks so like Valerie at her age. Her skin is milky pale. Her eyes flit past Jon's along the shadowed street. Valerie was already pretty ill by the time she had reached Nita's age. She had her silent days, and her shouting, out-of-reach days. By then Jon had become her protector, the role that Peter points out he still has. "Can I go to Andrei's this afternoon?" Nita asks.

"I thought we were going shopping for Peter's birthday present," Jon answers.

"Andrei and me are doing something."

"Andrei and I. Does it involve deception and death?"

"No." Nita smiles for the first time since Jon woke her with his usual kisses. She wants Jon to guess her new project. Last week, she and Andrei made a mud trap, a hole covered with a thin layer of leaves. They made Jon walk into it, but they let him change into his old shoes first.

"You're making a rope trap that pulls dads upside-down into trees."

"No," Nita says, delighted. "A bomb shelter. In the garage."

"How does Andrei think up this stuff? I want you to come

111

help me find Peter a shirt." Nita and Andrei have been best friends since they were fourteen months old. They met in a motion and music class, clutched together in a dance that was part ballroom, part wrestle. They seem to understand the pressure they are under to defy gender stereotypes. One month they're making up stories and devising costumes, the next they're building traps and shelters. Andrei, a graceful, kind boy whose parents are at the World Bank, was for years smaller than Nita, until suddenly, in first grade, he shot past her. Andrei doesn't seem to care what games he plays, as long as he plays them with Nita. When she doesn't show up at his house on Corcoran, he taps on Nita's front door. When Jon or Peter opens, Andrei comes in without a word and goes to find Nita, leaving Jon to tend to Andrei's friendly nanny, Monica.

"Peter wants Tony Lamas," Nita reminds him.

"I know, but I can't buy him those. Boots won't look the way he thinks they will. What he needs is shirts that he can wear out to dinner."

"You choose. I'll contribute," Nita says. Her standard contribution is now fifty cents. She has learned to buy her way out of obligations, to use words like *contribute*, and to speak in two-word declaratives, Peter's speech pattern. Jon, professor that he is, tends to speak in circuitous turns of phrase, such as *tends to speak in circuitous turns of phrase*, when *is wordy* would do the trick.

"I guess I can go by myself," Jon concedes. He's worried that, if he isn't careful, he and Peter will end up with pretty much the same wardrobe. This happened five years back, when they were on a raw silk kick. He was hoping that Nita would help him choose a shirt or two that he wouldn't have chosen himself. "Why don't you and Andrei both come? We'll go by Sonny's Surplus." Stimulants, bribes. Jon resorts to all the tricks Peter never employs in his negotiations with Nita.

"Can we buy a grenade? We have the money."

"A grenade," Jon hears himself saying. "In case losers who don't have bomb shelters try to get into yours and you have to blow them away?" Nita tilts her head appreciatively. Jon wonders if he needs to explain that the grenades aren't live, just husks. Nah. Nita knows. She and Andrei love the surplus store, with its camouflage clothes, its ultraviolet lights and posters, its knives and cans of mace, its no-nonsense tents, tarps, and sleeping bags that would keep a person snug in the snow. The mud trap had been dug with a collapsible shovel. "No, you can't buy a grenade. How about binoculars?"

"I have to ask Andrei," Nita says, as if Andrei would ever not do anything Nita wants to do.

"*A cheval,*" Jon says, finishing his muffin. They ride up 31st Street toward Dumbarton Oaks. Nita pulls over.

"I want to try riding without training wheels."

"Okay," Jon says, suddenly unprepared. "Not here. Let's ride off-road." He wants her to have grass to fall on, but grass will be bumpier to ride on. Should he choose an area with a grade, or a flat? He wishes he had the cell phone and time to call Peter.

In Montrose Park, a tall man is doing tai chi. Nita bumps along the grass past him. A couple in matching knee braces play a slow tennis match on one of the courts alongside Dumbarton. Big crows stand nearby while Jon gets out his tools and removes Nita's training wheels. His heart pounds. Large, bumpy Osage orange fruits make an obstacle course of the lawn. Jon searches for a route down the gentle slope between the scattered trees toward the jungle gym. Nita won't get that far. If she does, she'll just brake. He holds Nita's bike as she climbs on. He wishes he could map her exact route.

"Give me a push," Nita says. Jon is about to give her much advice, but instead gives her the tenderest launch in history. She creeps forward across the lawn, shoulders tense, elbows out. The handlebars oscillate. Nita stiffens and stops pedaling.

Jon starts forward to catch her, stops himself. The grade pulls the bike forward. The front wheel stops wiggling. Nita's feet give the pedals a tweak. She coasts, picking up speed, her hair rising like a fragile brown windsock. Nita is almost to the jungle gym before she finds her brakes, teeters, and leaps free of the falling bike. She runs back up to Jon, yelling. "I did it! Did you see?"

"I saw!" Jon yells, running. Then she's in his arms.

JUNE

The Competition

"BIRTHDAY CAKE is for one-year-old babies to squeeze and mash onto their faces," Bailey says. He's driving Louisa out to his daughter Bess's in Chevy Chase for his birthday party.

"What do you want instead?" Louisa asks.

"Oh, I don't know." But Bailey does know. He wants to kiss her. The thought came upon him quite powerfully when Louisa floated down the long staircase, announcing she was ready. Bailey was looking out the front window at the twilight. It has been a long time since he waited for a woman to dress. He hadn't known how much he missed that until he was waiting for Louisa—waiting, then appreciating her choice of dress, coming to her side, smelling her perfume. He only just stopped himself from taking Louisa's arm as they headed out. She is lovely and, he must remind himself sternly, all but engaged.

"It won't be as bad as that," Louisa tells him. "Just pretend it's Stevie or Laura's birthday."

"True. They'll be the main attraction."

"Remind me who's going to be there."

"Let's see. You haven't met Bess and TJ, Dee's parents, or

Dee's brother, Blake. Stevie and Laura, my grandniece and nephew, and their parents, Mike and Jess. Or," he says, with a tiny hesitation, "Marsha."

"She the one who wants to marry you?"

"Is that what Dee told you?"

"Yes."

"Marsha's a good friend."

"Dee says she's a catch."

"She is. I suppose I'm a fool. But she and Caroline were so close. I don't want to be with someone whom Caroline knows so well."

"Knew."

"Right. Caroline kept watch over Marsha after Marsha's husband died. Now I check up on her. I suppose she's checking up on me, too."

"Does she work?"

"She's on the boards of Sibley Hospital and the Washington Ballet." They pass the art deco facade of the Uptown theater, the Broadmoor apartments.

"I have a hard time conceiving of that as work," Louisa says. They drive a quarter mile, turn again before pulling into a semicircular driveway of a badly proportioned colonial house with the standard array of now fading azaleas and rhododendrons. Louisa finds herself unaccountably nervous. She was pleased when Bailey invited her to his party. She looked forward to finally meeting those family members she had only heard about. She especially wants to meet Valerie, the family's burden and yet, somehow, its center. Louisa has never met a crazy person before, only regular neurotics. She has in her head Hollywood notions of maniacal laughter and long, scraggly hair. She's also curious about Bess, Bailey's oldest daughter, who lives in this conventional house with her husband, TJ, and, for another year, their seventeen-year-old, Blake. How did Dee, so free and original, come from here? How did Bess grow up in the elegant Dupont house and end up, with all her money, in such a McHouse? Louisa is piecing together the Allard clan, studying their history, analyzing their branchings. Her interest centers on Bailey. She and Bailey talk about everything, except Chris and Caroline.

Bailey ushers Louisa past pillars, through the front door, onto the checkerboard foyer floor. With the lightest of touches on her arm, he keeps her just a step in front and to his right. This is the sort of gesture that draws Louisa to him. If only Chris had Bailey's way of looking after her first and himself second. A little boy, whom Louisa quickly decides is Stevie, Bailey's grandnephew, slides across the polished floor and climbs right up Bailey's long legs. Stevie was the one who had a fever the night Louisa met Jon, Peter, Nita, and Dee. That was more than two months back. The little guy climbs Bailey as if he were a jungle gym.

"Stevie, this is Louisa."

"Hi," Louisa says to the curly-haired boy, who has made it all the way to Bailey's shoulders. "Who's this?" she says, bending down to address a shy toddler who arrives a full minute after her brother and docks against Bailey's calf, sucking her thumb and hiding. "What a pretty party dress, and fancy shoes."

"This," Bailey says, "is Laura. Laura, this is Louisa."

"How old are you, Laura?" Louisa asks. Laura maintains her grip on Bailey but holds up two sticky fingers. "You beauty."

"So nice of you to keep an eye on Papa for us," a voice says. Louisa stands to face a well-groomed, confident woman in her early thirties, with Bailey's long limbs and Jon's good looks. Could this be Valerie? Valerie, who has been in and out of psychiatric facilities since girlhood? She looks like one of the well-heeled country club women who arrive at her mother's ranch, from as far as Missoula, to choose a Gordon pup.

"I don't keep an eye on him," Louisa tells Valerie. "I just

eat up his ice cream." Valerie laughs and hugs Louisa hard.

"We adore you," Valerie says. "Me, Bess, Jon, *and* Papa." The embrace does not loosen. Valerie's face is so close that Louisa sees individual pellets of mascara on her lashes.

"Thanks," Louisa says. Suddenly Valerie pushes Louisa away, takes Bailey's hand and pulls him further into the house. Stevie is riding on Bailey's back. Louisa steadies Laura, who sits down abruptly on her diapered bottom as Bailey is pulled away from her. "I've got you," she tells the girl, who is trying to decide whether to cry. "Do you want me to pick you up?" Laura studies Louisa for a moment, her tears thinning to nothing, nods. Louisa lifts her up, the girl's legs gripping her above the hip.

"Everybody!" Valerie calls. "The birthday boy is here!" Bailey looks back at Louisa, his eyebrows lifted. This is what Dee has described, Louisa realizes. Valerie's actions are strangely off kilter.

"You've met Val and Laura, I see," Dee says, coming to Louisa's side. "The strangest and the sweetest of us. Come meet the rest." She leads Louisa into the dining room, where the family surrounds a buffet table.

"I'm Dee's dad," TJ introduces himself. "Honey," he says to Bess. "Come over here and meet Louisa." Bess is as correct as Valerie is off. If anything, Bess is a little too decorous, making Louisa wonder what's really going on behind her placid smile. She plants her hands on Louisa's shoulders, presses her cheek to Louisa's, and kisses the air to the right of Louisa's temple. Louisa still carries Laura, who now uses Louisa to hide from everyone else.

"Are you hungry?" Bess asks.

"I am, thank you," Louisa says. She sees how Dee formed her own exuberant personality in contrast to her mother's unreadable calm. Kelley comes up beside Louisa, his arm encircling her waist.

"Have a relleno," he says. "Aruba peppers from our garden."

"You hold Kelley. I'll take Princess," Dee says, transferring Laura and putting Louisa's arm around Kelley's slim hips. "I'm not possessed."

"Possessive," Kelley tells her.

"What a lovely house," Louisa tells Bess. Kelley does feel muscular and handsome against her side. Hip candy.

"Dee says you're her new best friend," TJ tells Louisa across the table. To Louisa's surprise, Dee colors as quickly as she herself does.

"We are. I mean, she is," Louisa says. To fill the moment, she hugs Kelley tighter.

"All the fun people are eating in the kitchen," Kelley whispers. "I'll take your plate and save you a seat." Laura reaches from Dee to Louisa, so Louisa takes her back. In the living room, Peter is holding court. Bailey stands by the drinks table with a woman Louisa decides is Marsha.

"We're not putting any pressure on Bailey about the gay marriage case," Peter says loudly. "It's just that, if his ruling isn't acceptable, he won't get to see his grandchildren anymore. Louisa, how are you?"

"Fine. What's acceptable?"

"Gay marriage must be marriage. No domestic partnership or some such."

"Makes sense to me. What are you drinking?"

"Cosmopolitan. I'll make you one."

"That's all right," Louisa says, and starts toward Bailey and the drinks. Suddenly Louisa feels something give right in the middle of her person, right where the important organs are. Tears spring to her eyes. Her breath catches on the way out, then rushes back in. She looks at Bailey. She sees Marsha, attractive, his age, standing with a drink in her hand, holding his full attention. Louisa has the urge to go to Bailey's side and secure him. She doesn't question this. The world is a more urgent place. That's all she knows. She pulls Laura higher on her side and walks toward Bailey. Before Bailey can introduce her, Marsha turns.

"You must be Mike and Jess's new girl. I've heard you're a miracle. Aren't you big now, Laura? When you're ready to peek out and say hello, I'd like to give you a kiss." Bailey tries again.

"This is Louisa Robbins. She is my—"

"Where are Jess and Mike?" Marsha asks Louisa. "I've seen Stevie and Laura, but I haven't seen mom and dad."

"I don't know Jess and Mike," Louisa says. "I'm Louisa. I live in the house with Bailey."

"Oh."

"Louisa is a friend of mine. You remember Peter's idea that I take in a student. Well, I put a note up at the law school."

"Delighted to meet you," Marsha says, recovering with admirable swiftness. "I'm an old friend of Bailey and Caroline's."

"You were Caroline's closest friend. Bailey often speaks of you," Louisa says, pulling out her church-supper manners and settling, deliberately, an inch closer to Bailey's shoulder. Marsha struggles to regain her centrality to the scene.

"I hope Bailey has at least given you an air conditioner."

"She has a *working* air conditioner," Bailey says. "She's in Claire's old rooms. You know, looking out on the garden."

"Yes," Marsha replies dryly. "I know."

"It's quite comfortable. Louisa's friend, Chris, comes down whenever he can get away from New York. He's an apprentice surgeon." Louisa wonders why Bailey is in such haste to bring Chris into this. Marsha brightens visibly. It is clear to Louisa, in that sudden black and white vista that appears when lightning strikes the plains, that Marsha is moving in on Bailey. Not in the slow, steady way she has been, during the years since Caroline's death, but in a quicker way. Louisa is also sure that Bailey is oblivious to Marsha's new purposefulness. As far as Bailey is concerned, Marsha will always be Caroline's friend. For a moment, Louisa wonders what all this has to do with her. She knows it has a lot to do with her.

"When," Marsha asks airily, "did you move in?"

"End of April." Louisa says.

"Leo and Henry depend on her," Bailey says. "Even Virginia speaks highly."

"I'm not going to leave anytime soon," Louisa says. "I don't think I could study anywhere with normal levels of noise and interruption anymore. I'm spoiled."

"She brings work home," Bailey tells Marsha, who again looks perturbed, as if she has to belch and can't find a moment to do so unobserved. "She spends half the night at Caroline's old desk. No air conditioning down there, but it's cool enough after dark." For a moment, the silence is thick as Marsha pictures Louisa working at Caroline's desk.

"Bailey brings me snacks and expert advice. That's about as close to heaven," Louisa tells them, "as you can get."

"I always liked Claire's sewing table myself," Marsha says. "I was the one who suggested Caroline try it out as a desk. She wanted to bring in one of those horrible metal-tops. Laura, is this your mother?" she coos as a slim pixie of a woman approaches, smiling at Laura and Louisa in turn. Laura disentangles herself from Louisa and transfers her perch to her mother. "Jess, this is Louisa Robbins, a new friend of Bailey's," Marsha says.

"Thank you for taking care of Laura," Jess says. "I was eating as much as I could, as fast as I could."

"Anytime," Louisa says.

"What a dear girl you are," Marsha says. "Now I must have a nibble." She heads for the dining room.

"This one's booster seat is all set up," Jess says. "Her dinner is ready."

"Are you hungry, Laura?" Louisa asks. Laura nods.

"Don't go far. We'll be right back," Jess says. "I want to talk to Uncle, and meet you." Jess carries Laura off.

"What would you like?" Bailey asks Louisa.

"Cosmopolitan, please. Marsha's very attractive."

"She was surprised," Bailey says, reaching for the shaker.

"I'm surprised you haven't told her about me, in all those chats."

"I have mentioned you. I must have neglected to mention that you were a woman. I suppose, in retrospect, I referred to you as 'the student.'"

"Why?"

"I don't know. I'll make it up to you by mixing you a double." He does, handing her a highball glass instead of a martini glass. Louisa takes her first sip and realizes that she and Bailey are in cahoots. About what, or to what end, she's not sure.

"You can make it up to me," she says, "in any number of ways." She is flirting. What does this mean? She supposes there is a disruptive element in her presence in the Dupont house, a threat to the ghostly dominion of Caroline. Marsha is Caroline's living representative, a sort of keeper of the memory. *Well*, Louisa thinks, raising her glass to Bailey, *I guess I'm the competition.* "Long life," she tells him. She settles an inch closer to him, wets her lips with her tongue, and drinks.

Trust

"So the net," Max tells Eve and her money manager, "would be about eight hundred thou, after capital gains. I'm talking theoretically." George, the investment man, looks at Max as if he's wondering what Max is doing here at Eve's yearly meeting in the Prudential offices, eleven floors above Farragut Square. Eve is wondering much the same thing, though it was her idea—well, hers and her therapist, Alice's—that Max accompany her to the yearly bean-counting. *Perhaps if you include Max in your business decisions*, Alice suggested, *you'll start to feel that he isn't an intruder there.*

Since her pregnancy, Eve has been having ever more acute boundary issues. She is trying to firmly establish what aspects of her life she wants to keep hers alone. At the same time, she is trying to permit Max to join his life to hers. To this end, she has begun to allow Max into her apartment for entire weekends and is thinking about letting him join her for workouts at the JCC fitness center. Now that she has agreed to marry him, she is trying to integrate Max into her idea of the future.

As far as her money goes, well, that's hers. There's no unresolved conflict. The money used to be her grandparents', and they gave it to her parents. Her dad, who builds office buildings that start out as enormous holes in the ground all around Richmond and end up as twenty- or thirty-story colossi with windows like reflective sunglasses, enlarged the family fortune, and he and her mom gave a chunk of it to Eve on her twenty-first birthday. Max really has nothing to do with that money. Eve's mind boggles at the thought that people get married and just throw all their assets and debt into one big sack, especially when one person throws in the debt and the other the assets. No wonder marriages in previous generations were nightmares, with husbands autocratic comptrollers and wives secret hoarders and spenders. Her own parents each brought a handsome dowry to their wedding feast, a civilized solution. Eve has never understood the instinct for class preservation better than she does now, on the verge of a lifelong bond to Max. She feels a strong affinity to other young men and women of means, even people she doesn't like, whose politics are anathema to her and who wear pastels in all seasons.

"Don't you think we should hold Central Fidelity?" Max continues. Max, never shy, is already acting as full partner in Eve's property. He's talking his way into George's decisions. "I mean, George, who knows what kind of mergers are in the offing in retail banking?" George straightens up in his chair. Eve has to smile. In ten years, she has never offered George so much as a hint as to what he should actually *do*. She has only told him how much she *needs*, and nodded politely when he delivers his monologues about which stock or bond she has too much of and why she should consider consolidating this or dropping that. Listening to Max, Eve feels like a proud mother on parents' day whose third-grader has just spelled a word correctly.

"I'm wondering what United Petroleum's going to look like next year," Max goes on. "Since the merger, there hasn't been much E and D." E and D? Where does he come up with this stuff? But then Eve reminds herself that Max is a potty financier. He spends his hours of night wakefulness in the bathroom with the *Wall Street Journal*. When Eve wakes up a degree or two and sees the light leaking pinkly out from under the bathroom door, she knows Max is in there, shifting his vast nonfortune from Tokyo to London to New York and back to Hong Kong, speculating boldly on currency, placing silicon chips on the high-tech ventures of pimply engineering dropouts. Here, in the light of day, sitting in the tipping client's chair instead of on the toilet, looking at real money and talking to a real investment man, Max sounds pretty good.

"What about our pharmaceuticals?" Max asks. "I like Abbott. Have you read about their new great white hope?" George's attitude toward Eve has long been one part paternal concern, one part male appetite. Eve has been a coconspirator, dressing up for George and allowing him to pamper her, to place his hand on the small of her back as he ushered her in and out of his office during her years of majority. Today, when she arrived with Max, George said, "You look—" "Pregnant," Eve finished for him. She hadn't exactly wanted George to know she was pregnant. George talks to her father once a month about market developments, and Eve hasn't told her parents that Max is more than the fellow she's seeing. On the other hand, Eve doesn't want sleek, silver-haired George—an aging bachelor who perhaps harbored fantasies of marrying her and going from Rosen family investment man to son-in-law in charge of portfolio—Eve doesn't want George to think she's losing her figure. It's one thing not to let George seduce and marry her, quite another to let him think she isn't a perfect ten. "This is Max," Eve said, introducing him with no qualifiers. George adapted to the new circumstances. The three of them got down to business.

They are mid-hour now, having counted the beans but not figured out which are the growers and which are the throwers.

They are going to have to comb out a hundred thousand throwers, given suburban Washington real estate costs.

"I think we might sell some GE and some Coke," George murmurs with a hint of satisfaction. He takes credit for the events of the last decades—back to the end of the Cold War, the reintegration of Germany, the uncertainty of the Pacific Rim economies, the relentless inflation-clipping of the Fed, the feebleness of the Euro—in short, the doubling of Eve's blue-chip stocks during her adult years.

Eve has dipped modestly into the portfolio before, mostly into the handy dividend income but occasionally into the real kitty. On her twenty-fifth birthday, she went right out and bought the Legend. The odd thing was, no sooner did Eve, quaking, call George and ask him to sell off the price of the car (sunroof, leather) than the market gave a little bunny hop, and Eve had just as much money as before. She dipped in again for a vacation to Spain and for the furniture for her apartment. But never has she contemplated reaching into the portfolio with both hands and grabbing an amount with as many zeros at the end as she must today.

"If we sell now," Max says, "before Sweet Potato and I tie the knot, we pay less in capital gains," he says. "Plus, we hedge against whatever's going to happen next year." She's going to have a baby. Well, she and Max are going to have a baby. So of course she'll need a house with a yard, a fence, swing set, window niches, an exercise room, an office, a nanny. She and Max currently qualify for about a ten-dollar mortgage, what with their public servants' salaries and Max's school debts, which he boasts of as proudly as if each monthly bill is a recognition of his working-class merit. They are going to have to pay a hunk of cash down on this house and lose out on part of that wonderful middle-class racket, the deductible interest payment. That's why they are here today with George, for Eve to dig deep, which pains her on the one hand and pleases her on the other, since at last she can turn a substantial proportion of that stock market bonanza into square footage and bedrooms with closets, before another of the *adjustments* Max has been gloomily prophesying comes along and snatches thirty percent of her money away.

George wears a poker face. "On the other hand," Max is saying, "we lose the ten points a year, and we gamble on area real estate, which feels mid-swing to me. Interest rates are solid but not wonderful. We'll go fixed, since we probably won't move for a while. Probably just as well to channel some equity into real estate." George nods. "When are we actually going to buy the house, Dream Kitten?" Max asks Eve.

"September," she says. "Why do people have open houses on Sundays? I can't even get out of my own house on Sunday."

"Let's do eighty thousand now and let the other hundred float," Max suggests. George looks at Eve. She waves assent with the back of one hand. The men go to the computer and George punches away. Max looks over his shoulder, grunting occasionally as they sell off this and that.

"Damn, look at IBM. Just when you think they're belly up," Max says. He talks as if chewing a cigar, his financier affectation. George is silent. "What do you want to do with the booty, Buttons? Three-month T-bills?"

"Sure," Eve says. She's selling stock so she can buy a house, but she doesn't feel the exhilaration she anticipated all these years. Max is doing the fun part with George. She knows what Alice would tell her: *If you want to be involved, go help them. Don't be passive.* But Eve doesn't have the energy not to be passive. Men. They're always getting between her and her money. She wants to have her own treasure chest. Only she will have the key to the big, rusty lock. Max straightens up, grinning.

"We've got our nest egg, Miracle," he says. He and George wait for her to thank or congratulate them. Eve feels sick, thinking of all that old capital turned into fragile new currency. Max has a satisfied look. George looks at Eve accusingly, as he always does when she forces him to sell. He's thinking of what the next year, the next decade, would have yielded, if only these troublesome human needs, shelter, companionship, hadn't interfered with his long-term objectives.

"You give yourself a decent commission this time," Eve tells George. The man is forever undercharging himself. On the other hand, Phil sends George a nice Christmas bonus, despite everybody's being Jewish.

"Max should have the commission today," George gallantly replies.

"Max doesn't get a commission," Eve tells George. "Max gets me and the house."

"That's right," Max says. He pushes his glasses back until they're stuck to his cheeks. He grins at George, then at Eve again. Despite herself, Eve is mad for him.

Walk the Aisle

JON MANEUVERS the weighted cart down the cereal aisle in pursuit of Nita's Sugar Pops. He returns faithfully to the Safeway on Corcoran the way another person might bring flowers to a cemetery. David Matthieson, dead six years now, cannot know that Jon shops here to honor his memory. Yet Jon returns to *their* store and finds himself at peace once again, having made that pilgrimage. From Bailey, Jon learned to listen to quiet inner voices, prescribing duty. From Caroline, Jon learned the art of silent complaint, even while doing one's duty. Today, most of Jon's emotional injuries are acting up. He feels guilt for having worked late and now delaying his homecoming by another hour, even if it is to do the grocery shopping. He feels he has neglected Sam. Yesterday, after a hurried visit to Valerie's, where he held the little guy to his chest for an hour, he left Sam bawling miserably. Then there are actual aches and pains, souvenirs of competitive athletic youth. Sitting all day is hard on his body now, harder than gentle use. The left rotator cuff, the left hamstring, the right knee, ache. His underlying metabolism is enfeebled by the day without a workout. His lungs shuffle like dusty cards. His old heart pads along in his chest, like a cat in a travel carrier.

He finds the Sugar Pops but not Peter's Grape Nuts, inventory being spotty at this store. He takes the hairpin corner swiftly at the end of the aisle, the cart momentarily up on two wheels. In high school, Jon already lived primarily for balance sports. Day to day there was the bike, weekends the kayak, winters the snowboard. For nine years now he's had a new balance sport, life with Peter Day. This new one requires momentum and continuous readjustment. He and Peter love each other, they move forward, and that is what keeps them from tanking. Above all, Jon must counterbalance his own swoops and falls. Depression usually, but not reliably, hits him in the mornings, a melancholy that assures him his true love, tough, brilliant David, died and left him alone. Euphoria lifts him suddenly in the afternoon, when his marriage to Peter, sweetest of men, his love for Nita and now Sam, his belief in his work, all assure him that he is fortunate beyond expectation. That Jon appears to be the same man in the morning and afternoon is a daily accomplishment.

He grabs paper towels, fancy and everyday napkins. Self-pity and love for David carry him through the store. Right after grad school, in the basement apartment on 15th Street, Jon lived with David, shopped for David. Those remembered four months with David are nothing Jon can balance against anything else. David was a sky out of which Jon tumbled. That intoxication has not been eclipsed in all the fine Peter Day years since. Jon's premonition that David would sooner or later be the death of him was rendered moot when David began to die himself, despite all the miracle medications. Jon last saw David in the hospice on Upton Street and was unable to stop himself from sobbing out devotion in a speech David said reminded him of the deathbed scene in Garbo's *Camille*. David, sitting in the ornate garden on the spring afternoon, gave Jon a looking over much as he had the very first time. They had met at a party in Glover Park thrown by Ben, one of David's college boyfriends. "Sit down, Jon. Blow your nose," David said that last day. Then he got angry. Jon was Bailey's son, capable of only duty, honor, and sacrifice, which, fun for a while, came with too high a price tag. After a mere four months, life with Jon had turned into a bad marriage, a ball-and-chain imitation of sad, straight coupledom. David insisted that he either had to walk out or be tied to a lonely boy sniffling by a window, full of wheedling romantic dissatisfactions. "I may be dying," David said from his wheelchair beside the lilacs, "but that's not why you don't know how to live."

Jon doubles back to the dairy section. The first time through he remembered skim milk, whole milk, yogurt, and sour cream, but he forgot mozzarella and cream cheese. Never, before David, had Jon loved with such secret powerlessness. Never had he known the cycle of hiding, choosing not to hide, then wishing he had hidden his devotion. If there was one self Jon had been sure of until then, it was the lover who knew how to let go. How wonderfully wrong he had been. He squeezes into the narrow produce section and parks by the watermelons. Jon had believed himself to be a thoughtful solitary, a creature of habit and deliberation. With David, he had been a reckless adventurer. It couldn't last. It did last. Then it ended.

The plums look good but don't taste like much, Jon discovers, sneaking one. He goes with nectarines and a few peaches. Suddenly he remembers Peter arriving in bed the previous night, a few hours before dawn, curling up beside him with an I-am-here kiss. Peter had been working on the novel, which wakes him lately. Jon kissed him in a similar, I-am-getting-up spirit when he rose at six. Would life with David ever have become ordinary? Just before they split up, Jon spent several nights shadowing David as he went about his amorous rounds. Jon would sleep in the back seat of his car so that he could report to no one whose house David emerged from in the deceitful dawn. Now, twelve years later, Jon's passion and jealousy have become so abstract as to be indistinguishable from mourning.

Jon looks over the lettuce options, the mesclun wilted, the romaine a little past its peak, too, so that the iceberg calls out, *Take me. I'm simple, American, and can be cut into big chunks and slathered with ranch dressing.* Jon waits for David, as if he might appear at any moment from behind the cantaloupes and sweep Jon once more against his pitiless chest. But no. Jon chooses a cucumber, a yellow pepper, and relinquishes, by degrees, his regret. David will have to forgive him. Jon is alive and well. He has Peter and Nita, whom he loves. Soon, he will have Sam. That's just the way it is.

Because Peter saved him. It wasn't until their second year together that Jon realized that Peter had quietly taken possession of him, while Jon was, as Peter said, convalescing from a broken heart. David was still healthy, then. One day, Jon was looking at the EMERGENCY STOP button in the elevator on the way to a dance concert at the Kennedy Center. He was late, of course. Peter was to meet him at the theater door with the tickets. Jon knew, the knowledge as sharp and sudden as a bee sting, that he had a man and a home. A month later, Jon and Peter were raising Nita. A year after that, he and Peter declared themselves one in a public ceremony complete with priest, family, and an array of ceramic gifts.

At first, the story of the girl baby who came to stay had a fairy-tale charm. It was as if a stork had dropped a little bundle into the tiny back garden of their house. Their lives were suddenly dismantled and the pieces scattered through all the hastily child-proofed closets and cabinets. Peter didn't write a sentence for two months. Jon ran from home to the university and out to Chestnut Lodge so Valerie could spend time with her baby. On top of all the usual exhaustion, the two men faced the whole battery of resistance—disbelieving looks on the street, medical insurance tangles, no cooperation or patience from childless couples at dinner parties. Gay men were just beginning to adopt children in numbers then. What, everyone asked in one way or another, were Jon and Peter doing with a baby? The men grew closer, and more practical. There were decisions to be made about who would do what at what hour. Peter didn't have the fixed daylight schedule; his main job was art. So it was Peter who got out of bed night after night, Jon recognizes, heading for the checkout lines. Now he is asking Peter to start over.

Jon quickly unloads from cart to conveyor belt. He exchanges a few words about the weather with the checkout woman. Then Jon makes a go at the *National Enquirer.* He scans as fast as he can, but as always, he can't find the stories from the cover before it's time to pay. Peter doesn't thrill Jon the way David did. Perhaps because Peter is never cruel to Jon, never leaves him in doubt as to how much he is loved. Jon has to work hard to accept this sustainable, good life. He has self-destructiveness in common with these movie stars in the *Enquirer,* who have money, fame, everything except lasting love. It's as if certain people, Jon among them, have a hard time tolerating happiness and certainty. Jon could be a diva-type, divorcing yet again, taking sleeping pills and being rushed to the hospital. Instead, he's a work-a-day guy. Whenever Jon becomes too self-pitying, Peter gives him a who-do-we-think-we-are look that settles him down. Peter has a gift for conveying calm, the way David had a natural propensity to engender havoc.

Jon pays, thanks the checker. He rolls his cart toward the exit. *See you, David,* Jon tells his old flame, the one not meant for marriage. *It could have been different.* The automatic door swings open, then closes behind him.

The E-mail Eunuch

LOUISA PLUGS IN her modem and connects to the GW
server. She's in her fancy office at Arnold & Porter, which has
everything including a window and a door. She almost wishes
she were in the computer lab of Lucy Carson Library in Missoula, where she spent college evenings, studying and hanging
out with her friends. She has never liked uninterrupted soli-
tude. She's been reading about bankruptcy and refinancing
mechanisms since nine, with half an hour for lunch. Now, at
two-forty-five, her contacts are sticky and her head wobbles
with boredom. Time to check the real, as opposed to the work,
e-mail. She can't connect to her account at GW using the
firm's computers, which for security reasons only talk to one
another. But there's no problem with her using the outside line
and her own notebook.

As the modem whines, Louisa wanders down the hall to
the bathroom. She pees, washes her face, and makes her way
back to her office, nodding to her fellow workers. No one
talks. She has never spent time in such an environment. These
people work all day long, even the paralegals, as if they have
taken a vow of silence. They goof around only at ritually deter-

mined intervals, morning coffee breaks, lunch, and then, for some reason, just after four o'clock. Everyone socializes with a vengeance for ten minutes. Then they all glance at their watches and head back to their cells, in time to bang the clocks and log another fifteen minutes before four-thirty. Work rules the roost. Louisa, who has always thought of herself as a fairly driven person, wants to tell everyone, *Hey! It's June! Let's at least put on some music!* Two messages, one from her brother, Riley, one from Chris. She clicks Chris's message.

> Louisa,
> I got my schedule. I'll be working till six, so I'll be home before you get here. What shall we do?
> There's opera in the park. *Don Carlos!* Check www.summer-stage.org.
> Love,
> Chris
> P.S. I've been thinking a lot. I think we should talk. Maybe we should see other people.

Louisa reads the message a second, then a third, time. She sits down, puts on her headphones without thinking, and plays her new favorite pop CD—well, new to her. It's years old. She starts to laugh quietly. Shakes her head. Damn Dee. What a goofball, sending her a fake message from Chris. Dee and Louisa swap e-mail nearly every day, *and* talk on the phone. Louisa has been complaining about Chris and telling Dee she wonders if he will want to see other women before he settles down. Dee has put all of Louisa's complaints into this forgery —about Chris's dragging her to hear music, about his work schedule, and about his restless eye. Pretty good. Dee has Chris's style down, the way he forgets to begin "Dear Louisa" but never forgets to end "Love, Chris," the way he always has information to impart and often writes on the run, without small talk. Louisa clicks Reply and only then, when Chris's real e-mail address comes onto her screen, does she realize that the message is not from Dee. How can it be, since it's from Chris's computer? No, the reason it sounds so much like Chris is that it is Chris.

She closes her screen until it locks. She sinks back in her chair.

✴

At exactly four, Arnold & Porter fills with voices. The espresso machine hisses. The water cooler burps as ice cold water dispenses. Louisa chats with Tom, the most attractive of the male summer associates, a Michigan man with a tall, sturdy frame, easy smile, nice eyes. *I could go on dates with Tom*, Louisa thinks. Tom asked her to come get lunch with him during her first week at the firm, and casually inquired about her status on the way back. Louisa told him she had a beau, and Tom nodded in a *Duly noted* way. Since then, they have been friendly. Tom has made periodic inquiries about Chris, just frequent enough to let Louisa understand that, should Chris cease to be her steady, he, Tom, would like to see her in the evening. He lives right near Politics & Prose and has invited her twice to join him after work, to get dinner and browse. The bookstore and Tom's eyes are an appealing combination. Now Louisa drinks a tall glass of water, Tom having his customary tea with lemon, and thinks how an evening with this broad-shouldered guy would be just what the doctor ordered. Then she remembers that Tom keeps his lemon in the firm fridge, bringing a new one each week and cutting it into sixths, using a wedge each weekday and saving the last wedge for Saturday or Sunday. He always works one weekend day, never both. Tom is a little bit stiff, even if he is the best-looking summer slave. Louisa is having trouble getting excited about the prospect of being able to see him in the evening, though she wouldn't give up seeing him each day.

"You here late?" she asks.

"Looks like it. I need to give Milkman the Bowdan memo tomorrow. Look it over for me? Then I can buff and shine it in the morning."

"Of course. There's just this one little spot on the left." Louisa, coquettish despite herself, turns her back to Tom, who obligingly scratches her left shoulder blade. "Lower," she says, then, "Oh, yes." She and Tom read each other's work. One of their little jokes is that, whenever one of them hands off a text, the other does a little scratching. "That's the spot," Louisa says, upping the ante and realizing, as she does so, that she's unlikely to play her hand.

The final hiss of the Krups machine marks the end of break. Louisa heads back to her cubby, still talking to Tom, thinking it's a shame about the lemon. He really does a fine job of back scratching.

She opens the notebook. The screen blinks back to life. Chris's message hasn't changed. She reads it once more. Does he really think they will spend the weekend together, pursue cultural enrichment, then have their talk? Does he really believe that he will sleep with her Friday and Saturday nights, then call another woman next week? Yes, he does believe all that. If nothing else, Chris is honest. He wants to make the transition from Louisa to whomever as, well, surgically clean as possible. Hence the e-mail format. Louisa clicks Reply.

Dear Chris,
I don't think I'll come up Friday. We had to bring Virginia to the hospital yesterday and she is coming home Saturday. Poor puppy has diabetes, as we feared. She's going to be fine, but Bailey is going to have to give her insulin. He might need my help.
Have a good weekend.
Louisa

She clicks Send, knowing now that she won't see Chris again, or at least not as his girlfriend. She waits for the rush of sadness and anxiety that comes whenever she and a boyfriend break up. There have been two real ones before, Ed in high school, Steve in college. Both times, when goodbyes were said—she broke up with Ed, Steve broke up with her—she experienced that sudden rush of fear, as if she were leaving a place to which she could never return, as if she were giving up not just this one boy, but intimacy itself. *Bye, Chris,* she thinks. Nothing happens. *So long, Chris.* She tries to conjure tears into her eyes. She must be hiding her feelings from herself. The only thoughts that move her are that she can quit reading bankruptcy law in one hour and that, since she'll leave on time today, Bailey will still be in the front room reading when she gets home.

Choco Milk

VALERIE IS IN the living room with Sam, watching *Days of Our Lives*. Sam's sleeping. Roberta is downstairs putting the clothes in the dryer. Valerie thinks nothing, really, except that the sound of the dryer beeping, Roberta's steps on the stairs to the basement, remind her of the day of the milkshake.

When Valerie was five and Jon was seven, she made him a milkshake. She mixed it up in her red plastic cup in the basement of the Dupont house. She started with the regular chocolate milk from the kitchen that Nellie, the cook, made for her snack. She went down the back stairs to the washing room. She turned the mop pail upside down, climbed it, stood in the empty stone sink, and reached for the can with lots of writing on it where Hank, the gardener, got the rat poison. She opened the can and dropped a few brown pellets into the milk, which she'd set on top of the washing machine. By the time she had climbed all the way up to the second floor where Jon was lying in his bed, reading, the pellets were melted away. "Here," Valerie said. "Choco milk." That was how she used to say *chocolate milk*.

Jon didn't drink very much before Ollie, the maid, found

the open can on the dryer and ran upstairs, grabbed the cup away, and called Caroline, who was typing in the sewing room. Caroline pushed her fingers down Jon's throat to make him throw up, then drove him to the hospital.

Valerie got so much love from Papa when Jon was in the hospital. Mama didn't give her so much love because she was at the hospital with Jon. But Papa kept telling Valerie that he knew that she loved her big brother, that they all did. He said that she should never feel there wasn't enough love to go around. Papa played with her all day long, didn't go to work at all, and at night had Nellie make pancakes, Valerie's favorite dinner, two nights in a row. Those were wonderful days, but then Jon came home from the hospital and Mama still didn't give Valerie extra love, just regular love. Mama didn't give her foot tickles, just gave Jon his medicine and read to him.

On TV, Rudy is telling Mary that he loves her and they will get married soon. Rudy is lying. He's not going to marry Mary. He's cheating on her with Mary's best friend, Ellen. Sam is asleep in the bassinet. Valerie stands. Her head hurts. She hears the dryer door clank in the basement. She looks down at the baby. Its tiny lips hold a little gray bubble. One of its eyes is a crack open, and the other one isn't. A sliver of eyeball shows, blue and gray. Valerie picks up the pillow from the sofa and lays it over Sam's face.

❊

Roberta is starting to fold the sheets while they're still warm, when something stops her. Roberta is not supposed to leave Valerie alone with the baby, even for a minute. But Valerie is absorbed in *Days of Our Lives*, and Sam is sleeping so soundly. Roberta figured she can run down, put a new load in the dryer, and be back upstairs before Valerie even notices she's gone. But you can never be too careful with Valerie. Last year, Roberta's sister Lucy dozed off for no more than ten minutes one evening. When she woke, Valerie had sneaked out the front door and taken a cab to the Dancing Crab, where she met Mr. Sam. No matter that Valerie had no money to pay the taxi driver. What was he going to do? Have her arrested? Once inside the bar, the men took over, paying for her drinks, one of them, Mr. Sam, taking her to his hotel and giving her Sam. No, Roberta is not supposed to leave Valerie alone, even though the doors to the street are locked and Roberta has the key in her pocket. Roberta climbs up from the basement, emerging from the kitchen into the living room in time to see Valerie place the pillow on Sam's face. Roberta runs, picks the baby up. Sam sputters, then cries with outrage. Roberta presses him, hard, against her starched uniform. *"Ay, mi nené,"* Roberta moans. She turns to Valerie. Valerie is watching TV.

The Decision

PETER IS ON the phone when Jon comes home. Jon knows something is up as soon as Peter stops washing dishes and sits. Peter never stops washing or cooking to talk on the phone. On the contrary, as soon as he makes or receives a call, he heads for the sink or the stove.

"So they're not sure," Peter says. Jon recognizes Bailey's unwavering baritone. "I think so," Peter answers. Bailey speaks again. "Would you do that?" Peter says. "All right. What was Val doing alone in the first—" Jon is suddenly alert. He looks at Peter. Peter raises a hand. "No," Peter tells Bailey. "The important thing is Roberta and Lucy told us. Jon just walked in. Hi, honey," Peter says, reaching out a hand for Jon's cold one. "Looks like we're getting Sam."

"When?" Jon whispers.

"Tomorrow," Peter says. "Because there's... Listen, Bailey. I'm going to hang up so Jon and I can talk." Jon hears his father asking a question. "No, I'll tell him." Peter hangs up.

"What happened?"

"Sam's at Bailey's," Peter says. Jon tenses, his shoulders, his jaw. "Everything's all right now. Valerie laid a pillow over

144

Sam's face while Roberta wasn't looking. But then she was looking and Sam's fine."

"God damn," Jon says. He leans against the wall. His hands are in fists. Tears squeeze through his closed eyelids. Peter stands beside him, takes Jon's cold hands in his own. One by one, he uncurls the fingers.

"Valerie didn't know what she was doing."

"She did," Jon says, jaw clenched. "She does."

"Bailey's going to drop Sam and most of his gear off in the morning," Peter continues. "We'll talk to Nita when she gets home from Andrei's. Jon?" But Jon is listening for the sound of a baby breathing across town.

Triple Word Score

"ORTS?" Louisa asks.

"Crumbs, fragments of comestibles," Bailey tells her. "As in, 'The rapid consumption of crumpets made for an abundant fall of orts.'" Bailey and Louisa are turned toward each other on the slightly hard sofa. The board is between them, their feet on leather hassocks. Ella Fitzgerald is on the stereo.

"Are we playing Friendly or Fiendly?" Louisa asks. "Friendly is where you don't challenge, you help your opponents if you feel like it, and everybody takes as long as they want."

"Fiendly?"

"Challenges, no helping. Two-minute turns."

"Let's play Friendly-Fiendly Scrabble."

"Why not? Is *ort* really a word?" It is Friday evening and neither Bailey nor Louisa have plans. Louisa wonders briefly whether she wishes she was on Amtrak headed to Penn Station and Chris, or hiding out at Cafe Luna with a sad book for company. But only briefly. Bailey has promised tuna melts in an hour. Louisa is quite fond of tuna melts. A bowl of cashews is beside the Scrabble board. On the end tables are the martinis, which Bailey mixes wet, with more than a few drops of vermouth and an initial snowy melting of tiny ice flakes from the vigorously shaken shaker.

"In Fiendly," Bailey asks, "do we rely on the Scrabble dictionary, or on some reasonable dictionary?"

"Scrabble dictionary."

"Well, I don't have one. *Ort*, and *orts*, are perfectly fine words. I'll fetch the *OED.*"

"I believe you."

"I thought," Bailey hesitates, "you were headed to New York this weekend."

"I changed my mind. DRAGON," Louisa says. "Twenty. What's the score?"

"You're trouncing me."

"Hardly. I'm up maybe thirty."

"Thirty-two," Bailey says.

"When's the gay marriage case up?"

"Five weeks. I've got work to do. May I try out a few ideas?"

"Shoot," Louisa says.

"I want couples to marry, not be joined in civil union as in Vermont. The word *marriage* is imbued with power, as are the words *husband, wife*, even *father-in-law*, as anyone who has been given one of these sobriquets will attest. On the other hand, if the courts insist on the word, the backlash may be so strong that couples could have a longer road to get their rights."

"Sure," Louisa says. "The whole debate about judicial power and social change. You try to force change on the public, it can backfire. Was *Roe v. Wade* counterproductive? Would a less far-reaching decision, followed by a campaign of public education, have prevented all those bombings and state restrictions?"

"Gay marriage has been coming up from the states for a few decades now, the public education campaign has been effectively conducted, and the moment is ripe for the extension of state reform to the national agenda. All consonants," Bailey adds.

"Take your time. There's a free A," she points out. "Why do people have such a hard time with it?"

"The Welsh don't, I suppose."

"Not a rack of consonants," Louisa says. "Gay marriage."

"The fear that to be gay is contagious, that children must be protected from examples of homosexuality. To make gay culture open encourages vice."

"Sad."

"Primitive. Is FAX an abbreviation? Of course it is."

"Let me see your letters."

"My, this *is* friendly," Bailey says, turning his stand.

"JACKS," Louisa says.

"Proper plural."

"No," Louisa says, "the game. What do Jon and Peter think?"

"I thought that was JAX."

"Not at all," Louisa says. Bailey sets out the letters and jots down his score.

"Jon and Peter are representative of the two schools of thought. Jon is a pragmatist who only wants federal law to recognize the Vermont model of civil union. Peter is a fist-shaker who wants the word *marriage*. Jon is a historian who knows what a reaction in Congress might mean. Peter is a novelist who believes that language shapes thought."

"I've got the opposite problem."

"You see a third strategy?"

"No," Louisa says. "Six vowels. I want to use at least three."

"I'm moving Peter's way as I get older. It's a myth, you know, about one becoming conservative with age."

"Thank goodness for that. I keep thinking of *Brown v. Board of Ed.* What if Warren had been a wait-and-seer?"

"He was. He had been waiting and seeing since *Plessy v. Ferguson.*"

"NAIAD. Double word score. Say you insist on the word *marriage*. What will the Supremes do with your decision?"

"Well," Bailey says, hunkering his chin left, and making his right eyebrow into a little ^. "Jon would say I'm forcing the Court into a confrontation over DOMA. Peter would say I'm opening their imaginations to the possibility of change."

"Yes, but what will happen?"

"I've checked my crystal ball. I believe that what will happen is the Court will tuck tail between legs and refuse to take the case. They'll let appeals courts take their cue from us, and wait another five years, until there are five or six more decisions, half invoking the word *marriage*, half letting the distinction between straight and gay stand. Another five years of public education. Then they'll take a case and rule in favor of the word. ROPE. Pitiful, but there it is."

"SCYTHE. Triple word score."

"Ouch. You were planning that."

"I have my crystal ball, too," Louisa says. "Where do you keep yours?"

"In the toolshed with the time machine. Tell me," Bailey asks her. "Did you plan on using that S when you showed me JACKS?"

"Sure."

"That's the fiendly side."

"Win-win," Louisa says. "Helped you out, set me up."

JULY

Night Shift

IN HIS SLEEP, Sam objects to something, shaking his head and saying, *"Grauept."* Peter prays, *Please, God. Let not Sam awaken before I get a little more writing time.* Sam opens his eyes, looks at Peter over the side of his basket, then closes his eyes again. *Thank you, Lord,* Peter thinks. It is three-fifteen in the morning. The Church Street house is blue with shadow. Peter begins again. Night fairies waltz around, keep him company. They whisper dialogue, suggest comma placement. Peter taps. New words twinkle on the screen.

In the week since Sam came to stay for good, Peter has had trouble finding his rhythm. He goes to bed and drops into unconsciousness without preamble right after dinner. Jon spends the evening with Nita and Sam, gives Sam his bottle, reads Nita her book, and tucks everybody in. Peter, having slept a blessed four to six hours, rises to the potent alarm of Sam's shrill wail at around two. After a change and a new bottle, Sam wrestles the Sandman with superhuman effort, fighting to keep his own eyes open and limbs wiggling. While Sam struggles, Peter powers up the computer, finds his spot. When Sam conks, the fairies gather and whisper, and Peter is off, sometimes for fifteen minutes, sometimes for four hours. The night shift is a fine and mysterious time. Anticipation of it whispers in Peter's ear, like an orchestral accompaniment, throughout the day of errands and loving his children and husband.

As for the novel, it grows in the heart of the night. At first the novel worried that it would be neglected for the baby boy. But Peter is tied to the house. Unexpectedly, Sam's presence makes Peter work harder than he has for some time. The novel now likes the baby.

Peter talks to himself. He smiles, grimaces in the glow of the screen. He has a twenty-hour beard. His eyes are full of stories.

❁

"Sugar?" Peter softly calls, settling on Nita's bed at seven. Nita sleeps in a pretty maple bed, which catches the light. A stack of books from the West End Library reaches almost to mattress height. *The Wind in the Willows*, which she was reading with Jon last night, is on top. Peter rubs Nita's back in circles. He loves her so much he feels a sweet ache in the middle of his chest. "Almost time to climb out. Radio?" She nods, her mouth and eyes closed on secret thoughts. For some reason, Nita wakes most placidly to the chatter of WASH. Peter switches on the morning show. He lingers beside her, mentally reviews the pages he has written. He sees snatches of text on the pale plaster of the wall. He lengthens his neck and generally tries to shape himself out of the Day family hunch that is creeping up on him with the years. The new pages are delicate, now that he is away from them. Will their meanings survive the daylight?

"Okay, Mouse. You open your eyes and climb out of the burrow. I'll toast your bagel." She nods. He kisses her temple, the top of her head. She smells small and hot. She smells of the sweet Australian papaya shampoo she chose herself at the drugstore.

The Arrangement

"I'M NOT GOING to free you," Louisa tells Leo and Henry, taking Virginia off her leash. "You will get yourselves squashed by a bus. You will harass poodles." The males listen and wait. Virginia walks and sniffs. The sun hangs on the horizon like a worn-out basketball. "Bailey allows you to run wild. But he's not as exposed as I am. He is owner, but not shepherd. Shepherd assumes greater risk than owner. Much of early tort law arises from this relation, going back to the Brehon Laws, as Phillips notes in his seminal *Jurisprudence of Land and Tenant*." Louisa finds it pleasant to lecture the dogs while walking them. Today she discourses along Dupont's southern edge. "Virginia has established a history of nonsilliness. She has earned what appears to be a margin of liberty, but is actually a reciprocal obligation." A whippet is taking in the view of Dupont Circle from where she stands in front of the Washington Club. She and her walker cross over to Dupont at the eastern Massachusetts Avenue entrance. Leo and Henry strain forward. *"Quod erat demonstrandum,"* Louisa says.

"Candy will look after them," Dana tells Louisa, coming up beside her. "I'm Dana." Louisa takes a little breath. Dana is nearly six feet tall, has a weave of gray and black hair, a wide, strong face, and a fabulous sleeveless suit of chartreuse shantung. She stores a pink *London Financial Times* away in a Newsroom bag.

"Sure," Louisa says. "Bailey talks about you and Sean all the time."

"Candy, will you watch the puppies?" Dana calls to a woman sitting on the lawn. Candy's nose and forehead are burnt pink. Her nest of hair is tied back in a bandanna. She wears pants and an evening gown in gray crepe under a blue sundress with a yellow daisy pattern. Candy holds out her hands. Louisa leads Leo and Henry over.

"Hi, Candy," Louisa says. "I'm Louisa." Candy won't look at her, now that Louisa is near. "If I take these boys off their leashes, they won't keep still." Henry wags.

"I'll watch them," Candy whispers. She reaches across to Leo and Henry. They sniff her freckled wrists with interest. Louisa unhooks their collars.

"Thanks," Louisa says. Candy takes out a comb and begins a vigorous grooming of Leo. He adjusts his position to make Candy's strokes more comfortable. When Henry bolts for Crown Books, Candy runs after him, leads him back. Louisa and Dana sit down on a north-facing bench.

"Candy loves dogs," Dana explains, "but doesn't accept handouts. This way we can pay her and we won't have to get up and chase Leo and Henry. What's Bailey up to?"

"Working."

"On a Saturday? Oh, the gay marriage case."

"Almost time," Louisa says.

"How are you two doing?"

"I'm enjoying myself. I've always liked old houses. You don't have to invent how to live in them. You just discover how it's always been done."

"Yes," Dana says. "You find those places to sit, those places where the furniture wants to be. Bailey's not too uptight?"

"At first," Louisa says, "we were both tiptoeing around each other. Now we relax."

"He's very fond of you."

"He's a lot of fun."

"Bailey says you're engaged to a fellow in New York," Dana says.

"I had a boyfriend up there," Louisa tells her. "We split up."

"I'm sorry. When was that?"

"A few weeks ago."

"You'll patch it up. Long distance is work."

"No," Louisa says. "It's over. We did better long distance than we did up close."

"Does Bailey know you broke up?"

"Yes. He said the same thing you said just now, that Chris and I will get back together."

"Listen," Dana says. "Would it be rude if you and I skip all the preliminaries, and I just tell you what I really think?"

"Okay," Louisa says.

"You should go out with Bailey."

"What?"

"A date."

"Bailey's older than I am. I'm Bailey's housemate."

"I understand that. You should go out with him some-time."

"Why?" Louisa says, her face suddenly hot.

"Well, first of all, because I know he's attracted to you, and he thinks very highly of you. Hell, that sounds like a business relationship. He doesn't think highly of you. He's drawn to you."

"How do you know that?"

"He told me so. Right there," Dana says, pointing to a bench about sixty degrees clockwise. "A month ago."

"What did he say?"

"He said he thought you were wonderful, but that you were all but engaged. He said he was too old for you. I told him nonsense."

"You did?"

"Sure. I said if he felt strongly about you, he should let you know. I said a person either is engaged, or isn't. I said, you never know what another person wants or thinks unless you ask her. You never know what options she thinks she has, and what she might be waiting for." Louisa smiles. "I was right. You weren't all that engaged. You don't think Bailey's too old for you."

"I don't, no," Louisa admits. "I think there are men who notice, and men who don't. Sensitive men, men who respond, and are considerate, and smart. And men who are just one of those things, or none."

"Yes."

"Bailey has all his senses going. He doesn't miss a thing, but he's not pushy. Capable, but not insistent."

"Exactly. So you do want to go out with him."

"Yes," Louisa says. "Actually, I do. But I didn't think that was possible."

"Strange, isn't it, the strictures we impose on ourselves."

"Just talking about it, out loud," Louisa says, "makes me realize how much I was holding inside. "

"What about a double date?" Dana asks. Louisa looks at her.

"Yeah, a double date," she says slowly. "Then, if this is all wrong, Bailey and I can just go back to where we were. It'll just be you three taking care of the lonely housemate, the law student who took your husband's class."

"Now you're thinking. Listen, Sean and I know this restaurant in Virginia. It's really an inn. Hell, it's actually just a house. We'll take Bailey there for a late birthday present. We'll tell him we want to invite you along."

"So Sean can get to know me, now that I'm not his student."

"Because I met you here," Dana says, opening her palms to Dupont Circle, and to Louisa, "and I like you, and I want you to come along. Which is all true." The women smile.

Shoe Trouble

"OH, COME ON!" Eve says. "Serge and Bacchus were Roman soldiers, who pledged loyalty to the death. You make them sound like surfing buddies."

"They were married," Max tells her. "They just happened to have the bad luck to be Christian under Maximian in Augusto-Euphrates. They had a ceremony in which their union was blessed by a priest in front of the congregation. They joined right hands. They walked the aisle. They were joined before God for all eternity. They kissed. They were crowned. They had a big party. Then they went home and got down all night."

"We don't know that," Eve says. "We don't even know if Serge and Bacchus were formally united."

"They were big, strong teenagers. You've seen the manuscript illustrations. There's no mention of wives or concubines. Their love was celebrated for hundreds of years. Trust me, they quaffed mead and did the wild thing."

"Be that as it may," Bailey says. "The young men were joined in a civil union, not a marriage." Bailey, Max, and Eve are in the conference room looking out at the Capitol. They are engaging in one of their informal debating sessions. Max plays the free radical, Eve the informed objector, and Bailey the wise referee. Today's discussion is of whether ancient history and anthropological study clarify the question of the legitimacy of gay marriage in our time, or if it's all very interesting but irrelevant. Max throws back his head and laughs.

"Read the Greek, man! The word for marriage *is* union," Max says. "Civil union? With full property rights and church sanction? I'll tell you what, why don't we call the transfer of a girl, a minor, from her father to another man, a contract which gives her no property rights, no civil rights to speak of, *slavery*, and call these same-sex unions the *only* marriages in feudal times. Let's agree that male-male marriage is the oldest egalitarian relationship sanctioned by church and state in Western civilization, while male-female marriage-of-equals was never seen before the twentieth century and is still the exception rather than the rule."

"That's pretty much true," Eve concedes.

"What about the argument," Bailey asks placidly, "that the male unions of the medieval church were the equivalent of modern corporate partnerships? The state argues that these ceremonies had nothing to do with marriage, which the Bible clearly indicates to be the coming together of man and woman for the purpose of procreation. Homosexuality is fornication at best."

"You wanna talk Old Testament? Sex with a woman from a neighboring tribe is an abomination. Spilling of seed is an abomination. We should not allow members of different religions, much less individuals from different *races*, to marry. Modern marriage is out of the question."

"Honey," Eve says, "the judge is not saying the good book should guide public policy. He's saying if you want to give a fair account of the place of homosexuality in the Judeo-Christian tradition, there's no way you can say gay marriage has any precedent." Bailey nods that this is a fair representation.

"Le Beau Serge and le buff Bacchus," Max says, rising and crossing the room, his pants low on his hips, "Polyeuct and Nearchos, Perpetua and Felicitas, all of these good people are rolling over in their graves, if they were lucky enough to get one. Bacchus died in agony after wearing out the executioners who flogged him. Serge ran a half-marathon in shoes with nails driven upward through the soles. The next day he got up and did an extra nine-miler. That *really* hurts. But when they went to stab him with spears, crucify him, and burn him alive over extra-slow-burning wet hay, Serge still had the courtesy to pray for them, saying, 'When you judge them, Lord, forgive them the tribulations which they have visited upon us.'" Max pauses by the window, hitches his trousers. "Do you think Bacchus went through all that so some doubting Thomasina in the information age, when all kinds of convincing documents from the world's great archives are finally just a click away, parchments from the Metaphrastes and the Antiquiors, from Mount Athos, the Bibliothèque Nationale, and the Vatican—"

"We get the point, Max," Eve says. She is seated in the room's only office chair, perfectly polished pumps pointing downward beneath her.

"—So some doubting Thomasina would dismiss their undying love, which neither Serge nor Bacchus would forswear even when they were crackling on the hibachi, as a limited partnership agreement?"

"Sweetheart," Eve tells him, "I don't know and you don't know what those brotherhood ceremonies meant, or whether there even was a historical Serge and Bacchus. We do know that marriage is supposed to be a male-female union for the purpose of procreation in every major Western religion for the last five hundred years. Let's just move on."

"I'll admit that the church is divided on the question of what to do with gay couples, and apparently has been since the beginning, when male love of Christ was elevated above all other attachments. Sometimes the church has tolerated, occasionally celebrated, and mostly persecuted gays, until today. Now all the major religious bodies—"

"Excuse me," Bailey quietly puts in. "Oral arguments are eighteen days off. I appreciate how far you've gone in exploring background. But let's not lose track of case law." Max and Eve ignore him. They have a wild look in their eyes. They have spent all their time reading about marriage for months.

"What about Ifeyinwa Olinke?" Max asks Eve. "Igbo tribe, eastern Nigeria," he tells Bailey. "What about We'wha, cross-dressing Zuni emissary to DC, 1890s?"

"Constitutional issues, Max," Bailey tries again.

"Silk Marriages?" Max continues to Eve. Despite himself, Bailey gives Max an inquisitive glance. "*Sou hie*, 'self-combers,' South China early twentieth century," Max briefs. "Financially independent women, paired for life in public ceremonies. Supported themselves spinning silk."

"All right," Eve says, rising and taking a slow walk toward him. "Certain non-Western traditions include same-sex unions."

"Yup," Max says, backing up until his head meets the window. Eve pushes against him without using her arms. She doesn't have to get all that close to accomplish this. In her third trimester, Eve is lovely. She has that meaningful front to her now.

"These may or may not have the same status as our marriages," Eve says. "We can't tell from the outside. The closer we get, the more we see ourselves."

"Heisenberg principle applied to anthropology," Max says.

"Break it up, you two," Bailey says. But Eve doesn't move. Her head is just below Max's chin.

"How can we know something as subtle as the real status

of a particular kind of public union in another cultural or historical moment?" Eve asks.

"We can't," Max says. "What is clear is that many civilizations have peacefully integrated gay folks into hetero communal life. Why can't we?"

"Exactly," Eve says, pushing off from Max and maneuvering herself into the comfy leather chair beside Bailey's. "Listen to Bailey, Max. That's our job. There's no point getting sidetracked. It just doesn't matter what Pope Leo the seventh's view of same-sex unions was in 970, or whether *hwames* were permitted by the Mohave to dance in fertility rituals in 1857. We don't need to go any further back than Black's definition of marriage. Gay people can't marry, because marriage is not for them."

"Tell me this," Max says, "Miss Limit-the-Context. How's your approach going to handle all these New Mexico couples?"

"The referendum is going to turn off the tap," Eve says.

"Nobody's going to rescind existing licenses," Max says.

"There could be just this one generation of gay marriages," Eve says.

"Thirty-five thousand or so," Max counters. Bailey looks from one to the other, as if watching tennis from beside Eve's service line. "That's eighty thousand people who are all going to get old, demand custody, medical consent, inheritance. *Times* said last week eight more states will rule reciprocal recognition in the next two years. *Federales* better get in line before we start looking stupid. Let us not forget 1967, when sixteen states had bubba laws." Eve and Bailey look to each other with annoyance as Max launches into his pseudo-Southern accent. *"Almighty God created the races white, black, yellow, Malay, and red, and he placed them on separate continents. The fact that he separated the races shows that he did not intend for the races to mix."*

"DOMA," Bailey says, too tired of this law to raise the topic in a complete sentence.

"Second section is gibberish. Section three overreaches. Whole puppy rests on invidious distinctions. We just plain rule it unconstitutional."

"I see," Bailey says. "Then call out the National Guard when the riots begin."

"The Supremes will back you up," Max says. "Congress will make noise, but won't do anything. The reactionaries will stump on the networks until they're satisfied. Choice-of-law will sink, like the eerie swamp creature it is, back into the muck of jurisprudence."

"Max," Bailey asks. "Do you really think a federal same-sex marriage law would endure, and not provoke a dangerous reaction?"

"Your Honor, I do," Max says. "Furthermore, I respectfully submit that there's only one way to find out."

Making Time

AFTER LOUISA backs the car out of the garage, which looks like it was built for a horse carriage, Bailey swings the wooden doors into place and locks them. He climbs in and Louisa exits the alley. Dana and Sean's invitation arrived addressed to the two of them.

> Dear Louisa and Bailey,
> Sean wishes to take you out for your birthday last month, Bailey. We want Louisa to come along. Pick us up at eight Friday. Regrets only.
> Dana

Louisa pulls up in front of a hydrant on Swann Street. Late afternoon heat shimmers off the car in front of them.

"Dana thinks that you're interested in me," Louisa says. She looks straight ahead. She hadn't meant to say anything, but suddenly she had.

"You are lovely. It's been wonderful having you in the house. I'll miss you when you leave."

"It's all right, if you are. Interested, I mean."

"I..." Bailey starts, turning to her. "You..." She looks at him.

"I think you're fine," she says. Bailey opens his door and walks up to number 1914. His knees tremble and his heart hammers in his chest. He presses the buzzer. He curses himself for walking away. He is a coward, as always. Dana and Sean come downstairs and emerge into the summer night.

"You look apoplectic, Bailey. What is it?" Dana asks, taking his arm.

"You told her I'm in love with her."

"Of course, you absurd man. Sean, sit in front." They get in and the car rolls off toward Connecticut Avenue.

"Nice to see you again," Sean tells Louisa. He describes where they are going. They'll cross to the Virginia side and head north toward Great Falls. She's having trouble concentrating on her driving, even before Sean starts asking her about school. "What are you going to take next year?" Sean asks.

"Intellectual property. International."

"I thought you were environmental."

"I was, but it wore off. I remembered that my interest in environmental was really my interview strategy. I knew I could make a credible case, with all my *Missoulian* clips. Truth is, I don't ever want to think about mining or water rights again. I want to see the environment protected. But environmental law is glacially slow. Regulation, reclassification. I can't live like that." Louisa is talking with that curious out-of-body feeling that comes from speaking ad hoc, while still thinking about Bailey and trying to hear what he and Dana are saying.

"True," Sean says. "By the way, my number's come up for teaching ethics this spring. What did you think of that course?"

"A little too Sunday school," Louisa tells him. "You could make it into something."

"Like what?"

"Why are you doing this?" Bailey asks Dana in a whisper. He is breathing again, more or less.

"The art of matchmaking," Dana says, at ordinary conversational volume, "is that of creating two realities, one for each lover. Your reality was that Louisa was ignorant of your feelings and unaware of her own. Hers was that you consider her pleasant but not a possible companion, because she's too young. Now, these ideas must yield to new ones. What exactly did she say to you? Never mind."

"The inn and restaurant is really just Bruce's house," Sean is explaining. Louisa passes the lions, crosses the Taft Bridge. Tree tops float just beyond the railings. Louisa can't understand Washington's bridges, which are built over trees and creeks, rather than rivers. She listens to Dana, that wild woman.

"This is where we are," Dana says. "You have admired Louisa from the moment you met. Only now do you have the courage to reveal yourself. Her New York beau was convenient, in that he provided an explanation for your honorable hesitation. He's gone now. You must approach Louisa with conviction."

"Oh," Bailey says.

"Bruce was five years ahead of you," Sean tells Louisa. "He got that sinking feeling at the end of his third year. You know the one. You're probably beginning to feel it yourself. Two semesters, then you're supposed to study for that funfest, the bar, before practicing law. Bruce took one look at that future and went off to cooking school in London."

"For her part, Louisa finds you a wonderful alternative to the boys her age. They have too many toys and too few emotions," Dana says, "at least emotions about other people. You represent a more genteel age. The danger is that you don't signify vitality and action. I can see by your face that you've already stumbled badly. Clumsiness later could be costly. I want you to practice. Now."

"Do you mind," Bailey says, "speaking more quietly?"

"Sean will drive back to town after dinner," Dana continues, as loudly as before. "We'll go to listen to jazz. You will be you, only slightly drunk." In the rearview mirror, Louisa sees Dana slide close to Bailey. "No," Dana says. "Don't be sneaky, and don't be lukewarm. Come on, now. This is serious." Bailey shifts slightly.

"Heads up," Sean says calmly. A sport utility vehicle, driven by a fist-waving, red-faced man, honks through a long Doppler shift. Louisa pulls her front left tire across the double yellow line to her own side of Military Road.

"Not bad," Dana says, settling against Bailey. Her eyes meet Louisa's in the mirror.

❁

Two tables occupy the whole of a brick patio, sided by rose trellises and fronted by an expanse of pasture. Two llamas graze, the closer one thirty yards away. Louisa hears the rip of grass. Further off is the vista of the Potomac. As Bruce serves the second plates, he tells Louisa the llamas are going to be pack animals when he and his boys hit the Appalachian Trail next month. The between-courses treat is aspic with raspberries and lime-and-chili-cured trout. They drink white wine sweeter than Louisa fancied fancy people would drink. Bailey, in his light gray linen, with the ochre and plum tie, his white hair lit by the candles, is darling. He has intensified, becoming more what Louisa wants. His awareness of her is continuous and undemanding. When she turns her head, he is there. When she doesn't, he is still near, talking contentedly to Dana. He rests his fingers on Louisa's hand from time to time. Suddenly, after the soup, which had a tiny egg on top, his foot, without a shoe but with a sock, settles on her own sandal-clad toes and rests. "Footsie," he says quietly. Her nipples press against her demicups. So she and Bailey are having a thing. She doesn't care what it is.

Bruce comes and goes with dishes that Louisa feels a

vague obligation to identify before greedily devouring. The sun has set and she can't see much in the candlelight. Each course is more delicious than the last. After the third glass of wine, she observes the scene peacefully. Sean wears a double-breasted aubergine suit, the kind of suit that Louisa would have thought too young for him. But in the candlelight, with no tie and his narrow shirt collar curled under, Sean's wearing the heck out of it. Dana's organdy gown shows off her shoulders and cleavage but hides her upper arms. Her hair, tied high with a strip of shimmering cloth, and the amber piece on the silver chain—not one of those opera star necklaces but still grand—are just what the late summer night, the tall woman, and the dress require. Bailey and Louisa are wearing pale blue, gray, white, an apt expression of personality.

"You're from Montana," Sean says. "Do you spend time standing on a rock in the middle of a river?" It turns out the trout in the aspic was flown in from out West. Why does Louisa like fly-fishing? Sean, who never leaves cities, is always trying to fathom other people's nature activities.

"Fly-fishing," Louisa explains, "is like creek walking. When I was a kid, I walked creeks in tennis shoes and shorts. Now I wear fishing gear and wade in rivers, but it's the same feeling."

"What keeps you from washing away?" Sean asks.

"I stay in the shallows—well, not that shallow," Louisa tells him. "The force of the water, even a foot or two, is like someone trying to pull you in for a swim. That's part of the fun."

"What about a boat?" Sean asks.

"You're always trying to get your line to some pool you can see on the opposite bank, or behind a rock halfway across," Louisa says, ignoring the boat question altogether. "You just know the big one is over there, waiting." She slips her sandal off, runs her foot up Bailey's ankle.

"It's beautiful," Bailey says suddenly, "balancing between water and sky."

"That's right," Sean says. "You fished the Alps, with Egon."

"Egon?" Louisa says.

"Egon and Mimi," Bailey says. "Virginia and Leo's people, before Caroline and me."

"What I don't understand," Dana says, immediately redirecting the conversation upon hearing Caroline's name, "is why the fish sometimes gets away by breaking the line. Why not use a stronger line that will hold the fish?"

"Tradeoff," Louisa tells her. "The thicker the line at the end right next to the fly, the less likely you are to fool the trout. If he sees the line, he won't go for the fly." She loses the other sandal, embraces Bailey's ankle with her two arches. He finishes his glass of wine.

"If the line is too light," Bailey says, "and you luck into the best fish in a strong current, your line just snaps. Then you lose everything."

"Tradeoff," Dana says. "I see."

After two sets of jazz at the Black Cat, Louisa and Bailey drop off Dana and Sean. It's almost three when they pull into the garage. The engine, amplified by the walls, suddenly falls silent. Louisa and Bailey walk hand in hand to the house.

Bailey first put his arm around her as they rode across Chain Bridge, Dana driving, Louisa and Bailey in back, on their way to the club. At the tiny table inside, Bailey kept his arm around her. Now Louisa's hand nestles in his. The dogs greet them, prancing and circling. Virginia follows Bailey into the kitchen. They prepare her evening injection. For a moment, as Louisa steadies Virginia and Bailey's eyes meet hers, Louisa wonders if this is just another night, the two of them in their new routine, taking care of Virginia, Bailey about to lock up the house. But after Virginia rejoins Leo and Henry outside, Louisa and Bailey stand quietly together in the pantry. They kiss, Louisa's kisses telling him, *Yes, go on.* By the time they reach the stairwell, Louisa is not wearing her sandals. She guides Bailey's fingers over her. They shed clothing, climb the steps. The air is warmer as they reach the landing. They climb again, toward the air conditioning. "Tell me," Bailey asks, as Louisa lays his shirt over the banister. "When did you know?"

"That I wanted you?" she asks. Her skirt puddles as she steps out of it.

"That I..." Bailey says, kissing her. She steps backwards up another step, reaching his height. "...have been loving you."

"Tonight." They reach the second floor. Louisa starts toward Bailey's room, hesitates, leads him toward her own.

"No," Bailey says. They turn again to the front of the house.

"What's this called?" Louisa asks. Bailey's hands pulls her hip to him as they walk. By the canopy bed, she reaches out her foot to cover his. "Still *footsie*?" There's nothing between them but cool air.

"This," he tells her, "is called *making time.*"

Bethesda

"IT TURNS OUT the way to choose a house," Max announces, leaning against the lintel through which Eve's parents have just stepped, "is to come to a neighborhood you've already ruled out, choose the house that has none of the features you're looking for, and make the largest financial decision of your life, in less time than you would spend picking a video." Lenore peeks around the corner, pulling Max by the arm. Eve follows with Phil, her father. She's irritated by everything—the house, which has shrunk and aged since she and Max agreed to buy it; Max, who is being himself; and her mother, whose instant and literal attachment to Max is excessive. Lenore met Max this morning, and already she's treating him like the son she never had. Her parents arrived at Eve's apartment at ten sharp. Eve's pregnant state made her mother blissfully happy because, as Eve discovered with Dr. Alice Shapiro, Lenore and Phil divide the emotional spectrum between them. Lenore takes care of enthusiasm, joy, and awe at life's mysteries. Phil does worry, pain, and looking at things squarely. Neither of her parents has much experience with anger or sorrow, though Phil may be adding to his repertoire now that Eve has picked Max for her life partner.

"Let's face it," Max says. "This house isn't Victorian, it's not colonial, and it sure as hell isn't Georgian or Tudor. We call it Queen Anne in front, Mary Ann around the sides and the back. Don't we, Little Buttons?" Eve winces at her nickname, which she usually loves hearing, even in front of friends. Max's fifteen or so nicknames for her are a shorthand in which he tells Eve how much, and in what ways, he loves her. He calls her Banana in front of her friends, and Eve is tickled and pleased. Not today. Little about Max tickles Eve today. Eve and Phil pass through the suddenly cramped kitchen, the den, the living room with the fireplace, the dining room with the built-in hutch. The house isn't cozy and dignified the way it was when she and Max decided, after four minutes, that they had to buy it, even though it was too old, too expensive, too close to Bethesda's congested heart, and had no garage. Now, her parents beside her, Eve can't imagine what she ever saw in the place. She must have seen herself, Max, and the baby living simply and comfortably.

"Your Aunt Mimi's house had a lot of character, too," Lenore tells Eve, her arm still threaded through Max's.

"Dentist," Max says.

"What?"

"The character who sold this place to us was a dentist. He had the dining room all fitted out. I hope it isn't haunted. The dentist and his wife have a six-year-old daughter. They said they wanted a bigger place, but I wonder if the girl wasn't hearing folks groaning and spitting late at night. Only a half bathroom down here," Max adds, throwing open the door so they can all admire the low toilet. Max is no more disheveled than usual, one shirt collar in his blazer, one out, one sleeve traced with butter from a dish that strayed too close to his orbit at lunch. Phil says nothing. Eve can see that her father's not happy that she's pregnant by this man who talks constantly and can't keep his shoes polished. Phil puts a premium on looking smart, prosperous, and inconspicuous. Down in Richmond, at Beth Ahabah synagogue, at Lakeside Country Club, Max is going to stand out like a hairless cat in a pet shop window. That's one of the reasons Eve hasn't introduced Max to her parents until this late date. When her father saw that she was pregnant, he took Eve's hands and kissed them, tears in his eyes. Now Phil looks around the old house in the cramped, postwar neighborhood and wishes, Eve guesses, that he were at work. Phil spends most of his waking life in an air-conditioned trailer next to one of the gigantic holes off Powhite highway, where his next building is going up and where he is in charge and in control.

"We made an offer the day we found the place. What was that, Radish, two weeks back? They made a counter offer. We accepted that night. Good thing, because they had two more offers the next morning. We knocked fifteen grand off the asking price," he adds casually, to show his future father-in-law that he knows how to hold on to a dollar. Eve steps forward and takes Max's hand. As she tugs Max toward the stairs, her mother finally relinquishes him. Eve feels distant from Max and is trying to love him. Max has no idea just how little Phil is impressed with his business sense. Fifteen thousand dollars is a sum that appears on Phil's company invoices next to items like grommets. Eve knows she has to love Max now or she'll end up seeing him the way she imagines her father does, as a fellow who doesn't realize he's bought himself a house with a slight western lean and lead paint on the walls and sills. How is a daughter supposed to love both her skeptical, dependable father and her generous, ungroomed fiancé? Eve's been feeling queasy all day, pregnancy discomfort and ordinary parents-meet-boyfriend nausea combining.

"How did you all choose your house?" Max asks Phil, as he leads the way up the rickety staircase. Eve winces at the *you all*. Max is working hard. She reaches up to take his hand so that she doesn't abandon him, ask her father what she's doing with this cornball, and just walk away.

"My friend Mort designed it, and I built it," Phil says.

"There was a little house by the lake when we bought the land, but we had it taken down," Lenore adds.

"Funny," Max says, stopping. "You just had the house taken down? Like drapes? Isn't that funny, Bunny?" Eve smiles tightly. The four of them reach the second floor. Max grandly indicates the long rectangular room, not large enough to qualify as a contemporary master bedroom. "This is my favorite detail," Max says, leading Lenore, who's delighted to be physically attached to him again, toward the twin closets in the back of the long room. "Ta da!" Max says, throwing back the closet doors, neither of which quite closes anyway. There are small windows in the back of the closets. The house is unusually shallow front to back, built on a long, narrow plot. Phil remains silent.

"Windows," Lenore says. "In your closets." Lenore feels Max is a good person. She told Eve so when she drew Eve aside for a chat at the apartment that morning. Max is the kind of man who talks about his feelings, Lenore explained, which Phil doesn't do. Eve is lucky. Will Max become Jewish? she wanted to know. Lenore is not born-again Jewish, the way her best friend, Caren-with-a-C, is. Still, Lenore goes to Torah weekends in the woods with Rabbi Beifield, and when she comes back she lights candles every Friday for a few weeks, until she forgets. Eve and Lenore were in the kitchen when they talked about Max's feelings and whether he was going to convert. Eve said Max was raised in the Ukrainian Church, which looks kind of like the Russian Orthodox church. Eve explained that Max loves his religion because it's so ancient and full of what he calls *bells and smells*. Eve and Max intend to raise their daughter, or son, in the two traditions. She, or he, will certainly be able to handle the concept of two Gods, Max says, since she or he will have two parents. Eve said two-religion households are common now, and though she has a problem with Christ and wishes she had fallen in love with a Buddhist, she's just going to have to let Yahweh himself take charge of convincing Imogen to be bat mitzvahed, go to Camp Kadima, join B'nai B'rith Youth, and work on a kibbutz after junior year, the way Eve did. Or Eugene. Eve's daughter, or son, will not be taught that anybody is divine, and definitely won't be told that anybody died for the sins she or he might commit once she or he is old enough. Lenore looked a little baffled by all this. Eve said that Max says there will be no place for sin in our house. *Only good, old-fashioned guilt. We'll have an ethnically Jewish-Ukrainian home, with a secular, Reconstructionist Jewish theology and ethics,* Eve told her mother.

"Let me show you the nursery," Max says now, leading Lenore by the elbow past the bedroom that was home to the dentist's girl until last month. This bedroom will be Eve's office. On the shady side of the house is another, tiny room. "Our sweet baby girl is going to nest here. Isn't she, Butternut? But not right away. We've been doing a lot of reading. In the end, I think we just have to go with the practices of every other civilization in history. Lenore, what do you think of the family bed?"

"I haven't read it."

"I mean the keeping of Baby in bed with Mommy and Daddy for the first year. Baby doesn't cry when she feels Daddy breathing, and smells Mommy, and listens to Mommy's pulse, which has been her soothing soundtrack in the womb."

"Really," Lenore says. Phil just walks right back downstairs. Eve abandons Max and follows her father. He continues through the kitchen and down the cellar steps. Eve finds him beside the water heater, looking at the north wall. The cellar is not finished. In fact, it's not watertight. There's moss on the wall, beneath the sooty window. Eve waits. Phil has been inaccessible since Eve's pregnancy was revealed that morning. The mortar in the basement needs pointing, Phil politely points out. "For the love of God! Montresor!" Eve whispers, picking off a chunk of mortar with her finger. Her father smiles.

"Yes, Fortunado," he says. "For the love of God." At bedtime throughout Eve's childhood, Phil read her stories. This continued long after she could just as easily have read them to him. He read her the books he had read as a teenager, not girl books about horses and fancy balls, but Poe, Arthur Conan Doyle, Edgar Rice Burroughs. Eve loves to spend time with her father, and her father loves to be quietly with her. Marrying Max, even now, when Eve is pushing thirty, poses two problems. How, Eve wonders, is she going to be with her father the way she likes to be? And how is her father going to get along with Max, when Max is so different from him in every obvious way? Eve remembers what Alice told her, that one's relationship with one's parents evolves after one's marriage into a mature friendship. Phil walks to the other side of the basement and looks over the house's wiring, a motley collection of the contemporary and the antique. Phil explains the different types to Eve, from the breaker box, on which the last owners had dropped a couple grand, to the ancient and apparently nonfunctioning knob-and-tubing, strung to the bottom of the full-measure beams like a teenager's electronics set. "I'll have Jack check the place and up-code whatever," Phil tells her. Eve doesn't suggest that there are electricians nearer than Richmond who could handle the job. "I saw trippers next to all the sinks. When are you moving in?"

"September, after the closing. Dad, you'll like Max. You'll see. He's just nervous."

"Well, he's a very energetic young man. I'll say that for him." Eve takes her father's hand. He looks at her. "He has one quality I require."

"What's that?" Eve asks, knowing what her father will say, but needing to hear it.

"He is crazy in love with my little girl. Crazy in love." Phil turns away, his eyes filling with tears, as they had that morning.

"Yes. He loves me, Daddy. And I love him."

"Now," Phil says with a generous sweep of his arms, "you've got yourselves a home."

The Way It Is

"WALKETY-WALK, walkety-walk," Jon says, ascending the steps. Nita holds his hands to balance herself, her bare feet on his loafers. This game is a vestige of her babyhood, when she would be walkety-walked up to her room, then changed to her pajamas and put down for the night. Now she does all the changing, tooth-brushing, and face-washing on her own. She comes downstairs and Jon walkety-walks her up for her bed-time book and goodnight kisses.

"The thing I don't get," Peter tells Sam, five months now and a whopping nineteen pounds, "is why anyone bothers to julienne carrots. What about just disking them? All right, it's not as pretty, but it takes less than half a workweek."

"*Gpmnt*," Sam says.

"And what's this business about cooking the salmon on one side? These filets are an inch thick. Frankly, it makes me a little queasy to think of the bottom side never seeing the broiler." Sam doesn't have much to say about that. He's standing in his Exersaucer and sucking on a felt-covered snail. The seat holds him upright and is ringed with toys he finds irresistible. The snail is his favorite, closely followed by the daisy, the frog, the ladybug, and the three caterpillars. He and Peter started cooking late, when Jon made it home and took charge of Nita. Sam is on his last half-hour of battery power before he will become extremely hungry, fuss, have a last bottle, and conk. Sam looks up at Peter and releases the snail, which springs to vertical on its plastic stem. He smiles.

"I love you, Sam," Peter says, and Sam smiles even wider. Peter says this as often as he thinks it, maybe fifty times a day. Sam may not understand the words, but he knows what Peter's eyes and voice are saying. Peter wants Sam to be as accustomed to this feeling, these words, as Nita is. "You're my sweet baby." Sam rocks from foot to foot and crams his fist, minus his thumb, into his mouth. "I respect your mother and your uncle Jon, but you know what?" Peter says. He's steaming carrot disks and keeping his eye on the rice. Other people time their rice, believing it a bad thing to lift the pot lid and check on it. Peter lifts the lid, adds water, and burns maybe one batch in five anyway. "If she tries to take you back, I won't let her. Not again. You're too old and alert to be stuck in a bassinet whenever she's just not up to paying attention to you. Lucy and Roberta do the best they can, but when your mother's in a state, they have their hands full. So that's that. I'll tell Jon tonight."

Sam takes a glistening set of knuckles out of his mouth and looks up at Peter solemnly.

❊

"Wait a minute," Nita says. "Charlotte's gonna die?"

Jon's been dreading this moment since Christmas, when Grant, Nita's father, gave her the book. Jon had hidden it behind a large fairy tale collection on the top shelf of Nita's tall bookcase. Last week Nita found it. What was E.B. White thinking, writing a children's book this frightening?

"Yes," Jon says.

"Why?" Nita asks, aghast.

"Well," Jon says, "because Charlotte is old, for a spider. She's had a good life. She's helped Wilbur win the prize for special pig. So Wilbur's safe."

"But Charlotte's not safe."

"No," Jon says. "We don't have to read the rest of the book, you know."

"I want to know what happens." So they read on, past the usual quota of two chapters, taking turns reading paragraphs, no matter how short or long. Jon has thought about how to approach the book since Nita received it. Grant, the idiot, probably just knew it was a "classic." The rules of parenting are simple and difficult. Know the terrain into which you are leading your child. Think about what effect your decisions will have. Grant is not up to this any more than Valerie is.

Jon delayed Nita's reading of the book. When she found it, Jon tried to talk her out of reading it. He told her it was very sad. He even gave away plot, which is not his usual practice, and said that one of the characters in the story, a nice one, dies. Nita shrugged. She said she wanted to read *Charlotte's Web*, everybody reads it. Andrei had read it. Besides, Grant had given it to her for Christmas.

> "I'm done for," Charlotte said. "In a day or two I'll be dead. I haven't even strength enough to climb down into the crate. I doubt if I have enough silk in my spinnerets to lower me to the ground."

Nita sobs painfully. Jon dries her tears with a corner of a bedsheet. He holds her close. Peter appears with Sam in his arms. He is about to ask Jon what the hell is going on. Instead, he stays in the doorway.

"*Charlotte's Web*," Jon tells him. "We're just finishing up." Nita looks at Peter through her tears. Her breath catches in her throat.

"Come kiss me goodnight," she makes Peter promise, "after we're done."

"I will," Peter says. He frowns at Jon and carries Sam back downstairs. Nita and Jon read on. Nita is not comforted by the appearance of the dozens of spiders who emerge from Charlotte's egg sack back home at the barn. The three little spiders remain behind with Wilbur when the others fly away on their silk balloons. This does not reconcile Nita to Charlotte's death. Jon tells Nita that sometimes, someone we love very much dies. We remember them, and go on loving them that way. The way Grandpa and all of them remember Grandma Caroline.

"Who died just before I was born," Nita says. "I don't care. I want Charlotte to live in the barn with Wilbur." When Jon tucks her in, she bursts into tears again.

"Is it Charlotte?" Jon asks, hating to mention the name. Nita pushes her face into the pillow. Jon sits back down beside her.

"I want Peter," she says when Jon tries to comfort her. *Great,* Jon thinks, as he heads downstairs. *Nita associates me with the cruel book. Peter is the good, comforting father.*

"We have to talk," Peter says, handing off Sam and a warm bottle in the kitchen. Only the stove light is on. Sam is on the verge of sleep.

"I should have just thrown the damn book out," Jon says. "But you know Grant will ask about it."

"I mean we have to talk about Sam," Peter says, heading upstairs. "I want to legally adopt him and Nita. I don't want another decade of your family 'understandings.' What if Bailey croaks, you get sick, and Val comes after both kids? And you're right. You should have hidden *Charlotte's Web* for five years, then hidden it again from Sam. That's not censorship. It's called parenting."

183

The salmon is dried out. The carrots are mush. The wine is slightly sour. Eating too late, with too much hunger and fatigue, is a chore. The baby monitor hisses static at intervals, as if expressing the tension between Jon and Peter.

"Want to dance?" Jon says, when they're finishing cleaning up.

"You're kidding," Peter says. "You want to have sex *tonight*?"

"It's been..."

"I know how long it's been," Peter says. "Well, actually, I don't. Do you know what time it is?" Jon does know what time it is. Athlete that he is, he doesn't consider sack time an additional strain. In fact, when he's tired and anxious the way he is now, when he and Peter just aren't in synch, making love seems like just the ticket.

"We don't have to take all night," Jon says. He won't look Peter in the eye. He feels as if he is inquiring about something inappropriate.

"Tired," Peter says. "Baby makes man tired."

"Husband likes to make love," Jon says, his face tight. "Just a thought."

"Oh, don't do that," Peter says.

"Do what?"

"You know. The I'm-a-healthy-man, why-doesn't-Peter-ever-want-to-make-love thing. As if there's something wrong with me, or I'm punishing you."

"Are you?" Jon asks.

"I just want to sleep. Is that a difficult concept? I've been with the kids all day."

"I see."

"Fine. We'll have a date," Peter says. "But you're doing all the work." Jon looks at Peter hopefully.

"You mean it?"

"Sure. Why not. I guess if I wait for a night when I'm not

tired, it could be eighteen years." Peter loves the way Jon always wants him. He wants to encourage this. Peter knows he'll get into it, once they start. He always does.

"I'll meet you in bed in twenty minutes," Jon says, smiling uncertainly, as if he's just won a raffle. He starts on the dishes.

"Bring a Power Bar, champ," Peter tells him, heading upstairs. "You'll need it."

August

A Cup of Coffee,
the Sunday Papers,
and Thou

THE HEAT invades the house after brunch, as noon approaches. Louisa and Bailey take the *Post* and the *Times*, coffee, and Virginia to Louisa's room. They use Louisa's room so they're not confined to the front bedroom, with the other air conditioner, all day. They make love again. They lie side by side.

"You're quite a guy," Louisa tells him. She imagines that a man can't hear that too often. She herself has never had so much opportunity to say it.

"For you," Bailey says. "I've never been before..." He falls silent. She kisses him. They read, Louisa on the chaise with the *Times*, Bailey on the floor beside her with the *Post*. Virginia lies beneath the window gnawing a rawhide bone. Leo and Henry are out back.

"How's the case?" Louisa asks.

"It's too big. Scattered from tax to due process to conflict of laws. There's as much sociology and theology as there is case law. I've got briefs from psychiatrists talking about how the children of gay couples are fine, from the Roman Catholic Church saying that gay marriage is not only sinful, but impossible. I've read strong arguments that marriage in state and federal statutes cannot discriminate against gays because it never considered them a distinct group in the first place. I've got equally well argued decisions proving that gay couples are entitled to marry, because marriage is a fundamental right. In short," Bailey says, cutting himself off before he becomes long-winded, "I know what I'm going to hear, roughly. I just don't know the most effective way to shape a decision."

"Look," Louisa says, holding up the wedding announcements. "These couples are all in their early twenties. What do they know about the world, or each other? What gives them the right to marry, and not Peter and Jon?"

"True," Bailey says. "What do any of us know, except whom we love?"

"Look at these two." She points to a picture of a black man and a white woman. "There was two hundred years of anti-miscegenation law against them. They couldn't have married until someone like you threw out all that."

"I know," Bailey says.

"Or these two," Louisa says, pointing out a description of a wedding of two residents in a nursing home, the woman eighty-three, the man nearly ninety.

"Fine. We'll just make this whole wedding section a footnote in the opinion."

"Why not?" Louisa says. "While you're at it, you can mention that convicted felons and child molesters can marry, and underage teens, with parental permission. That, in short, everybody but gays and lesbians can marry."

"The religious right argues that marriage is about procreation. But people who can't have children marry all the time."

"I almost like that argument," Louisa says, "because it's so silly. That only men and women can marry, even if they aren't fertile. That straight sex is okay, because it's like practicing making babies."

"If making love is about only procreation, then we are animals."

"Happy animals," Louisa says. She leans over and kisses Bailey behind the ear.

"Happy because we are free. Free to make love and babies. Free to make love without making babies." He tilts his head back and pulls Louisa's lips to his.

"I like babies."

"Babies are nice. Yours will be magnificent. But lovemaking is more than that. Lovemaking is a kind of glue that bonds couples, all couples, together."

"You make it sound a little industrial," Louisa says.

"No," Bailey says, tilting his head, raising his hand to his chin. "I mean, making love makes us love each other."

"I know what you meant. Why don't you write that?"

Natural Law

SAM IS ALL BABY. First of all, he has that hair style, conservative, wavy, light brown, thin in the pillow zone. He has that
ruddy, round, smiling and smile-inducing twenty-one-week
way about him. He finds the faces that go with voices, then realizes that, when he makes expressions, the face floating a foot
or so in front of him makes expressions right back at him. He
has the knee pudgies, which create a powerful need to squeeze
in even infant-shy visitors. You'd think, looking at Sam, that he
has nothing to do but sit around all day and eat like a miniature
sumo wrestler, waited on hand and foot by two men and a big
sister. He has the disproportionately large blue eyes that close
all at once when he's had enough bottle, enough being awake,
enough exercising his neck muscles, his running-in-place legs,
his rapidly flailing left arm, his right held stiffly by his side. Yes,
Sam is in the blush of babyhood now. When Sam complains in
short broken laments, like a stuttering cat, and is completely
intransigent in his refusal to settle down with a bottle, Peter
says, "Oh, stop being such a baby!" As if he could.

Sleep deprivation works two ways, making Peter either
giddy and giggly, or short of patience with everyone except

Sam. Generally, Peter is giddy with Sam at night and short of patience with Jon in the morning. Now it's Wednesday afternoon, and Valerie is coming for a visit, Lucy driving her over, Jon at work, Nita at school. Peter is pissed. Even when not exhausted and overwrought, Peter finds Valerie trying. Today, he is more than a little irritated by this arrangement, in which Valerie can drop by anytime with an hour's notice. Peter would really like to have a quiet hour with Sam before he goes to pick up Nita. Sam wears his light blue cotton suit with the bunny embossed on the chest. Sam is on his quilt on the living room floor, practicing that baby yoga position, Looking Straight Ahead While Lying Face Down, in order to converse with the rectangular grill of the heating vent in the wall two feet away.

Lucy opens the storm door. "Hello, Mr. Peter. Hello, Sam," she says. Lucy's efficient figure, her hennaed hair in a bun, her white uniform, all please Peter, as if she were arriving to stay indefinitely and help him with every little thing. Valerie is a step behind Lucy, blinking rapidly in the sunlight, looking like anyone, properly dressed, not talking to herself. Sam pivots toward the women.

"Hi, Peter," Valerie says. Peter takes a quick second reading of his sis-in-law. He's wary, knowing that it is when he lets down his guard and gives Valerie the benefit of the doubt that she really does a job on him. That's when she says the cruelest or strangest things. That's when she acts most dangerously.

"Nice to see you up and about," Peter tells her. Valerie has the hectic eyes Peter knows to be the flip side of long despondency. She tosses her purse on a chair, kicks off her shoes, and falls to her knees, close to Sam. Peter is immediately beside her, following the rule that he will never be further from Valerie's children, or anyone else's children, than is Valerie herself. Lucy declares *qué grande* Sam has become in the seven weeks since his move to Peter and Jon's house. Lucy heads for the kitchen and gets to work. There's no point trying to stop her. Peter hears her load the breakfast dishes, hears the squeak of vigorous rubbing as she bleaches stains out of the countertop. Hears Lucy speaking Spanish to Voltaire while she freshens his water and refills his bowl with food. If Peter ever decides to throw in his beliefs about domestic help, he will offer Lucy a yearly salary, and she will bring him *empanadas* and coffee with condensed milk in his study while he writes. She will tend to the children, hush the children, drive and tutor the children, and they will all tiptoe around him, while he writes. She will admire him quietly from across rooms, while he writes. He will occasionally ask her, *Lucy, what did I ever do without you?* This is all she will require of him, while he writes. Valerie lifts Sam and places him, facing away from her, on her knees. Sam balances, feeling the air with his fingers. Peter stands by.

"Lloyd says I can take Sam home soon," Valerie says.

Here we go, Peter thinks. Dr. Lloyd Jones would no more say such a thing than give Val her own prescription pad.

"You don't want me to get better. If I did, you wouldn't get to keep Nita or Sam." Valerie's voice is placid, even sweet, as if she were offering Peter the gentlest reprimand. "Jon will live with me. He'll help me take care of Nita and Sam."

"You can always count on Jon," Peter says. "But Jon and I live here. We're not going to argue today, are we?" Valerie has forgotten him. She lifts Sam high and flips him around, then holds him on her knees, facing her. Sam gives her a big, lopsided smile. The smile fades slowly when he doesn't get anything back. Valerie looks at Sam as if she is trying to solve a riddle. Peter's arms ache with the double work of wanting to reach out, and of resisting. Lucy comes in, wiping her hands on a dish towel.

"Miss Valerie, we can't stay such a long time today. You know you must not become tired." Peter looks at Lucy. "Let

Mr. Peter hold Sammy. Sammy is so big now." Lucy lifts Sam from Valerie and Peter stands to take him. Full diaper, he notes. He marches upstairs and puts Sam on the changing table. Sam begins conversing in Gruntspeak with the invisible audience floating around him in the air. Unlike Nita, Sam is happy on the changing table, considering it a frolicsome time for frog-kicking, back arching, and wrist sucking. Nita always felt put upon by temperature change, however subtle, and would scream her displeasure. At first Peter had been reduced to changing her in the bathroom, after running the shower for warmth. Valerie comes into the room and stands close beside him.

"You shouldn't have a baby. Lloyd says gays are illegal." Again the voice is gently teasing. Peter flushes with surprise, as if a sane adult were attacking him in some perfectly ordinary way. His hands alone maintain their distance from the barrage, methodically cleaning Sam, salving him. "You're not allowed to get married. You can't have children. You really shouldn't live in this country." Peter pushes the old diaper into the Genie, bundles Sam up, clean and dry. "My son is a gift from God," Valerie says now, Sam holding one of her fingers and looking at her ring. "I have to keep him away from you," she adds, and Peter feels his face harden. Valerie, he reminds himself, doesn't know when she's speaking out loud. She is just trying out voices, playing with words, to see what will happen.

"Why don't you sit down with Sam?" Peter asks Valerie, guiding her across to the glider by the window. Valerie sits. Peter carefully settles Sam onto her shoulder. "Lucy?" he calls. "Could you warm up a bottle?"

"I come," Lucy calls. Peter studies the beauty of Sam and Valerie, she holding her baby with rapt attention, Sam settling in, gazing up at her. Valerie's fine fair hair, Jon's hair, only longer, hangs across her cheek. She has an innocent, unlined perfection that Peter remembers seeing in photos of Jon when he was sixteen. Valerie never ventures outdoors. Her hair, her nails, her skin are taken care of at Andre Chreky Salon, on Tuesdays, when she's well.

"Everything is fine?" Lucy asks, arriving silently in her nurse's shoes. Voltaire is in her wake. Lucy looks closely at Peter, as if to surmise what has led him to trust Valerie so far. Valerie takes the bottle and gives it to Sam. Sam sucks ravenously. Valerie turns the nipple, adjusts Sam into a more comfortable position, as well as anyone could. Sam hugs his bottle with the whole of his rounded forearms — like Popeye, Peter thinks.

"Everything," Peter says, "is fine."

Lady, Godiva

"When it comes to riding," Dee admits, walking Godiva as stiffly as if showing, "I'm a reactionary. I don't know why. I just hate newfangled ideas around horses. I want everything to be just the way it was at Reddemeade Farms when I was a little girl—traditional riding habits, Caldene tweeds, Regent boots. As for technique, I'm down with manege step patterns, and no funny business with mouth position, thank you very much."

"I just want to have a good time and get back home without getting lost or bruising my butt too grievously," Louisa tells her. Louisa feels like she's back in high school, riding with her friend Julie, except Julie didn't ride English. Louisa, in her jeans and T-shirt, slouches back in the saddle. Lady, the lanky chestnut, pauses to nibble at the grass. Ahead of her, Dee, in beige jodhpurs and a sleeveless pipe shirt, posts broomstick straight, holding Godiva up like a mount on parade.

Louisa follows Dee into the woods on Western Ridge Trail. Dee borrowed the sisters Godiva and Lady from Reddemeade and trailered them to Rock Creek. She and Louisa are midway through their ride. Louisa bounces along under the trees, watching for low branches and wondering how to tell

Dee about Bailey. She knows she should talk to her today, that the longer she waits, the more Dee's feelings will be hurt. Dee slows across from Candy Cane Park, the jungle gym and swings striped like giant candy canes. Kids climb the ladder and push themselves down the unslippery slide. Adults stand around talking to one another and calling out warnings. Godiva snorts in the heat.

"I love Bailey," Louisa says.

"He's the best," Dee agrees, hands quiet. Louisa's arms and hands are all over the place.

"I mean I'm in love with Bailey," Louisa says, her voice ungraceful and young. Dee doesn't turn her torso an inch. Her velveteen cap makes her look a little like a monkey.

"Have you told him?"

"Yup," Louisa says, realizing that Dee thinks she has a crush but Bailey doesn't know anything about it. "We've been together for a couple weeks. I'm telling you first. Not even my mom knows." Dee stops posting and just thrusts with her horse's stride. Even in this simple motion, she looks like money.

"You mean *together?*" Dee asks, still not turning to look at Louisa.

"Yeah." Dee pulls Godiva to the slowest of walks. Beneath Louisa, Lady's bones lift and fall, first one side, then the other, like a giant machine winding down. Then Godiva is still, and Lady beside her. It is strange to be without forward motion. The candy canes on the far side of Dee appear to be moving minutely backwards. In the haze of the day, Dee's muscular arms stand out against her white blouse.

"Which room do you—" Dee falters. Dee, who can say anything. "Where do you—"

"We stay in the front room." *Stay,* Louisa thinks. *Why not "sleep"?*

"Bailey and Caroline's room," Dee says.

"Bailey's room."

"Wow." Dee takes her cap off, pulls a white kerchief from her pocket to wipe her brow. She pivots to look Louisa square in the eye. "He better not treat you like just another girlfriend. I mean when you leave, he better not—"

"I don't know if I'm going to," Louisa says. Dee blinks.

"You've got another year of school."

"I might stay in the house."

"Sure," Dee says. "You want to?"

"Hey," Louisa says. "You're not listening. I said I'm in love with Bailey."

"I know. He's my *grandfather.*"

"I think he's in love with me."

"Oh," Dee says. She looks confused. Godiva is walking again, Dee looking back into Louisa's eyes. Lady and Louisa catch up.

"Dee, I know this is a lot to take in."

"Yeah."

"Bailey is who I've been waiting for."

"Grandpa."

"Yes. I didn't know at first. Ever since I met Bailey, what was it, three and a half months ago? Ever since, I've felt like he was the one I'd been waiting for. At first I thought I was so happy, just having a real job and living in a real house in DC, not living like a student. Having you, my new best friend, to talk to. And Bailey, always there, always thinking about me." They parallel the creek. Lady breathes deeply, and Louisa takes a deep breath herself. "I knew Bailey was making me happy, but I thought that was because I broke up with Chris, or rather I suddenly realized Chris just wasn't there, never had been. I thought that was what was going on this summer. I was giving up on Chris, working, getting to know you and Bailey. But then—"

"Then Bailey happened."

"He did."

"How?" Dee asks, sounding a little like her old self.

"We went to that restaurant in Virginia with Dana and Sean. I told you about that place."

"I wondered what happened. When you talked about that night, you had a kind of hushed tone. I thought it was just the food, and being out with your professor."

"I didn't know what happened myself. I knew Bailey and I…"

"Wait. You slept with Bailey that night?"

"It started at dinner. Then we went to the Black Cat. We got home in the middle of the night."

"You slept together."

"We fooled around in the car on the way to the club," Louisa says, feeling odd to be telling Dee about it. "He wasn't shy."

"Fooled around how?" Dee asks. *I'm not going to tell her,* Louisa thinks.

"Bailey is wonderful," Louisa says, and nothing more for twenty feet or so. Dee takes the hint. Maybe she doesn't really want to hear details. "I thought maybe it was a one-time thing we would keep secret. I thought maybe we'd regret it and stop. I talked to you about that dinner. I didn't want to give away Bailey's secret. I would have told you, if it was just mine."

"Okay."

"But it's real. Even though we've only been together three weeks."

"Are you sure? I mean, Bailey's the best. Nobody knows that better than me. But he's—how old is he?"

"Sixty-seven in April." The two women walk the horses in silence for a minute. They come to a crossing. The trees give way to the water. They lift their boots, Dee tucking her shiny black ones up by her butt, Louisa splaying her ratty brown ones high to the sides. Godiva and Lady take their time in the cool creek.

"That's what I wonder about," Dee says when they are side by side on the bank. They start off under the canopy.

"I want to be with him," Louisa says. "I'd want him if I could only have him a year. Instead, I feel like I'll have him forever." They ride quickly. When they slow again, they are in a field. On the other side of it, a line of evenly spaced, bright cars travels along Western Avenue. Lady and Godiva suck and blow. Dee looks slightly warm. Louisa's T-shirt is soaked. She blinks sweat from her eyes. "You don't," Louisa says, catching her breath, "think I'm wrong?"

"No, you love him," Dee says. "He loves you. That's all that matters." Godiva and Lady turn a slow circle through fifty yards of seed grass.

Transition

"THERE'S ALWAYS a moment in birth stories," Max says, and the whole birthing class turns to look at him, "when the helper runs into the hall, yelling for a doctor."

"That shouldn't be necessary," Terrie, a labor and delivery nurse at the Childbirth Center, tells him. "One of us will always be with you during active labor. Plus, there's a call button."

"But this moment tends to come," Max says, "when the laborer is laboring, the promised epidural has not been administered, the baby is crowning, and there's no one around." *Laborer* and *helper* are Childbirth Center terms. They are inclusive, avoiding *wife, husband,* and *partner,* none of which might apply.

"That just doesn't happen at George Washington. People will tell stories. Don't believe everything." Terrie continues where she left off, talking about the advantages and risks of different anesthesia regimens. She emphasizes that no one should have a fixed idea about how the birth process is going to go. She talks about Flexibility, Options, and Choice, FOC, as if this were a commonsense acronym with appropriate associations. "Just stay with FOC," she says. Eve is doodling on the folder they've been given, creating a medieval map. She has drawn a pregnant woman in profile. The woman's belly contains an ocean in which there is a baby, a creature with a fish's tail and the head of a bull, a dolphin wearing an apron, and a whirlpool pulling everything downward.

"I'm the bull fish, right?" Max asks. "Virile hairy swimmer that got you in this situation? You're the pregnant woman but also Flipper. Gentle and sweet, helping the baby, wearing an apron." Eve sketches on. The snub-nosed, web-footed infant soon tows a sign across the water, MY OTHER CAR IS MOM.

"Any questions before Transition?" Terrie asks.

"Just one," Max says, as if he's been waiting for this chance. Eve glances at him grimly, pen suspended. "Why doesn't everybody get an epidural right away? Aside from FOC?" Terrie returns ever so briefly to the earlier topic, pain tolerance and timing constraints. She glances at the clock on the wall and plunges into transition, ignoring two new raised hands. As dilation occurs and the body prepares to push the baby out, the mother pants, loses track of time, develops tunnel vision, and screams whatever comes into her head.

"Think of transition as being locked in a closet with just one light to concentrate on," Terrie says.

"This is positive imaging?" Max whispers. Eve turns over her folder and writes:

transition

imogen
between the hangers
and the hats
next to the board games
below the scarves
put on your party dress
head for the light

"Nice," Max says. "Spare, strong."

"I don't want a critique," Eve whispers back. "Why don't you practice holding my hand and saying, 'You're wonderful, honey.' That's what your job will be."

"I'll do that."

"You'll say that you love me. That our baby loves me. That you love our baby. That everything's going to be just fine."

"I'll be there for you. Right now, I feel like we need another stanza."

Terrie announces a break. All the women eat muffins while the men drink coffee and talk baseball. Max joins the women. Eve has a new friend, Linda, whom she met the day before, the first day of the two-day class. Linda is carrying twin boys.

"I'm not bigger," Linda is telling Eve, as they do the pregnant women's comparison. "I'm wider."

"Your arms are thin," Eve says enviously.

"You're carrying high," Linda counters. "I love that." Linda's husband, Tom, comes over.

"I've been thinking about names for your twins," Max says to Tom, "as per our discussion. Romulus and Remus are out, not only because they were raised by wolves, but because of Uncle Remus." Tom agrees. "Castor and Pollux have sound associations of castor oil and pollution. Unfortunate, because Castor was a champion horseman and Pollux a top-draw boxer."

"We're going to name them Mark and Michael," Tom says.

"Nice," Max says. "Mark is Roman, meaning 'of Mars,' but with Christian associations. Michael is Hebrew, 'Gift of God.' Only named angel, besides Gabriel, in the canonical scriptures."

"Mark is Linda's dad. Michael is my uncle."

When they sit back down, they are up to Birth on Terrie's outline. The class watches a movie in which a mother has a typical labor, not short, not long. Her helper actively supports her by massaging her shoulders, saying nice things, and counting during the pushing. All the couples in the class cry when the baby girl is delivered, set on the mother's belly, and begins nursing.

"She knows how to suck," Eve says, tears rolling off her nose.

"She's full of adrenaline," Max says, sniffling. "She won't nurse like that again for a day." Max has read a shelf of books about pregnancy, birth, and nursing. He is of the knowledge-is-power school. Eve is of the I'll-learn-as-I-go school. Terrie turns the lights on and asks for questions.

"I thought it was funny the way the woman made her husband brush his teeth," one of the young mothers says.

"A lot of women get hypersensitive to smell," Terrie says. "Also bright light, scratchy sheets, drinking water that's not cold. Anything might bother the laborer a lot. The helper's job is to fix the problem, not question it."

"Can I bring music?" another woman asks.

"The Childbirth Center encourages personal music," Terrie answers. She refers to the Childbirth Center as an autonomous being, in a way that Max finds Orwellian. "Easy Listening doesn't work as well as New Age." Terrie has strong opinions. The best place to buy the books and music she likes is at nearby Borders Books. They have comfortable chairs and smoothies for the very pregnant. They have a play area for the already born kids. An example of appropriate music, which she plays for the class, involves a lot of repetitive native singing of many lands, overdubbed with glory-alleluia synthesizers. As far as books go, she particularly recommends a popular pregnancy book Max read and immediately hid from Eve—a book full of strict dos and don'ts, which defines cheating as eating a low-fat brownie once a month. Kim the Bold, as Max calls the other talkative member of the class, says she wants to take a shower during labor. Terrie is all for showers.

"Showers can just melt that discomfort away, before it becomes pain," Terrie says.

"I don't want to take a shower when I'm in labor," Eve says. "It's bad enough to be in pain, dry, in a bed."

"Every laborer finds her own path," Terrie says. "You may change paths, once you're in labor. Helpers should bring bathing costumes."

"This helper's going to dress up as Triton," Max whispers.

"The Childbirth Center," Eve whispers back, "encourages the bearing of the trident, but discourages the donning of the seaweed garland."

Show Time

BAILEY AND LOUISA wend their way to Logan Circle and ride south on 11th Street past two-story bungalows fronted by matchbook lawns. It is quiet and almost cool at eight-fifteen. Louisa, on Caroline's ladies' Raleigh, rides with her skirt tucked beneath her.

"How you feel?" Louisa asks.

"Unprepared. This could be the most important morning of my working life," Bailey says. He rides his old ten-speed. He sits tall, hands on top of the handlebars.

"You've been ready for years," Louisa says. "Now you're on the right bench at the right time." She has taken the day off to see Bailey in action. Already, as they ride through the rising heat, Bailey undergoes a transformation. He read into the night. For weeks he tested out his and his clerks' ideas on Louisa. She listened, and argued the anti–gay marriage position as much as the pro. Now Louisa doesn't feel excluded by his concentration. Her presence is not forgotten.

"What I like," Bailey says, "is the way it all comes together in an hour of argument. Thousands of pages, thousands of hours, condensed to the spoken word." They cross into downtown, the stone and glass blue in the early light. The Asiana Deli is already busy. They lock up their bikes and sit at the counter.

"So this is how history feels," Louisa says. "A day like the rest."

"That's what makes it so hard to get a hold of. We'll hear the oral argument today and issue a decision in a few months. Then we may hear the case again *en banc*. The Supreme Court will hear the case, or a case like it, in a few years. Their decision will be reflected in state law. If there is change, when will it have come? With the first civil union in Vermont? When the last state accepts gay marriage?"

"Today," Louisa says. "It will happen today."

❁

"All rise," says the bailiff. The three judges enter from the left, cross the dais. Patty Wells, a middle-aged woman with curly brown hair, Bailey in the center, last Martin Roland, a younger man with a sour expression. With his cheerful yellow bow tie peeking from beneath his robe, Bailey sits taller than the other two. He looks around the marble ceremonial courtroom, with its high ceiling and podium for the lawyers. His eyes seem to take account of each of the hundred or so people in the gallery.

"Hear ye, hear ye," the bailiff says. "The United States Court of Appeals for the District of Columbia Circuit is now in session. All persons having business before this court and the Honorable Judge Bailey Allard..." Jon and Peter hurry in and tumble into their seats, which Louisa has saved. Jon wears a summer suit in a dusty slate color. Peter has on a sports shirt and a Snugli with Sam in it. The first case of the day, a drug case, begins. Louisa and the men don't pay a lot of attention.

"How are you?" Jon whispers.

"Enjoying myself."

"There they are," Peter says, pointing out Thomas Wilson and Daniel Love, and their son, Tony. Wilson, seated in the second row, is a round-faced, balding man. He has a timid expression, wears a wedding band, and seems surprised that all this fuss has come of it. Love is a slim, graying fellow. Tony is about four and is wearing dress-up shoes and a blue sweater against the air conditioning. Peter whispers to Louisa that Tom and his husband, Dan, met at a volleyball game when they were freshmen at Wesleyan. They've been together ever since. How does Peter know? Louisa whispers. Read it in the *Blade*. College sweethearts. Adopted Tony through their church.

"What are you doing for lunch?" Jon asks. Louisa wants to have a late lunch with Bailey, after he conferences with his clerks. Bailey is planning to have a talk with Jon and Peter about his relationship with Louisa soon, maybe even tonight. Louisa has sworn Dee to secrecy.

"I'm just going to hang out in the courtyard, then go see Bailey," Louisa says. Peter looks at her for a long moment, as if something is just occurring to him.

"Chambers are down a floor," Peter says. "Left out of the elevators, end of the hall."

"He showed me this morning."

"Groupie," Jon says.

"Let's just say I'm saving today's docket for my album."

Finally, Peter stops looking at Louisa. The first case is over. The clerk announces *Love and Wilson*.

✳

"Appellees argue," Ms. Holmes argues, "that the Court has already recognized a fundamental right to marry. Yet the federal constitutional right to marry is a due-process right, affirmed in *Washington v. Glucksberg* and based on a history and tradition test. That test cannot credibly be used to legalize homosexual marriage." Ho-mo-sexual, Holmes says, giving even weight to the *o*s. Louisa has the uneasy I-told-you-so feeling that comes from having correctly laid out the battle plan the government's counsel will follow. She's pleased to have predicted the IRS strategy and to have helped Bailey develop counterarguments. She wants the case to be well argued on both sides and for Bailey to depend on her as much as he depends on his clerks. Max and Eve sit together at a table along the left wall of the courtroom, their legal pads in front of them. The IRS has half an hour and is past the midpoint.

"The Court's most detailed discussion to date of the right to marry is found in *Zablocki v. Redhail*. The *Zablocki* decision, which links marriage to legally permissible sexual relations, procreation, and child rearing, again highlights the heterosexual nature of the right to marry." Holmes, tall and businesslike in an Ann Taylor suit, knows how to modulate her attack. She is taking the IRS off the hot seat and will then argue that DC had to reject Love and Wilson's married status. Over the last weeks, Louisa has dissected Holmes's brief, carefully studied amicus briefs from professors of legislation and statutory interpretation, the National Association for the Research and Therapy of Homosexuality, the Parents and Friends of Ex-Gays, the Christian Legal Society, the National Legal Foundation, and the Roman Catholic Diocese. But Louisa has not *heard* the anti position articulated. She's struck by what easy listening the conservative position is, Holmes interpreting old decisions in a straightforward way. She looks past maverick state courts and methodically points out that there is no indication that the Court intends recognition of same-sex marriage. Holmes downplays the possibility of heightened scrutiny and whether the state has an interest in restricting marriage to different-sex couples. Holmes goes instead with the argument that the IRS was just doing its job; that the state of residency is the relevant one for marriage status; that Love and Wilson aren't married in DC; and that DC has the power to reject the effect of laws, including marriage laws, from other states, which DC finds offensive. This is true not only because state governments traditionally have such power, but also because DOMA declares that no state shall be obligated to recognize marriages that are not the union of one man and one woman. Louisa calls this the Which-part-of-NO-don't-you-understand? strategy. Then Bailey is talking and everyone is listening.

"The argument could be made that the District of Columbia has no business refusing to recognize one group of another state's marriages. Does Full Faith and Credit allow a state to selectively disregard another state's marriages based on judgments about the *quality* of the other state's policies?"

"Yes," Holmes says, not missing a beat.

"Why?" Bailey asks, smiling. Holmes looks up from her papers, squares her shoulders.

"The court may select between conflicting laws using a better law analysis. They may also apply interest analysis, Second Restatement, or comparative impairment analysis." The speed of Holmes's response is what counts here. She's still in the driver's seat, and she's said almost exactly what Bailey predicted she would. Suddenly Patty Wells, a.k.a. Civilization, chimes in.

"Why doesn't the place of celebration rule determine the status of Mr. Love and Mr. Wilson?" Wells's long neck and high hair give her a Nefertiti look. "If the District can void this marriage, why not the licenses of couples who marry after short acquaintance in other states? Or couples who return to the bride's or groom's home state to marry with no intention of establishing residency?"

"There have always been exceptions to place of celebration," Holmes says.

"Yes, but these were narrowly construed to block recognition of underage spouses and of bigamous and incestuous marriages." Wells looks to Roland. His cheekbones have shadows beneath them. He frowns at his own folded hands, as if interrupted from his thoughts by this whole court session. Bailey has told Louisa he and Wells will be talking to Roland, even when they appear to be talking to the lawyers. Roland is sure to write a dissent.

"It is in keeping with this narrow construction of the public policy doctrine that the District of Columbia does not recognize the marriage of Mr. Love and Mr. Wilson," Holmes says calmly.

"Despite the DC City Council having voted to accept New Mexico's licenses?" Wells asks, crossing her arms now and leaning forward in an *Oh, really?* pose. Bailey said he's going to let Wells carry the argument. Presiding, he says, is mostly the art of keeping one's mouth shut. Besides, Roland listens to Civilization better than to Bailey, or to any other male.

"Acts of the DC City Council do not have the force of law," Holmes answers.

"True," Roland suddenly says. "Acts of the Council are rather like the declarations of colonists petitioning the mother country. But what," he asks, his voice filling the courtroom, "are these acts, if not expressions of deeply held public belief?" Louisa keeps score in her mind, with a column for each judge and lawyer. One for Wells, who has apparently persuaded Roland on the Council question.

✺

"As Ms. Holmes argued," Wells tells Mr. Triano, attorney for Love and Wilson, "no state shall impose on a sister state any law that runs counter to that sister state's established public policy." It's time for the pro position. Louisa finds much of court protocol endearing, such as the way the judges occasionally refer to the states as sisters, as if the opposing positions are in regard to a pinching fight under the dinner table and the decision will be about which state started it.

"Yes," Triano says, brushing sweat from his lip, "but—"

"But what you're saying," Wells continues—Louisa also gets a kick out of the way the judges constantly interrupt the lawyers, who clearly aren't used to it—"is that DC, under Congressional oversight, may have the right to choose between its own policy and that of another state. Yet it may not have the power to arbitrarily disregard law of another state."

"Exactly," Triano tries again. "Here—"

"You argue that the exclusion of same-sex couples from marriage in DC does not reflect public belief," Wells goes on placidly. "Therefore, it must be a choice of law based on un-demonstrated state interest."

"Which runs counter," Triano says, unable to contain the quote a moment longer, "to what Justice Black called 'the strong unifying principle embodied in the Full Faith and Credit Clause, looking toward maximum enforcement in each state of the obligations or rights created or recognized by the statutes of sister states.'"

"I'm glad that's where you were going," Bailey says, inviting his fellow judges and all two hundred or so in the courtroom to smile with him. "I thought for a minute you were going to ask for DC statehood right now." Louisa smiles with the rest. Bailey keeps the discussion focused and shuts down minifilibusters, all without imposing himself. Triano, handsome and compact, Superman in a blazer, now talks about the difference between heightened scrutiny and *just looking really hard at something*. Louisa has read at least four or five times why gays aren't entitled to heightened scrutiny. They're not historically disadvantaged enough, they vote too much, they can't be picked out in a crowd, some combination of these questionable suppositions. Triano has been hitting three main points. One is that Love and Wilson's marriage should be recognized in DC, since DC has a long tradition of reciprocal recognition (*and without all this litigation*, Louisa wants to jump up and add. *Who ever heard of bringing your marriage license down to city hall, with the lines they have there, and saying, "Hi. We got married in New Mexico. But the thing is, my husband and I are ho-mo-sexuals. Is this thing good, or should we just tear it up?").* Two is that Council voted to recognize same-sex marriage licenses issued in other states. This one has been overly harped on, as far as Louisa is concerned, like one fine piece of china used every time guests come over. Three, the most effective one, is that DC, by granting the men guardianship over Tony, already recognized the integrity of the Love-Wilson family. So the state now has a strong interest in recognizing the men's marriage. Triano is hitting his stride, tilting his head back, speaking with a nineteenth-century oratory bravado.

"In *Meyer v. Nebraska*," he says, "the Court recognized that the liberty protected by the Fourteenth Amendment consists 'not merely in freedom from bodily restraint but also the right of the individual to contract, to engage in any of the common occupations of life, to acquire useful knowledge, to marry, establish a home and bring up children, and generally to enjoy those privileges long recognized at common law as essential to the orderly pursuit of happiness by free men.'" *Whew*, Louisa thinks, as Triano gasps a breath. "Implicit in the establishment of a home is the right to marry. Through marriage, two adults declare to their community and to the state that they are in a committed relationship and that they are ready to assume the responsibility of raising children." As if to illustrate that point, Sam wakes up on Peter's chest and begins to complain to the court about the absence of a bottle in a high, airy *wahwahwah-wah*. Triano pauses. Love and Wilson look back sympathetically. Peter recognizes the state's compelling interest in his exiting the courtroom. Triano continues.

"The superior courts of Massachusetts, Vermont, and New York have allowed *both* members of same-sex couples to be legal parents. In each case, the individuals had a committed relationship with their partners. Allowing adoption was clearly in the best interests of the child. The Vermont court made explicit that the paramount concern should be with the effect of laws on the reality of children's lives." The reality of Tony's life, as far as Louisa can see, is that he's got about ten more minutes of sitting and reading his books before he's going to start squirming like an octopus. He's been well behaved so far, reading and then exchanging books with Dan, who has a canvas Tree Top Books bag full of them. Triano winds up his argument, his back to all the people in the room. *Why not let lawyers argue in three-quarters profile,* Louisa thinks not for the first time, *and eliminate this rear view?*

"If the court considers the basis for the state's classifications, sex and sexual orientation," Triano says in a concluding tone, "and the right that is implicated, the right to marry, each in isolation, the court might overlook the important fact that in this case *both* the right in question *and* the basis for the state's classification are constitutionally significant." *Huh?* Louisa thinks.

"Hold on a second," Roland pipes up. Another convention of court is the informality of the judges juxtaposed with the ornate language of the lawyers. The more power you have, the more you can speak in ordinary English, according to the system. "You're saying that the men are in a group that doesn't get scrutiny, and the right in question isn't one that warrants scrutiny, but somehow when you put the two together, that warrants scrutiny? I don't understand."

"Well," says Triano, drawing a deep breath, "even though the court concludes that classifications drawn on the basis of gender or sexual orientation do not, in themselves, call for heightened scrutiny, there is no doubt that such distinctions create the *types* of classifications about which courts are particularly concerned."

"So we add up bits of quasisuspect until we get suspect. Is that the idea?" Roland interrupts. Triano leans over his podium for a moment, as if counting to ten.

"I would argue," Triano says quietly, "that the state must

demonstrate that discrimination against Mr. Love and Mr. Wilson serves a governmental interest, narrowly tailored to a valid objective." *They've come to that place,* Louisa thinks, *where you either acknowledge that gays are getting a raw deal or you don't.* She checks out the portraits on the paneled walls, some of judges dead a hundred years, others painted in the last decade. The older the portrait, the smaller the judge's head, the darker the canvas, and the more frightening his expression. Thirty feet to Louisa's left is an old guy, gavel raised, eyebrows twirly, about seventy percent life-size, looking meaner than a junkyard dog. There aren't any women from the olden days. But right next to Louisa is Sylvia Matthews, first woman appointed to the district court. Post-WWII portraitists are stuck between a rock and a hard place, wanting to make an artistic statement, but knowing the courthouse isn't the Hirschhorn. Judge Bazelon was done pointillist. One artist even dared paint a judge on the far wall *smiling,* with impressionistic robe, shirt, and tie.

Triano heads down the homestretch. "Judge Carter of the California Supreme Court declared in 1948, 'We must not legislate to the detriment of a class, a minority who are unable to protect themselves, when such legislation has no valid purpose. Nor may legislative power be a guise to cloak prejudice and intolerance.' This was nineteen years before Chief Justice Warren wrote, 'There can be no question but that Virginia's miscegenation statutes rest solely upon distinctions drawn according to race.' Today, we once again face a wall of prejudice and intolerance. Let us not wait another nineteen years. Let us break down this wall and march into the land of promised freedom, where men and women who love one another may receive recognition, through marriage, of their commitment to one another, to children, and to the communities in which they live. Thank you," Triano finishes.

He gathers his notes and turns, and for the first time in twenty minutes, the public gets to see more than the back of his head. He turns out to have wavy, caramel-colored hair, a tiny tie knot, and a chin dimple.

❋

Amelia, Bailey's secretary, knocks on the open door. Louisa is a pace behind her.

"Come in," Bailey says. He and the clerks are sitting in the conference room, Bailey having already met with Patty and Martin while Louisa read the paper on the lawn between the courthouse and the Canadian embassy. Eve is about as pregnant as a woman can be without actually going into labor. Max is bent over his own scrawled notes. Amelia makes no move to leave.

"Amelia, Eve, Max. This is Louisa Robbins, my girlfriend." This gets Max's attention. He looks up and peers at Louisa. "She's at GW Law, entering third year," Bailey says.

"Hi," Max says. "I didn't know you had a girlfriend, your honor."

"Max, it was none of our business, until now. Excuse me if I don't get up," Eve says. "You're the woman who's been feeding Bailey all those good objections to gay marriage, and objections to the objections. He said you were a housemate."

"I am," Louisa says. Bailey comes over and gives Louisa a kiss. If Bailey finds the situation awkward, it doesn't show. "I know you want to go over the case. Bailey asked me to stop up and say hi."

"How long have you two—?" Max starts.

"Max, can it. Nice to meet you, Louisa. Interesting morning, I thought."

"Fascinating," Louisa says. "I'll leave now. Nice meeting you all. I hope you're feeling well, Eve."

"I feel like a mobile home being relocated. You know how they always wobble back and forth on the highway? That's how I walk. But thank you. Only another couple weeks."

"Have you been going out all year?" Max asks.

"Zip it, Max."

"I'll be right with you," Bailey tells his clerks, and Amelia, who reluctantly withdraws. Bailey and Louisa go next door to Bailey's office.

"Well?" Louisa asks.

"I write the opinion. Patty concurs. Martin writes a dissent. How was I?"

"You were very dignified and dapper."

"Was I on track?"

"Wells brought Roland partway around."

"Think so? He's not talking much. I didn't monopolize?"

"Just right," Louisa tells him. "Holmes was excellent. She made precedent seem ordinary and sensible. Triano played the right notes, but a little too loud. You reined him in when he was wandering. Nice work."

"Now, we write."

"Better hurry. That girl in there looks like she doesn't have too much time for revision."

OCTOBER

Say "Ah"

Jon, Nita, and Sam wait just outside the group practice, one of a dozen medical offices in the building on Massachusetts Avenue, almost to the Maryland line. There are four doctors in the practice, perhaps ten patients and their parents in the waiting room. The receptionist sits in a white office glassed off from the carpeted room full of toys and magazines. Just inside sits a friendly woman, her sniffling five-year-old daughter, her busy three-year-old son, and a very unhappy baby boy, who is burrowing his head into his mother's bosom and crying in a tired way. Jon has brought Sam and Nita in for after-school checkups and has no intention of letting them catch a virus here. The woman understands.

"Definitely stay in the hall," she says. "I always do that when we're all healthy." Several mothers and one father look alarmed and start discreetly gathering their children closer to themselves. One woman picks up her daughter and comes into the hall.

"Now everybody's going to come out here," Nita announces. "Why don't they have two waiting rooms, one for sick kids, one for kids who aren't sick?"

"I don't know," Jon says. "That's a good idea. I'm sorry

your baby isn't feeling well," he tells the woman who, on closer inspection, looks a bit frazzled. Her hair, her clothes, the circles under her eyes, all indicate a long week, though it's only Wednesday.

"Nina, my oldest, had a bad throat last week. Now my little baby has another earache. I hope he doesn't have to get a tube."

"My friend Andrei got a tube," Nita says. "He thought it would make him deaf, but it didn't."

"Where's Mom today?" the woman asks, smiling. Before Jon can answer, the woman rises with her baby to chase down her three-year-old, who's prying a leaf off the rubber plant in the corner. A small wave of adults stand to pull their children out of the path of the woman and her sick baby. Finally, everybody's settled again.

"I don't live with my mother," Nita says, before Jon can decide how to intervene. "I live with my two uncles." Nita waits for the woman to ask more. When she doesn't, Nita digs in her backpack. She pulls out her spelling and math. Jon makes one of his quick calculations. He'll never see this woman, or any of the rest of the customers, again. The friendly mother may be ushered into an examining room any minute. Yet, Jon feels compelled to enlighten this small public.

"I'm Jon," he says at room-reaching volume. He even edges Sam, in his stroller, close to the door. "My partner, Peter, usually brings the kids in. This is Nita and little Sam." Propaganda. Peter is getting a massage, but of course Jon doesn't mention that. The tired mother introduces herself, Sheryl. She's a little flustered by her assumption that there was a mother in the wings. What wears Jon out is having to be charming at such times, so that the woman and all the others in the room will decide that gay men are just fine as fathers. He and Sheryl talk for ten minutes about everything except gay men raising children. Nita kneels on the hall carpet to do homework, which she has in quantities Jon doesn't remember getting until seventh grade. Jon and Sheryl talk about how much fun the fireworks display on the Mall was last summer, though too late at night, as always, for families. They're partway into suburb-versus-city life — Sheryl and her husband live near Glen Echo — when Dr. Scott's and Dr. Lewis's medical assistants appear simultaneously and usher both Jon and Sheryl and their broods into the inner complex. Jon wheels Sam in his stroller. The woman carries her little one, shepherds her other two forward with her hands and knees. Before they part in the examining room area, Jon lifts Sam, who has just woken and is blinking at the white walls.

"Nice meeting you," Jon says. "I hope your baby feels better very soon."

"You all have a good day," Sheryl says. She looks more relaxed now, as if she's learned, or unlearned, something.

"Twenty-one pounds, five ounces," Russ Lewis says. "Aren't you a jumbo. Nita, climb up on the scale. Don't jump." Russ is adept at the parallel exam. He has the two charts open in front of him.

"Mr. Potato," Jon tells Sam. "I bet you're going to feel even heavier now that I know what you weigh."

"Can I do my own?" Nita says, not waiting for permission before sliding the weights around.

"What's he eating?"

"He has cereal and jar foods twice a day, three times if we are especially conscientious. Formula. We graduated to a fast-flow nipple. He can drain a bottle in about three minutes."

"Watch yourselves. This is how the keep-the-youngest-a-baby-forever stuff starts. Ease off on the formula, up the cereal and pureed fruits and vegetables. I covered this with Peter last time. No meat or dairy for another six weeks."

"Mea culpa," Jon says. "I promise I won't still speak to Sam in baby talk when he's in middle school."

"I'll hold you to that. Here's a tooth," Russ says, his finger exploring.

"Yes, that's the first one. Sharp when applied unexpectedly. Is it unusual to have just the one coming in, without its match on the other side?"

"Quite uncommon, Jon. It indicates bike-racing aptitude."

"I got two teeth at once," Nita says. "On the bottom."

"You remember, do you? Sixty-seven pounds," Russ tells her, lifting her up with a weightlifter's grunt. "What have you been eating, gravel?"

"No," Nita giggles. Russ deposits her on the exam table. She wanted to marry Russ for almost a year, after Peter and before Andrei. She always tries desperately not to cry when he gives her shots, her lip trembling, a silent tear or two squeezing out. Russ saw her through her first tough six months, when he was new in town and she had reflux. Russ looks in Nita's throat and ears.

"Good Lord," he says. "I can see right through." He holds up a hand on the far side of her head. Nita giggles.

"Can not."

"Test me," Russ says. This is an old routine. Nita holds up three fingers on the side Russ isn't. He peers into her ear, surreptitiously checking Jon's poker cheat, three fingers extended out of Nita's sightline. "Three," Russ says. Nita giggles even before the cool stethoscope lands on her chest.

✸

"How's the morale?" Russ asks. He's checking Sam's hip joints, vigorously bicycling the boy, who lies on his back. "Peter was not a hundred percent sure about all this." Peter made the last visit, and as always, told Russ everything. That he wasn't sure he was ready to raise a second child.

"We had our ups and downs," Jon says. "We're not youngsters."

"No, but you're rich as Croesus. Buy a little help."

"I'd love to," Jon says. "Peter won't even talk about it."

"That man," Russ shakes his head. Russ's own wife is a divorce lawyer. His three have been in daycare since their first months of life. Russ occasionally proselytizes gently for the positive effects of early socialization, but then undermines his own argument by admiring how few nasty colds Nita gets and bemoaning his own children's run of infections, caught at daycare and passed around all winter and spring. "Well, Sam is a fine lad. I want you to let him grow up at the ordinary rate. No fruit juice. We don't want to make a sugar junkie out of him."

"I'm not a sugar junkie," Nita says, sucking her lollipop and waiting expectantly. She's having a hard time sharing Russ with Sam.

"You," Russ says, lunging toward her, hands out. She squeals. He hugs her, then lets her slide slowly down his white coat until she's standing. "How's this one accommodating?" he says to Jon.

"Nita loves Sam a lot. But sometimes she wishes Sam took up a little less of our time."

"I remember when my brother was born," Russ says to Nita. "I went over to my friend Jeff's house and refused to come home."

"You moved in with your friend?" Nita asks.

"My father came and got me after one night. But it took a long time till I really liked my brother. He was always getting my mom's attention."

"I like Sam."

"I'm glad," Russ says. "He likes you, too. He just doesn't have a lot of ways to show it yet."

"Oh," Nita says. She turns and looks solemnly at Sam, as if waiting for him to speak.

The Letter *B*

HENRY ACCELERATES from a dignified trot to an all-out run. He bows and arches, bows and arches, a cartoon dog on a cartoon road. Leo and Virginia follow side by side at a leisurely trot. Bailey and Louisa ride the towpath a dozen yards behind the senior Woofs.

"What did he see?" Bailey asks.

"Henry doesn't need much reason to run," Louisa tells him. They've been out over an hour, chatting, watching Virginia to see if they've gotten her insulin right. Virginia's the confident marathoner she has always been.

"How far are we from Fletcher's?" Louisa asks.

"Ten minutes." Bailey says. Louisa rises on the pedals of the Raleigh.

"Are you ready to eat? I say let's stop there." Louisa speeds up. Bailey matches her and allows himself to wonder if she will have him, really have him, not just for another year, not just for an adventure, but for a husband, with all the glorious plainness and permanence of that state. It has been three months now since their first kiss. They have settled into familiar ease. Louisa has learned that Bailey is not always fascinating. He's learned that Louisa has long quiet spells. She's back in school, and says she is comfortable telling her friends that she and Bailey are living together. But she hasn't introduced him to anyone. He has told Jon, Valerie, and the rest of the family that he and Louisa are together. But all of them, even the usually no-question-too-personal pair, Peter and Dee, have received the news with quiet acceptance and not pursued the topic. It's as if they are all waiting to see if Louisa will bolt or Bailey will panic. Bailey loves to make love to Louisa as, he truly believes, and this frightens him, he never loved making love to anyone. Louisa has told him, not teasingly but directly, that he is everything she wants in a man. But for how long? He rides after her.

⊛

Louisa is a skillful sandwich maker, and this, she claims, is the extent of her cooking. Louisa constructed today's sandwiches after breakfast with care and precision. She found ripe avocado, leftover steak, red onion. There is iced tea in the thermos. Bailey leans on his elbows on an old blanket. Louisa reclines against him. They are between the towpath and the river. The sun fires the brown and rusty leaves, which fall when the breeze comes. Beneath the blanket, the earth is cool with the next season. A young couple walking by registers the difference in Bailey and Louisa's ages and looks away. Bailey smiles. "Should I wave to them, and tell them yes, I'm old enough to be my girlfriend's grandfather?" he asks.

"We make them nervous," Louisa says. "Does that make you nervous?"

"I don't like being the old one. I wouldn't object if I were the young one. As it is, I want to tell them to move along before I demonstrate my mobility by kicking them with my antique foot." Louisa kisses Bailey's knee. The dogs take turns at their water bowl. The river is high. A castle-tall cottonwood leans across the dark green water toward Virginia.

"Why don't you come home with me for Thanksgiving?" Louisa asks.

"I'd like that. Or we could have your family here."

"My brothers? With all the Allards? Bold."

"It's time the families start getting used to us," he says. "You just tell me how you want to do it."

"I'll think about it." Virginia beds down on Bailey's far side. Bailey finishes his sandwich and lies back, using his sweater for a pillow. Teenagers ride by, shouting about something they saw on TV. The voices float overhead like clouds. Bailey dozes deeply—*napture*, he calls it. Each night, he and Louisa sleep in arm- and back-wrenching tangles, unwilling to compromise intimacy for anatomy. These knotty nights leave them silly and sleep deprived. When he wakes from his nap, Bailey looks at his watch, unsure how long he and Louisa have dozed. Probably just a few minutes. Paddlers in kayaks on the water are silhouetted against the sun. Louisa's chin is on Bailey's chest. He strokes her fine hair. "Are you chilly?" he asks. When Louisa answers, he knows he should let her be for another quarter hour.

"I don't want to ride home," Louisa murmurs, still dreamy. "Let's take a cab."

"Or a rowboat," Bailey says. He feels her smile against his breastbone. "Will you marry me?" he asks. Under the edge of his hat, as straight as the roof of a house, he studies Louisa's eyes when she lifts her head to look at him.

"Yes," she says. There is no fright in her, no sudden drawing back.

"I want to spend my life with you," Bailey tells her. "I feel as if it's a whole life, even if it isn't. I suppose you know what I mean, even at your age."

"I do," Louisa says.

"I feel I have a whole life in front of me, since you're with me. I know that people will call me selfish to be with a woman your age. I could become a burden to you next week or next year, hold you back with illness. I could trot along healthy, until one day I just drop in my tracks and leave you holding the bag, or the baby, the bills."

"What's all this letter *b* business?"

"So you are awake," Bailey says. "When you said 'yes' you weren't dreaming that I was a young man. You will be the girl left holding the *b*s." Louisa frowns.

"I want the money right away, let me be clear about that," she says. "You must disinherit your children at once, so we can have one of those tabloid court battles, in which they accuse me of bewitching you, and I wear too much eye shadow, show the jury a lot of leg, and squander millions before they can tie it up in escrow."

"That goes without saying."

"You mentioned babies. I want two."

"Naturally. How else am I going to shock and dismay my cousins, colleagues, and cronies?"

"Bailey," Louisa says, her expression now solemn and fearful. Where is the easy smile he saw only a moment before? "Do you really think we can do it?" Bailey looks into Louisa's eyes, the river behind her. His head inclines into his left hand. He forces himself to think, hard. If he and Louisa marry in a year, and Louisa finds a clerkship somewhere in the area, and they have two children as soon as Louisa is done with clerkship, and his health follows the trajectory of his grandfather and father, she will be a happy, almost middle-aged woman with teenagers when he is suddenly too old to get around or dies. She must believe and he, too, that fifteen or twenty good years together outweighs the thirty, forty, even fifty years she might accrue with a man born in her decade. In truth, Bailey can say that he and Louisa love each other with a force and simplicity he knows comes along only once in a lifetime, or twice. Who knows if either of them, even Louisa, at her age, will ever find a love like this again? There are the dark unknowns, such as that not every woman lives a long life. Louisa may not have fifty more years, with anyone. How can the two of them say to the gods, to each other, *No, not enough. The fifteen or twenty years you offer us is not enough.* Wouldn't that be misguided? In a year, if they are wrong and all this is just novelty, joy in bed, the fun of defying expectations, they will know that, too, and they can call the whole thing off.

"We can do it," Bailey tells Louisa. "If you will take all the chances with me, the good luck chances and the bad luck chances, we can do it."

"Good," Louisa says, not a hint of laughter in her eyes. She sits now, facing him. "I think so, too. I thought you might not think so. I thought you might just be in love with me. That would be fine, I wanted that to be fine. But I just can't stand the idea of not being with you. If you told me to go, that it's for the best, that it's the only way, I would leave. But it would break my heart."

"Never," Bailey says, taking her in his arms. Virginia, with her diabetes defining the lines of her dog's life more sharply than before, looks at the two of them. Louisa, weeping, settles her head to Bailey's neck. Bailey recognizes what he hasn't before—how completely Louisa needs him, the weight of that.

Amy

"I'VE GONE from *Penthouse* pet to *National Geographic* mama," Eve complains. She and Max stand in front of the mirror in their bedroom in their new, old house. Max holds Amy. It is five in the morning and they have broken the cardinal rule of night parenting: Don't both get up at once.

"You're magnificent. Your belly is like a tent, lain on the ground but not yet tucked away. Your breasts are gourds, heavy with nutriment for the tribe. Your hair—"

"Is falling out. What's with that? I thought the little surprises were supposed to end when Amy came out. And please, no more about tents and gourds." Eve takes Amy from Max, and Amy nurses while Eve walks. Breast-feeding while walking is one of Eve's special moves. She finds it easy, but other mothers are astonished that it can be done. Max walks to keep company. It is a warm October night after an Indian summer day, and nobody's wearing any clothes, except the one diaper. Amy is two hours shy of seventeen days old. She is not on a schedule that distinguishes night from day.

Eve finished helping Bailey draft his gay marriage opinion ninety hours before Amy was born. Max wanted to call their baby Imogen Diversity. Or Imogen Tolerance. But Max likes Amy Rachel, too. Eve said Amy was clearly Amy, as soon as she met her. Imogen turned out to be her practice name.

"That's a good girl," Max says. "Plough through the fore milk, glean the hind milk. Antibodies, simple sugars, the fat of the land."

"Max. No fat of the land, please. Aren't you sleepy?"

"My eyelids hurt, I'm lightheaded, and I feel a little jumpy," Max says. "But I'm not sleepy in the conventional sense."

"You're welcome to lie down. I'll let you know when it's your turn again."

"I like walking with you and Blossom. We're nomads, heading for the next watering hole. The sheep and goats fan out before us in the moonlight. The camels cough and sway. Above, stars embroider the velvet sky." This is all part of Max's idea why Amy screws up her face and bleats when Eve stands still or sits. Max thinks Amy thinks that she is the child of nomadic herdspeople. When she isn't being jostled, Amy thinks she may have been left behind on a dune in her swaddlings. Only in motion, in Eve's or Max's arms, in the car or in her bouncy chair, does Amy feel that she's traveling with her people.

"Max, are we going to resume our active social lives?"

"We don't have active social lives, Buttons."

"Okay. But we did have jobs. Can you believe that there are people in this country who are trying to keep couples like us, couples who are trying to build homes and raise Amys, from getting married? I mean, I thought I was outraged before, but I didn't understand how hard this was going to be. Now I'm outraged. I can only imagine how outraged I'll be when I get a little sleep."

"You'll be alertly outraged. And you'll have years of work ahead of you, on cases that haven't been filed yet. Married gay couples whose marriages suddenly are invalid when they move to a new state. Gay parents whose custody is suddenly in jeopardy. Your outrage is only a tiny bud right now. Like Blossom."

"When's Bailey going to issue?"

"Next couple of weeks. You know how judges write. Now that we're gone, he's probably down to a couple paragraphs a day. Thank God he's got Louisa."

"True. By the way, should we be offended by that relationship? I know we adore Bailey, but isn't there a little letch-factor when a man in his sixties takes up with a woman in her twenties?"

"Switcheroo time," Max says. Amy smacks her lips and makes exploratory reaches with her hands. Eve detaches Amy's embouchure with her thumb, raises Amy vertical, switches her, and situates her near the left nipple. Amy has the narrow face and expressive, slightly pursed lips of a French woman reading a slim novel at a café table in the 1950s. Until she begins frantically bobbing her head and opening and closing her mouth. Then she resembles a baby bird. Max cradles her head, with its wisps of black hair, and steers her in to the nipple.

"Belly up to the bar. It's payday," Max sings to his daughter. Eve looks at him. "I've been listening to a lot of WMZQ since we've been home," Max says. "Country music perpetuates a pastoral, nationalist myth with disturbing ethnically and racially exclusionary undertones. But it's fun to listen to. What were you saying about Bailey being an old satyr?" They walk into and around the pyramid of boxes in the nursery, which at the moment is largely a staging area for unsorted infant clothes and large, primary-colored plastic objects. The crib is filled with gift boxes, some opened. The changing table, with its parabolic foam pad, its wooden diaper holder, its Tupperware of cotton squares in water for light daubing, and its dispenser of unscented, alcohol-free baby wipes, is the only equipment fully deployed. Eve, nursing, carries Amy out in the hall and down toward her office, also partly unpacked. Luckily, the departing dentist and his wife left the curtains.

"I was just saying that I know marriage is an adaptable institution that fits teenage sweethearts, middle-aged second-time-arounders, octogenarians, and also people of differing ages," Eve says. "I still have a problem with old men and young women. It's not like you see women Bailey's age carrying on with guys Louisa's age. Why is that?"

"Theory is that old-male, young-female has biological and sociological advantages. Clearly, it perpetuates patriarchy. I'm starving," Max adds. "Are there any Pop-Tarts left? Perhaps the root of the pattern is to be found in the Oedipal rejection of maternal love. Boys can't be with women who look too much like their mothers. But why should girls feel they can be with father-age suitors? Consider the fairy tale record. Lots of stories about princes whose fate is held in the balance by shriveled hags, what we'd call today crones, or wise women. Under duress, the young man gives the old gal the tiniest kiss, and at once the golden-ager is transformed into an apple-cheeked virgin. Show me a fairy tale about an old man transformed into a prince by a princess. Doesn't happen. The young woman just marries the geezer, who happens to have all the power and money."

"*Beauty and the Beast*," Eve says. "Beast turns into a prince. I think we've got a couple Frosted Strawberry left. Would you get me a glass of milk?"

"Exception that proves the rule," Max says, finding his robe and heading downstairs. The treads and risers creak like the timbers of a ship. He pours milk and toasts Pop-Tarts. "Besides," he shouts, "Belle lives with Bête in his nasty form for ages. She teaches him not to growl. She trims his hairiness. Basically, she learns to live with male ugliness. The princes never have to do that."

"So Bailey's off the hook?" Eve looks at Amy, suckling

away. She feels a little burst of happiness and sadness. Happiness because Amy is lovely and hers; sadness because Amy will never be sixteen days old again.

"Bailey," Max says, ascending, "is in love. You okay? Just having a cry? Blossom makes me cry, too. Here, let me hug you both. Better? Have a little bite. Watch out, the frosting's hot. No, you can't saddle Bailey with being an exploitative, groping cradle-robber. He's just a country boy lookin' for a country girl."

"Even if Bailey is just in love," Eve says, "can't I be judgmental and feel superior?"

"Oh, judgmental and superior." Max says. He takes a bite of Pop-Tart and a swig of cold coffee. "To regard others critically and to feel that one's own situation, decisions, or actions are in some way more noble, or simply more comme il faut, than theirs, is one of the great satisfactions of a reflective life."

"Okay," Eve, with a milk mustache, says. "I'm going to bed." Amy is asleep. But if Eve lies down with her, she'll wake up. She must be kept in motion for another twenty minutes.

"I'll take Blossom for a stroll. Maybe help Caitlin do our street."

"Caitlin?"

"Papergirl."

Tailless Lesser Apes

"I HAVE NEWS," Bailey tells Sean. They are at the zoo, in front of the peacocks. A pin-headed male stares across a cement moat. The peacock's head is in profile. He uses one eye, then turns to use the other eye. "I proposed."

"She accepted?" Sean asks.

"She did." They walk on, past tapirs and bongos (antelope, not drums), before coming to rest on Olmstead Walk. Elands, ibex, and white-tailed deer all hang on Bailey's words. "It was as if she had been afraid I wouldn't want to be with her."

"But you convinced her," Sean says. "Dana owes me ten bucks. Let me buy you some popcorn."

"Why?"

"I said you would propose this month. Dana thought it would be between Thanksgiving and Christmas." They walk on.

"Did I move too fast?" Bailey asks, perhaps because they have paused in front of the cheetah enclosure.

The cheetah, fastest land animal, a long-legged spotted swift-moving African and formerly Asian cat (*Acinonyx jubatus)* about the size of a small leopard. Blunt non-retractile claws, often trained to run down game. Capable of only short bursts at seventy-five miles an hour . . .

Bailey calms himself. The cheetahs are hidden.

"Not at all. Dana thought you'd still be —"

"Working through my feelings about marrying again."

"Yes."

"I don't know what Caroline thinks," Bailey admits, shaking his head. He locates a cheetah asleep in a pile of oak leaves. The tree, wrapped in hemp up to six feet, serves as a scratching post. "She doesn't talk about it. She's decided that Louisa is my business."

"Bailey. Have you ever considered targeted psychotherapy?"

"So I can stop talking to Caroline? No." They head for the Education Center. Sean buys popcorn. "I have less time with her now, of course. She knows this marriage will mean a change." Sean starts to reply, and has a fistful of popcorn instead. "Reptile Discovery?" Bailey asks. Off they go.

It's cool and shadowy in the building, with its thick glass cages and echoing interior. The rooms are lightly trafficked by boys and their parents. The *Micrurus fulvius tener* is a pretty thing, like a painted walking stick. Red, black, yellow, white rings. Copulation occurs in Southern Arkansas and Louisiana to western central Texas from October to May. The female can store sperm in her oviducts for seven months.

"You've met the mother?" Sean asks.

"Nora's coming for Thanksgiving."

"Always good to meet the mother."

"Yes. To know how Louisa will look when I'm ninety-seven."

"Speaking of which," Sean says, "when are you planning to issue the marriage decision?"

"I'm done. It's just hard to let go without Max and Eve to force me. I depended on them."

"How are the new clerks?"

"Deferential. They're no use, yet."

"What's it going to say?"

"Oh, you know. That Love and Wilson have as much right to marry as anybody. That DC must recognize valid marriages in sister states, especially since Council already voted to do so. That DOMA doesn't make a lot of sense."

"Are you going to hear it *en banc?*" Sean asks.

"Don't know yet." A golf-bag-size Komodo dragon is stretched across a Zen garden of white sand.

"Well, hurry up and issue your decision. I put it on my spring syllabus. Great Apes?" They head through bird-twittering twilight. Bailey is wondering where Louisa is studying. She could be lying in bed. She could be in the library, cradled by the arms of the armchair. Bailey has not had this double consciousness, in which he is perpetually mapping his loved one's location, since Caroline died. It is one of the pleasures of love he had begun not to remember. "I'll call Dana in Berlin as soon as I get home, and tell her the good news," Sean says. After the cool serenity of Reptile Discovery, Great Apes is a zoo. Gorillas hoot and swing, or sit quietly engaged in complex interactions. Strong odors predominate. "What the framers had in mind was to create little monarchs," Sean announces.

"Framers again. You don't mean me."

"Judges. Court is a counterweight to popular will, since people often vote for all kinds of malarkey and mayhem. Judges are a nod to benevolent kings and queens. Why else appoint them for life? Admits the unlikelihood of true democracy perpetuating itself. Problem is that sometimes the judges are unprincipled tyrants."

"You think gay and lesbian marriage will survive the reaction?"

"Laws will go down state by state, with some holdouts. As with the antimiscegenation laws. Nobody's going to secede over this. There's a natural life span to prejudiced law, roughly equal to the political life of those who write it or run on it. Gibbons?" Sean suggests. He and Bailey head back outside and under the orangutan overpass. A couple of them gaze down, long-armed, with orange shag-carpeted bellies, monk's tonsures, and wide, ingenue eyes. The men look upward as long as possible, craning their necks as they walk. The white-handed gibbons are slender tailless apes, a couple of feet tall, with curved upper backs, as if from too much reading in poor light. Gibbons swing rapidly through their enclosure with a casual economy bordering on criminal negligence. They miss one another by inches. "Of course the easier and surer path might be Vermont. Marriage in all but name."

"That's what's holding me up," Bailey admits. "That and a basic unwillingness to give up what I've written. I don't want to be the guy who championed the wrong strategy."

"You don't have any choice. Love and Wilson are already married in name. Barsugli, Beaumont, and McWhinney in New Mexico get the distinction of shaping strategy, however it goes. Giraffes?" They walk. The baby stands at an awkward forward tilt, like an incorrectly adjusted tripod. "Besides, I don't like the idea of all-but-name. It takes away the blessing. Just as the state's resistance functions psychologically to clarify lovers' duty, in the end city hall must give its blessing. Citizens, that is to say children, require resistance, then a blessing. The state has replaced the recalcitrant fathers of Shakespeare's comedies of love. Gays need to be blessed just as much as straights."

"Mind if I quote you?" The baby giraffe's ears are being licked by her mother, as if she were a tall kitten.

"Mind? I never read one of your decisions," Sean says, "without signing it."

Date Night

PETER, JON, NITA, and Sam come into what is now Bailey and Louisa's front hall. Nita wanders back to the kitchen. Jon hands Sam to Louisa, who kisses him here and there. He smiles his tooth at her. She sets him on the rug. He rolls to the side, gets to his knees, then moves backwards with a series of arm pushes until his feet begin kicking the wall.

"Interesting," Louisa says. "Is that crawling?"

"He's stuck in reverse," Peter says. "He can back up, and he can pivot on his belly. This means he can get anywhere. How's the visit?" Nora, Louisa's mother, is in from Montana. Peter and Jon are about to meet her, before they head out for their Saturday night date.

"I thought Mom would look at Bailey the way she looks at dogs she's thinking might not be pedigree. I thought she'd look at me sadly," Louisa says. "But she's fine. It's a regular, get-to-know-you visit. Bailey gave her a tour yesterday—walk downtown in the morning, Old Ebbitt Grill for lunch, out to Monticello for the afternoon. Mom's been to Washington, but never with a historian. Come meet her." Louisa scoops up Sam and leads the men back to the kitchen, where Bailey's semi-homemade pizza (store-bought dough) is being served. As they crowd into the kitchen, Peter remembers the night he and Jon showed Louisa the Dupont house, before she decided to move in. A scant six months later, she and Bailey are informally engaged—no ring, no date for a wedding, but lots of public displays of affection and talk of the future.

"I hear they've been keeping you busy," Peter says, meeting Nora.

"Bailey has me on a schedule," Nora says. "I told him I'm taking tomorrow off." Nora is closer to Peter's idea of a mother-in-law than is Louisa. Louisa is, well, young. Peter knows there could be no one and nothing better for Bailey than Louisa and a second marriage. He and Jon don't have to worry about Bailey being lonely. They can drop off both Nita and Sam when they go out for date night, knowing Bailey has Louisa to help. But there's a nagging part of Peter that doesn't like change, and he keeps thinking things were just fine before. Somehow, he and Jon are slightly less central than before Louisa's arrival.

"May I hold Sam?" Nora asks Peter, and Louisa. Nora has that outdoorsy, suntanned look of a Western woman. Nora takes Sam from Louisa and blows raspberries in his neck. Sam laughs. Nora is like a young grandmother, who hasn't lost the skills or muscles of motherhood. Louisa leans into Bailey's chest where he stands by the counter. *Make one like this*, Nora's eyes are saying to her daughter. Louisa and Bailey are in such love that Peter is reminded of his and Jon's own headiest days.

"No, we've got to be going," Jon says in answer to Bailey's entreaties. The plan is for Peter and Jon to sit down to a proper dinner in a restaurant with soft lighting and no highchairs. They will talk about this and that. They will look at each other and remember when it was just the two of them.

❁

But they stop in "just for a minute" at Kramerbooks & Afterwords Cafe. No sooner do they enter the bookstore than Peter finds himself face to face with a small but prominent display of the newest novel by his cherished rival. Jon makes his way to the history section, so he doesn't see Peter stop in his tracks. Peter buys the book and heads to the café to read. He half hopes the book will be very fine, so that his own novel, several months from completion, almost a year from publication, will have a target, or distant horizon, or mountain to shoot for, journey toward, or climb higher than. The other half of his hope is that the book will suck eggs, so that he won't have to worry about coming up short in the perpetual competition, even if it is a competition that only Peter himself, Jon, and perhaps the rival, know about. Part of Peter's shock is that this guy's book is *already out*, not even two years after his last one. It was supposed to be Peter's turn. Fair's fair.

Thing is, Peter *likes* this guy. Ten pages in, he's already beginning to forget that he's upset by the book's existence. Fifteen pages and Peter's enjoying himself, marveling at how the damn book is put together. Peter knows the man from a single evening's memorable conversation. He keeps tabs on his rival via friends, without communicating directly. He knows the man doesn't have a new baby to care for. He just sits around all day and writes. He is like Peter in many ways—gay, not a teacher, thirty-eight. He is unlike Peter in other ways—not married, no kids, West Coast. When they met, they had already read each other's first books. They felt an affinity, and spoke of it. Peter always keeps the man in the back of his mind. He and Peter read each other more closely than anyone else reads either of them. They are pen pals, three thousand miles apart, exchanging long letters in the form of books every few years. Or, in this case, after only twenty months.

Peter orders beer and nachos. Halfway through his snack, he looks up to find Jon with a nineteenth-century social history book.

"I couldn't find you. Why didn't you tell me—" Jon starts

to ask, helping himself to a chip. "Oh." He sees the name on the book (one of those first initial period, full middle name, surname names). Jon sits down, orders wine and a salad, and studies the dust jacket, which features an erotic Renaissance painting. The kind of cover, Jon thinks, that will sell. "How is it?"

"Good. Don't want to talk about it."

"Right," Jon says, wondering how the publication of this novel will affect his evening. Will Peter be capable of conversation? Will they just have appetizers here, and then go have dinner as planned? The rival can put Peter into moods of elation and bonhomie when he thinks he is part of a circle of like-minded artists who all nourish, support, and influence one another. But reading this man can also make Peter feel out-gunned, and can make him wonder why he bothers to write at all. Jon could have sworn he remembers Peter reading a good but flawed book by the same author less than two years ago. Just because the guy knocked out another one doesn't mean there's less room for Peter's own, which should be finished any month now. Peter may feel trumped if the book is too much like his own, if he and the West Coast double seem to be chasing the same squirrel. One thing's pretty clear. Jon has about as much chance of getting laid tonight as of seeing a movie.

"Shall we just eat here?"

"Do you mind?" Peter says.

"No. I'm surprised. I thought—"

"I know," Peter says. "I really wanted to have a—"

"Romantic?"

"—nice dinner with you," Peter says. "With a Scotch, first. I can't believe I forwent the Scotch." Jon settles in at the table, hoping for the best as far as Peter's mood goes. Both men read. Before Jon has finished his salad, Peter orders another beer and a steak. Jon orders the sea bass.

"We can go out tomorrow," Peter says. "We'll bring the kids over to Mike and Jess's."

"Two nights in a row. That would be youthful," Jon says. He reaches for Peter's hand, which is clutching the novel, rather hard.

"I'm sorry," Peter says. "I shouldn't have ordered without discussing a change in plans."

"That good?" Jon's eyes flicker toward the new book.

"I like it."

"Yours will be even better," Jon says.

"I'd better go home and write it."

"That would be relaxing and fun," Jon says. "For me, especially."

"I'll tell you what." Peter closes his book, a finger inside. "Let's have dessert here. We'll go to the Circle, read for a few minutes, head home. Then we'll do"—Peter looks into Jon's eyes—"whatever you want to do."

"Hmmm," Jon says.

❁

The water of the fountain is blue. Not the bright aqua of a spotlit fountain, but a cool, jazzy blue, at nearly eleven. The October sky is reflected upside-down in the water, the clouds pouring off the lip of the saucer above the inscription, SAM-UEL FRANCIS DU PONT, REAR-ADMIRAL. Jon and Peter have settled onto one of Dupont's benches. Across from them, a young woman with a guitar sings about love. Pot perfumes the air. This is turning out to be a satisfying date night after all, Jon recognizes. Peter continued reading for half an hour once they reached Dupont. But luckily, he is in his we-are-all-brothers-in-art state of mind. The new book has given Peter a sense of serenity rather than of panic. It's as if, reading the rival's book, Peter feels he has advanced his own work. Against the odds, this Saturday has become dreamy. Jon rests his head on Peter's shoulder. Peter's leg warms his.

"Maybe we should get married," Peter suddenly says. "Who knows how long Bailey's decision will be in effect."

"A recommitment ceremony?" Jon asks.

"No. Pledging eternal love once ought to be enough," Peter says. "I want that real marriage license. For one thing, it might come in handy, if—"

"Yes. It might. You don't have to go into all the tragic scenarios in which being legal might be important."

"You mean little problems like medical consent, custody of our children? Small matters, such as home ownership and becoming suddenly destitute? Okay, let's forget all that. We still should get married. We deserve the recognition. We pay taxes."

"Definitely," Jon says. They listen to the fountain, and the singing. "When?"

"Soon. What does Bailey's decision say?"

"Requires DC to recognize New Mexico licenses, effective last week. Doesn't require DC to issue brand-new licenses."

"Oh."

"That will come. In the meantime, we go to Santa Fe, get hitched, come back, and pick up a license."

"I want to get married here," Peter says. "DC is where we live. I want this place"—Peter points his forefingers beyond Dupont Circle, south beyond the yellow and gold leaves hanging in the streetlight to the White House, south and east to Capitol Hill—"to recognize you and me." He now points his thumbs directly to the two of them, as if there might be some confusion.

"You've been thinking about this," Jon says.

"I hold Sam responsible," Peter says. "When that boy showed up, and turned my world upside-down and even more wonderful, I realized I wasn't going to be an almost-father this time. I was young before. I accepted being an almost-dad, almost-husband. Now I've wised up. I know I'm real, you're real, and what we do is important and difficult. I want to be recognized for who and what I am. By the damn DC and federal government. Even by your extremely slow family."

"That's fair."

"Overdue."

"Yes," Jon agrees. He really *does* agree. But there's a part of his brain in which he accuses himself of agreeing completely with Peter because their evening is going so well and they'll be home in bed soon. The woman with the guitar finishes singing. The small crowd gathered around her applauds, then there's a flurry of cigarette and joint lighting. A man and a woman pass, speaking in loud, postcinema voices about the movie they've seen. Jon tries to figure out which film, based on what they're saying, but he can't concentrate on film criticism because Peter kisses him. A long, sweet kiss.

"Nice," Jon says, at last. "What for?"

"Because you let me read on date night," Peter says. "Because you're handsome. Because"—he kisses Jon again lightly, looking into his eyes—"I love you."

"I have an idea."

"I'm sure you do."

"No," Jon says. "I mean about what you said."

"Marriage."

"We sue DC."

"We do?"

"For the right to marry here," Jon says. Peter looks up at the mild night sky.

"We'd lose. I might not handle that well."

"I love you, too. Lord knows," Jon says, that smile starting on the left side of his mouth, "I don't want to lead you down a garden path." He kisses Peter, pulling him close. "Thing is," he says, pausing for one more kiss, "I believe we will win."

Dupont Circle's fountain splashes down with a faint ringing sound, like that of distant bells.

Acknowledgments

Deepest appreciation to Janet Silver, my gifted editor and friend.

Thanks to Deborah Levi, Melissa McWhinney, Paul Wolfson, Susie White, Sean Murphy, Louise Milkman, and especially to Allison Jernow and Anne Beaumont, for insight into the life and work of the law clerk; to Susan Murray, Beth Robinson, and Mary Bonauto for their inspiring argument before the Vermont Supreme Court, which I had the privilege of hearing; to E. J. Graff for her invaluable account of the history of marriage in Western culture, *What Is Marriage For? The Strange Social History of Our Most Intimate Institution*; to David Shapiro for a thread through the labyrinth of federal procedure; to William Eskridge for his published works, particularly *The Case for Same-Sex Marriage: From Sexual Liberty to Civilized Commitment*, and for his anecdotal account of the history of same-sex marriage litigation in DC; to M. A. Sheehan for a grounding in the DC judicial system and DC politics; to Larry Kramer for his published insights into the problematic status of the Defense of Marriage Act; and to Walter Kittredge and Jude Mullé of the Harvard herbaria for their help identifying the trees.

Thanks to Charlotte Sheedy, superb agent and encourager. Hugs and kisses to my fast-reading, fast-editing friends and family, John and Marian, Alex and Lauren, Egon and Maureen, Dan and Ann, Andy and Alice, Eric and Susan, Janet B., Joe and Bob, Marck, Brook, Caroline, Mike, Paul M., Claudia, Sean and Stella, Lisa, Tim, Ben and Ray, Debra and David, Kevin and Bob, Nicole, Bruce, Sean and Julie, Annie, Françoise, Juliet, John T., Peggy and Burton, and Andrei; to Michael Schade, who knows Dupont Circle best; and to the professionals, Alison Kerr Miller, Anne Chalmers, Elizabeth Van Itallie, and Walter Vatter for bringing the book to life. Appreciation to Marie Arana, Cheryl Chapman, Bob Compton, Jim Concannon, Jon Garelick, David Kipen, David Mehegan, and Oscar Villalon for all the fine new books I've had the privilege of reviewing. Gratitude to Monroe Engel, Bill Wiser, Marjorie Mussman, Marcus Schulkind, and Jeanne Traxler, gifted teachers, giving spirits.

First and last, love and thanks to my wife, muse, and prime reader, Patty Gibbons.